Mid Witch Two

DJ Bowman-Smith

Illustrated by
DJ Bowman-Smith

Edited by
Anna Sharples

Pen Archer

This book is dedicated to all the women of maturing years who felt the fear - and did it anyway.

Foreword

Hello Dear Reader,

Firstly, thanks to each and every one of you for connecting with Lilly the Mid Witch. So many of you took the trouble to leave a review or rating for book one - once again I must ask for your support so that Mid Witch Two does not sink into the depths of Amazon - never to be seen again. Reviews mean Mid Witch Two will be visible on the Amazon store and more readers can connect to the story.

Also, if you have not signed up to my mailing list please do. There is a free short story on there about Lilly and I will keep you up to date with my writing life and the progress of the next book.

Many thanks,

Deborah

www.djbowmansmith.com

Chapter One

We are warm in bed. Ink lies on her back next to me. Long, black greyhound legs hooked over, daft doggy grin on her snoot. Outside, a dull January day dawns. I fidget, and Ink drapes her head over my legs to keep me in place a few moments longer. This time of year is my least favourite. England's changing seasons are delightful, but I'd like to get rid of January. Spring has not begun, the excitement of Christmas is over and bleak New Year resolutions fill the air.

I drag myself out of bed – not easy with a greyhound clamped onto you. Ink harrumphs, stands, circles and lies in the warm patch. I take my faded pink dressing gown from the hook on the back of the door and put it on. Hanging beneath it is a red kimono my son, Jason, gave me for Christmas. Brightly embroidered with peonies and exotic birds, it probably cost a fortune. Unlike this old gown, which looked cheap even when it was new. I give the kimono a pat and go downstairs. In the kitchen, I stoke the fire in the old range cooker with logs. Put food out for Ink and Claudia, the cat, and rinse their water bowl. I fill the kettle and the fire crackles as last night's embers re-light. It's another cold, damp morning. At this time of year, I try to keep the fires burning.

Roused by the sound of dog food, Ink gallops down the stairs. The back door opens for her, and she mooches into the garden. She can do that: open doors. That's because she's a witch's dog, and I am a witch. I know this now as a positive truth. As real as the colour of my eyes or the beat of my heart, magic is within me – new and strange.

Standing on the back step, I feel the star etched in the stone. Cold lines of starlight tingle the soles of my bare feet. I have lived in North Star Cottage all my life, and I love it here. Recently, I became a witch, and now the energy of my home and the surrounding woods seeps into me. If I had to describe it, I would say I am growing magical roots. There is a bond between myself and this place and all the witches who lived here before me.

I snap my fingers in front of my face and watch sparks float. Today, they are green and blue. Every morning I do this. Just to check. 'I am Lilith, the last of the Blackwood witches,' I say, and Maud the magpie swoops from the bare branches of the apple tree and lands on my shoulder.

As well as a kimono, I have received two pairs of crocks. Ink loves them. She likes all my shoes. Crocks on – one blue, the other pink and both left feet – I set off with a dog poo bag. This is one of my New Year resolutions: deal with shit (actual and metaphorical) straight away and don't let it fester. This year, I will not pretend everything is okay. I will stand up for myself. This new attitude is less witchcraft and more menopause. These days, I'm less conforming, less biddable, less *nice*. My desire to please and placate has fucked off with menstruation.

Thin strands of coloured fog float about the garden as I pick up the poo, deposit it in the bin and fetch logs from the shed. 'They ought to sell dressing gowns that are worn in,' I say to the magpie on my shoulder. She gives my ear a friendly peck. I can't imagine doing the morning chores in the kimono. I should find a dressing gown in a charity shop. One that is worn in but not worn out. A halfway point between this old thing and the frightening newness of the posh one. A dressing gown more like me.

After filling the log baskets, I trundle in my left feet to the garden gate and collect my post from the little box. There's nothing much. Two late Christmas cards, some flyers for a new pizza takeaway in Marswickham, an official-looking brown envelope – probably a bill – and a large white envelope bent in half. In the kitchen, Maud flaps onto the top of the dresser. I wash my hands, make tea and fix myself a bowl of muesli. Today, the witch ball that hangs in the kitchen window looks like nothing more than a football-sized bauble. I peer at the silver surface while waiting for the tea to brew. No dark shapes or fleeting shadows. Good.

'Alexa,' I say, 'play Classic FM.'

The Alexa bot complies with cheerful Mozart. This is a Christmas gift from my daughter, Belinda. I wasn't sure at first and would have left it forgotten in the box if she hadn't insisted on setting it up. Very useful for the radio, the weather forecast and timing cakes.

The Christmas card is from my friend Cressida. We planned to go out on New Year's Eve but she cancelled. Secretly, I was glad. I had nothing to wear. And the last time I went to the Enterprise Hall at the University, I had an awful time I'd rather forget. It's a great card, though: a picture of a greyhound in a Father Christmas outfit with the caption 'Santa Paws'.

I prop it on the dresser and settle Ink, who has eaten her food and is scratching her bedding. I bought her a nice, smart bed for Christmas, which I thought would look tidier than her pile of blankets and old towels. But she'll only sleep on the pet bed with the old stuff on top. Silly dog. I get her cosy and snug by the range, and she tucks in her nose for a nap. It has started drizzling and greyhounds don't do rain, so there's no need for a walk. I ask Alexa about the weather and am told there will be blue skies this afternoon.

As I clear away breakfast, the kitchen door opens. Claudia saunters in, shakes off the rain, turns her nose up at her food and snuggles in with the dog. The little black cat can also open doors. She's less good at closing them. She leaves that to me.

The large envelope contains my final divorce papers. I pull them halfway out to get the gist and push them back in. That's it. I am no longer Mrs Turner. How does Mike feel? Happy? Sad? Or vaguely vacant, like me. I poke the document between some cookbooks on the dresser.

Next, the official-looking letter. This is closely typed from a solicitor's firm called Thorisson's. When I've read the first line of each paragraph, I slot it with my decree absolute.

My heart hurts. I thought the cottage was safely mine. Now this. I open the kitchen door and stand in the cold, rain-washed air. I wanted to begin the New Year with a clean slate but Mike is taking me to court. He wants half of North Star Cottage. I have not read the letter carefully, but it seems he has some evidence that I am not the rightful owner. When will it end? Mike is not content with divorce. No, the selfish bastard has to try to take the only thing (apart from the kids) that I really care about. He's a relentless shit.

Ink grumbles. She's unimpressed with the draft. I shut the door and open the other Christmas card. It's an invitation.

Please attend Allingshire County Hall at 9am on January 6th for induction. Bring a packed lunch and a notebook.

And that's it.

Honestly, I'd expected something more exciting. But then life's not like the movies. Owls haven't dropped letters down my chimney inviting me to a prestigious school of magic. No. This is real life. County Hall. Packed lunch. Biro and pad.

On the kitchen table is my new diary. I mark the date in, even though it is tomorrow. I wish there was more information. Is this the first of a few weeks of training or a few days? They could do with a witch website. www.ww.com?

This news sets me in motion. I shower, dress and get the new stacker boxes from the cupboard under the stairs. Not only am I going to take down the Christmas decorations, I'm going to have a big sort-out. I find a charity plastic bag and haul all the boxes of unused decorations into the lounge. The plan is to discard at least half. Isn't that what the de-cluttering programmes advocate – getting rid of half to make room for a better life? Mind you, I've never seen Christmas decorations as a decluttering theme.

Brian, my son-in-law, took my daughter away the weekend before Christmas, and I looked after the twins, Sophie and Amy. Since I've been on my own, I don't bother much with decorating the cottage. A few baubles on a branch. Bit of tinsel here and there. Jug of holly. Poinsettia from the supermarket. The twins were thrilled to be given free rein, though, and turning my lounge into a tacky Santa's grotto kept them busy all weekend. We even went into the woods and dug up a small fir tree. I've watered it every day.

'Well,' I say to the tree, 'time to take you home.' Most of the baubles are on the lower branches where the seven-year-olds could reach. With the radio on, I ask myself if each decoration makes me happy. Apparently, things that don't must be let go of. If the neat police are to be believed, it is the only way to stay sane and tidy. The trouble is, most of this stuff has memories. My childhood and that of my children. I cry over cotton wool snowmen and squashed paper chains Belinda and Jason made. Blowing my nose on a crumpled paper napkin depicting robins in hats, I decide this job can wait another year. Anyway, the attic has plenty of room since I cleared it out. The charity bag is still empty when I drag the tree outside and onto the wheelbarrow.

The rain stops, and Ink follows me into the woods. I dig a big hole and plant the tree in a different spot from where I found it. One where it will have the chance to grow and spread. Since I've got the wheelbarrow with me, I collect sticks for kindling. I used to do this with my mother – pick sticks up in the woods. She was also a witch, although I never knew until recently. Now, my memories of her are different. So much that she did was witchcraft. The way she patted the trees and thanked them for the wood. The herbs she pinned to her garden coat to ward off evil. How she could grow anything. I replicate these many small actions as if she is here, teaching me how to be a proper witch.

Dark clouds bring the twilight early. 'If it doesn't rain, I'll come back tomorrow with the watering can,' I tell the fir tree. Ink trots beside me as I push the barrow along the dirt track. Being out of doors always makes me happy, and since I learnt they are mine, the woods feel like an extension of the garden. And like in the garden, I feel safe here. When the moon is full, I wander, listening to the night creatures and watching for the soft swoop of owl wings.

This evening, something tugs at the edge of my mind. Watchfulness steals over me, and I glance into the shadows behind as if I am being followed. Ink keeps close, ears pricked and hackles risen.

I stop.

Without the noise of the wheelbarrow on the path, silence surrounds us. No bird song or the rustle of small animals in the undergrowth. It is more than the quiet. There is a stillness too. Nothing moves, and my heart beats heavy in my chest.

'Always trust your instincts, Lilly.' These are my late mother's words, loud in my head. If I'm honest, I've spent my life ignoring her gentle advice.

Not today.

I run.

One stride on the path and another into the leaves, and my two left feet send me falling. I twist my foot and hit my face on the side of the wheelbarrow.

It is almost dark when I wake. The forest is noisy again. Rain patters through the branches, and a blackbird scolds my magpie in the beech tree above. Ink lies beside me, keeping us both warm.

I stagger to my feet. The wheelbarrow is overturned. I must have hit it hard to knock it over. Tentatively, I feel my bruised face. Slightly nauseous and lightheaded, I pick up my phone from the pathway. The screen has cracked. I put it in my pocket. I'm only wearing the pink croc. The blue one lies on top of some brambles. I limp over to retrieve it, and green eyes gaze up at me.

'Hello, Fox,' I say. She sniffs my hand to check I am alright and then slinks away without a backward glance. 'Thank you,' I say as she disappears into the wood. She is my secret familiar, and I know she had something to do with banishing whatever was after me. The last time she turned up was when another witch tried to steal my powers.

Maud perches on top of the sticks as I wheel the barrow home. She opens her wings for balance when we go over a bump. Ink trots in front. Apart from my sore head, everything is normal again – rain, birdsong, tree branches rustling.

At the cottage, I leave the wheelbarrow in the log shed. My head pounds, and I'm keen to get inside. Unusually, the kitchen is cold. The fire is out even though I left it burning merrily. It's much later than I realised. I re-lay the fire in the range and light it with a spark I snap from my fingers. I never seem to have any matches. All I want is sleep. I'm covered in mud and leaves, and my mind is clogged. I need a nap, and then I'll sort myself out. So I lie down on the dog's bed by the warmth of the cooker. Ink does not mind and snuggles up. A short woman and a long dog. 'Just twenty minutes, Inky dog. Then I'll take a shower.'

Chapter Two

In the morning, it takes me a moment to remember why I am on the kitchen floor with my dog and cat. Winter sunlight streams through the window. It's a good job I live alone. I mustn't go into the woods wearing two left shoes. One of these days, I'll break my neck. There is a niggle at the back of my mind about something I should have taken with me. Something important.

When I get up, my head thrums. A drink from the kitchen tap helps clear my thoughts, and I remember the creeping fear when I was in the woods. I breathe in. In the garden, Maud is hopping about happily in the apple tree, and the sky is a beautiful blue. It strikes me how late it is – and what day it is. Monday. I should be at Allingshire County Hall in Barrington for the witch induction thing.

Fuck!

Still covered in mud and leaves, I rush for the shower. It's only when I get out that I have the chance to examine my face. I look like I've been hit with a shovel. Hard. I am black and blue from temple to jaw, and my left eye is swollen and bloodshot. But more pressing than anything is that I am late. So very fucking late.

I don't bother drying my hair, just screw it up in a bun and pull on the first dress I grab from the wardrobe. Galloping down the stairs, I hear knocking. The last thing I need is a visitor.

Cold air blasts through the cottage from the kitchen, where Ink has opened the door and is greeting Grant Rutherford with her skinny wriggle dance. She dashes back and forth between the two of us. Look who's here! Look who's here! She's delighted. I wish I felt the same.

'Come in and shut the bloody door,' I say, grabbing dog food from the fridge. Late or not, these animals need feeding.

He touches the doorstep star with his fingertips and

comes in. 'Lilith,' he says, 'I've been sent to find out why you haven't turned up. You made a pact.'

'I know.' I put the pet bowls on the floor.

'What the fuck happened to you?'

'I fell over. Banged my head.' I touch my hairline, where a scab of dried blood has formed.

'My god, are you okay? How?'

'I'm late...'

'You should have been there hours ago.'

'Well, concussion will do that. Make you late.' And a bit confused, to be honest. I search around for Big Bag and check my phone. The crack is a small line at the bottom edge, it still works, which is something. I put boots on, which is not easy in bare feet. My hands are shaking.

'Let me ring the Coven. I'll explain you've had an accident.'

'I'm fine.' I pull on a coat and hat. 'Honestly, I'm fine.' I check the kitchen clock. If I'm quick, I will make the bus.

'At least let me give you a lift,' he says, and the hairs on the back of my neck stand up. Getting in the car with him is not my ideal plan. Then again, at this point, nothing is ideal.

'Lilith, it's okay. I'm a safe driver, and I've got to go back to the office, anyway.'

I am acting like a teenage girl. Handsome Mr Rutherford is unlikely to want to have his way with me on the back seat. Those days have gone. My mind is in a time warp. I'm a saggy, middle-aged woman that nobody notices, and he's only here because the Coven has allocated him as my protector or some such shit. We might be roughly the same age, but he is way out of my league. If I ever was in a league.

I take a deep breath and let it out slowly. Isn't that what you're supposed to do these days? Breathe? Isn't it supposed to fix everything?

'Is that what you're wearing?'

I look down at myself. I am, in fact, in a nightie. An old one that was Belinda's. Two cute bears in nightcaps declare they are 'Snuggle Ready'. This knackered old thing was probably on a coat hanger because I dried it on the hooks over the range.

'Put some actual clothes on, Lilith. It'll make a better impression. And dry your hair; it's freezing out there. Another fifteen minutes won't make any difference.'

Condescending prick. I throw the coat over a chair and kick off the boots.

Upstairs, I take off the offending nightie, dry my hair and brush my teeth. Slap a fresh HRT patch on my bum. I might be slightly concussed, but at least I'm not hormonal.

Soon, I am back in the kitchen in thick tights, a more suitable warm dress and a jumper. My long grey hair is dry and loose to conceal a bit of my poor face, and I have attempted to dab foundation over the worst of the bruising.

Grant drops a sandwich and a bottle of water in the top of Big Bag and hands me a cup of tea in a travel mug and a handful of digestive biscuits. 'I've stoked the fire,' he says, opening the door for me. Ink is wrapped up in her fleecy blanket and Claudia is beside her. I put the biscuits in my coat pocket.

Grant's car is parked in the lane, and I try not to spill tea on the leather seats as I climb in.

'Have you got your wand?'

I hand him the cup and rush back to the cottage to get it from the pocket of the garden coat. Is there something else I've forgotten? Nothing comes readily to mind.

He's playing with his phone when I get back and carries on while I put on my seat belt and stuff my late mother's wand into Big Bag.

The travel mug is in a holder on the dashboard. I'm still queasy. Even tea is unpalatable today. He tucks his phone inside his jacket pocket and drives off smoothly. I wonder who he was texting. The Coven, to tell them what a disorganised idiot I am and that I am unfit to be a proper witch? Or Theo, if she's still his lover? Or is he on social media, telling his many followers about every aspect of his perfect life? Glossy photographs of a healthy breakfast and artisan coffee alongside his workout statistics. Prat.

I'm not on social media. Well, I have an unused Facebook account Jason set up. But what the fuck would I post on it?

Slept in the dog's bed. #coveredinmud

Almost turning up to a meeting in nightwear? #winter-laundryproblems

I've put a new hormone patch on my bum, but did I take the old one off? #middleagedmadness

'So,' he says as we turn onto the main road that leads to Barrington, 'any particular reason why you don't drive?'

'No.' What can I say? My ex-husband always talked me out of it because he was a controlling bastard.

'You should take some lessons.'

'Bit late now.'

'You're not incapable.'

I fold my arms. Easy for him to say.

He drives on in silence, changing gear precisely, easing through the traffic and only speeding up when the road is clear. I sneak a look at him. Today, he is clean-shaven and wears a smart dark grey suit. Nothing flashy. No tie. But then he doesn't need one. His neck is great. Is he still shagging the oh-so-capable Theodora Grimshaw? The bitch.

The traffic in Barrington is awful, as usual. When he eventually pulls up outside Allingshire County Hall, I have butterflies. No, not butterflies, more like stones that are sinking fast. Last time I was here, things did not go well. Today, I wanted to make a new start.

The building looms, all Victorian brickwork and fancy windows. 'Where do I go?'

'Through the main doors. Someone will find you.' Grant leans closer and I shrink back. He holds his hands up. 'It's okay,' he says, 'I just wanted to get this.' He pulls a leaf out of my hair.

'Er, thanks. And thanks for the lift.' Briefly, I look into his dark eyes. He nods, and I get out.

A few tourists are milling about inside County Hall,

appreciating the architecture. I make my way to the welcome desk, although I have no idea what I might say. Before I get near, the same woman who greeted me last time I was here appears. 'Ms Blackwood?' she says.

'Yes.' I'm impressed that news of my divorce has already reached the Coven. I will have to get used to using my maiden name.

'This way, please.'

I follow her up the sweeping staircase. She is wearing a fleecy onesie patterned with parrots. I should have come in my nightie if bedwear is in fashion. It looks cosy and warm. Unlike the get-up she had on last time. Must be chilly when you need the loo, though – having to strip it all off.

We climb two flights. At the end of a long corridor, she opens a door. 'Have a nice day, Ms Blackwood,' she says as I go in.

I take a seat at the back of the small, empty classroom. Have I missed everything? I check the time on my injured phone and see it is lunch. Not just late, then. A whole morning late. Hungry, I eat the sandwich Grant made me. It's cheese and salad, with cherry tomatoes all sliced neatly and just the right amount of mayonnaise. He even bothered to grate the cheese. A much nicer lunch than I would have made for myself. Perhaps I should have told him about the thing in the woods.

There are voices in the corridor, and six girls enter. They are in their late teens and early twenties. They chatter away and seat themselves in the front. Another young woman comes in. She's in her coat and looks flustered. The others turn to her. 'My train was cancelled,' she says to no one in particular.

'The South Allingshire Line?' says one girl.

'Yeah. Did I miss anything?'

They introduce themselves and chat. Some of the girls cast a glance at me. But here, at the back, middle age renders me invisible. Soon, they begin talking about the invitation they received from the Coven. Turns out everyone had a unique and magical experience. Two girls heard music when the envelope opened, others saw a watermark of birds that flew across the page – and the girl from the late train told of a sparkly mist that smelled of flowers. They are excited and delighted. Perhaps the Coven didn't bother to give me a magical experience because I'm old. Or, and this is what really concerns me, am I not magical enough to have triggered it? I will tell anyone who asks that I saw a moving watermark as that seems the most common.

A woman, smartly dressed in a trouser suit, briskly makes her way to the front of the room. She's about thirty, although it's hard to tell these days. The young lady who just arrived stands. 'Hi, I'm sorry I'm late. The trains. I'm Della Green,' she says.

'Imogen.'

I stand and am about to speak when the woman, Imogen, says, 'You're Lilith Blackwood. I know.' She marks us off on the register and switches on her computer. Imogen must have been at my trial. I sit and try to pay attention to the presentation on the board.

The young witches in front take notes. I do the same, glad I have pen and paper at least. Well, I have last year's diary and a green biro. Not ideal, but better than nothing. The afternoon drags on. The young witches have questions. I'm not even following what's going on. I'm more concussed than I realised. At the end of the session, Imogen gives me a shove. I have fallen asleep with my head in my arms, and everyone has gone.

'Are you alright?' Her voice is crisp and without sympathy. I sit up and wipe drool from my chin.

'Yes, sorry. Banged my head.'

'I've printed out the particulars of today's presentations,' she says, tossing a wad of papers onto the desk. 'Please read them carefully.'

I gather them up. 'Thank you.'

'You missed registration this morning. You'll need to be here early so that we can get that straightened out.' She looks at her watch as though I'm holding her up.

'Yes. I'll be here.'

She nods and leaves, and I find the ladies' room and have a pee. My reflection in the mirror is not a pretty sight.

That's the trouble when you nap when you're older – your face stays asleep.

Chapter Three

The next day, I am organised. I have moved Alexa to the bottom of the stairs – where she is able to hear me from the kitchen and upstairs – and used her as an alarm clock.

Warm, sensible dress paired with thick tights, boots and a

coat. Sandwich in a plastic box. Small flask of tea. Proper notebook. Black pen. Again, I have the sense of not remembering something. In any case, it's too late now, and I push the thought aside. As per Imogen's instructions, I am early for the registration process. Once inside the large oak doors of County Hall, I hang about at the bottom of the stairs. The place is empty and I'm surprised the doors were unlocked. I wait, and when no one comes, I decide to go to the classroom I was in yesterday.

Perhaps it's because I don't drive, but directions are not my strength. I can always find my way in the woods and countryside, but streets, roads and large buildings always turn me about. The carpeted corridors all appear the same. Some have paintings and others have huge antique mirrors in elaborately carved frames. The speckled surfaces reflect my bruises. They've turned a shade of dark green, and blue-black circles have formed around both my eyes. Too sore for make-up, I am shiny. A zombie in a layer of aloe vera gel.

When I got back last night, I made myself read the printouts. Most of it was dull exposition about the history of witchcraft, which felt entirely lifted from a Google search. The important information was on page one. This said I was to tell NMPs – non-magical persons – that I am attending a course in business studies. It will take two weeks, followed by a basic compatibility test. Whatever that means. The actual initiation will be on the night of the Spring Equinox.

In two weeks, I will be safe in the Coven's fold. After the

incident in the woods, I know I need their protection. It's rattled me more than I care to admit.

Meandering along a corridor, I recognise the door to the library where I was taken to pledge my oath. Hoping there will be someone I can ask directions from, I go in.

Bookcases reach the high ceiling, and grey winter light seeps through long, narrow windows. There is a hush in here different from the rest of the building, and as I walk toward the round table where the Allingshire Coven's Grimoire rests, I hold my breath. The book is shut. The many entwined animals and plants carved into the dark red leather are beautiful, lifelike and tactile. Before I can stop myself, I trace my fingers over their embossed forms. The creatures – all of them witches' familiars, I'm sure – liven and flee from my touch until only three remain: a hound, a fox and a magpie. A little faded cat wanders into view, walks across the cover and disappears. Fox, hound and magpie face me. Expectant. Waiting. As if I have an answer to a question.

I am about to speak when I hear voices in the corridor. I step back and turn to face the nearest bookcase as the door opens.

'Ahh, there you are!' It is Ida Carmichael-Grey with another woman I have not seen before.

'There was no one about, so I thought I'd wait here,' I say.

'Indeed.' She glances at the Grimoire.

The woman behind her steps forward. 'So sorry. The trains...' She casts a beseeching glance at Ida, who ignores her and stands to one side.

'This way, please, Ms Blackwood.' The woman takes me to a cramped, windowless office in the basement. 'Please take a seat,' she says, draping her winter coat around her chair. After the timeless elegance of the old library, her workplace is ugly. I hope she doesn't have to stay in here all day.

'I'm Gina.'

'Lilly.'

Balanced on a stack of box files is a cheap electric kettle. 'Let's have some coffee, and then we can press on. So sorry. Have you been waiting long?' She spoons instant granules into mugs and hands me one. Her desk is so cluttered I debate whether it is more impolite to put the mug on top of everything or to move stuff out of the way. In the end, I plonk it down and hope for the best.

'I didn't really know what time I was supposed to be here. I was just told "early". Obviously not that early.' I laugh. 'Wasn't sure what to do. Wandered about...'

'Best not to,' – she finds her glasses and puts them on – 'wander about around here. Always best to quell the urge.' She's not joking. I think of the Grimoire and the moving animals.

Gina smiles for the first time. 'So, you're a midwitch?'

'Apparently.'

'Must be nice. Now your magic has finally arrived. When did you expect it to start?' She waits, biro poised.

'Oh, I didn't know. About witchcraft or anything, really. This is all new to me.'

She writes.

'So, you didn't know you would one day become a witch even though you come from one of the very oldest witch families?'

'No.'

'You didn't guess even though your mother was a lifelong witch?'

'I never knew.'

'About midwitches?'

'About witches, magic, any of it.'

She scribbles my answer with her eyebrows raised. Am I on trial? Again?

'You have a witch's familiar, a dog, is that correct?'

'A greyhound, yes.'

'Black?'

'Yes.'

'Any others?' As she asks this question, I see again my creatures on the cover of the Grimoire.

'A bird. A magpie.' I don't know why I always keep the green-eyed fox a secret. Claudia, my cat, doesn't count. Even the Grimoire knows Theo stole her magic.

'Good,' says Gina, closing her file. 'That's the preliminaries cleared up. Just a few guidelines to go over, and I'll let you go on your way.' She reaches for another file, finds a booklet made from thick cream paper and hands it to me.

'Now, we must work through this together. Do ask me if there is anything you don't understand.'

I hope it's not too complicated. My head feels full of wool. On the front is a flying crow and a crescent moon. The words 'Strength in Unity' encircle the image. She reads aloud;

'The Allingshire Coven was founded in 1598 for the protection and guidance of witches and those of lesser magical abilities local to this area. The Coven endeavours to protect its members from threats, both magical and mundane, as well as providing fellowship.

'Membership will be granted after a novice has completed a training period, known as the guidance, can demonstrate an understanding of magical safety and agrees to uphold the principles and rules of the Coven.

'Upon initiation, each witch will be required to offer a percentage of their power to the Coven's collective source, hereby enabling the Coven to function in a protective capacity. The amount donated will depend on the individual. Individuals with a higher magical spectrum will provide more, and those with a lower magical spectrum will provide less. All donations, great and small, are gratefully received at the initiation ceremony.

'The guidance and initiation cannot be completed without the participant's endorsement for the following Coven statutes.

'Every initiate must understand the difference between grand magic, small magic and forbidden magic. Without proof of understanding, joining the Coven will be postponed and/or forbidden.

'Grand magic may only be performed in groups of 8–13 with permission from three High Witches of this Coven.

'Small magic must be conducted away from the notice of non-magical persons (NMPs) at all times. Witches believing they have drawn the attention of NMPs must contact the Coven immediately with details.

'Forbidden spells are strictly prohibited.'

I turn the page, but there is nothing on the other side.

'The last page is blank for your signature,' says Gina. On the messy desk is a cracked pen pot. I take one out.

'No, Ms Blackwood,' says Gina, plucking the pen from my fingers and dropping it back into the pot. 'We require a magical signature.'

'Magical?'

'You need to use your wand.'

From the adjacent room, a voice calls out, 'Sorry I'm late. Traffic was hell. Bloody trains.' The door bursts open and in comes Theo with an armful of files. 'Could you be a darling and process these for me...' Theo stops, and we stand there. 'Oh,' she says. Theo has a new short haircut that emphasises her cheekbones. She's wearing slim-fitting grey trousers and a black turtle neck sweater. Christmas has not expanded her figure as it has mine.

'I'll pop back tomorrow when I have it with me,' I say, stuffing the booklet into Big Bag. Theo holds the door and shuts it behind me. I stand in the corridor, heart pounding. I'm not entirely sure how I feel. Angry? Sad? Scared?

Lost again, I start walking. The corridor leads to the staircase. At the top, I rummage in Big Bag for a tissue. I don't know why I'm crying exactly.

'Ahh, Ms Blackwood, there you are.' It's the young woman who shows people the way. Today, she's wearing shorts, tights, white knee socks, high heels and a fluffy sweater. 'Let me take you to the classroom.'

'I don't want to go,' I say, dabbing my sore face with the tissue. 'I want to speak to somebody. Somebody in charge.'

The girl stands where she is, her body moving subtly in time to the beat of music only she can hear. I point to my own ear, and she plucks out the earbud just long enough to hear my request.

I follow her through another maze of corridors. How big is this place? Somewhere at the top of the building, she taps on a door, opens it and gives me a little push. Ida Carmichael-Grey sits behind a large oak desk. She closes the lid on her thin, expensive laptop and presses her lips together. 'Yes?'

Like a child in the headteacher's office, I wish I was elsewhere. 'Why is she here?' I blurt, wiping my runny nose.

'Who?'

'You know bloody well who! Theodora Grimshaw!'

'Theo is a member of the Coven and one of our office officials. A role she has had for many years.'

'She's still here after what she did to me?!' And my cat, I almost add.

Ida turns her attention to her phone. 'Ms Blackwood, the Allingshire Coven endeavours to provide fellowship for all its members. Good, bad, old, young,' – she looks up – 'indifferent and mediocre. All witches, whatever their ability. You are not yet a member of the Coven. When you are, you may go through the proper channels and seek retribution, if that is what you so desire. Excuse me. I have more pressing matters to attend to. Fiona!'

The girl comes in. 'Take Ms Blackwood to her class, please, and no more nonsense.'

Chapter Four

The day goes slowly. I sit at the back of the class and try to concentrate on what Imogen is teaching. Mostly, my mind wanders. At lunch, I sit alone at my desk and eat my sandwich. I read the handout sheets about global witchcraft through the ages. The dull presentation and Imogen's monotonous voice are so boring. I doodle in the margins – a fox, a hound, a magpie and a faded cat. Claudia never did anything magical – apart from opening doors. Yet I knew she could and probably would. Her pale presence on the Grimoire this morning bothers me, perhaps because it confirms her lack of magic. Magic that was stolen. Poor cat.

I get out the booklet Gina gave me this morning. On the last page, small letters at the top invite me to place my signature *here*. I hold my hand over Big Bag and summon my stumpy little yew wand. It looks like an old stick – which, of course, it is. But pulses run up my arm and my fingers tingle when I hold it. I'm fascinated to know what a magical signature looks like. Do I write with the wand? Tap the page? However it's done, I have a terrible feeling about signing this. Since my magical abilities surfaced, I pay more attention to my instincts. Well, I try to.

Approaching voices make me stuff everything into Big Bag. The other students return. There are two new girls who tell the others they are late because they were on holiday. Imogen comes in, takes their names and declares that everyone is here. She says there is one more presentation and then we can go early. More papers are handed out, and she starts her monologue. Her words roll together. I've often heard it said that education is wasted on the young. Not this education, though; the faces of the girls in the front seats are attentive. I can't make head nor tail of anything Imogen says, and I am almost asleep when Elaine puts her head around the classroom door and says, 'Could I speak with Lilly?'

In the corridor, she leads me to a window where the winter sun shines, holds me by the shoulders and scrutinises my face. 'Lilly!' she says, giving me a gentle shake. I would like to go to sleep more than anything. Perhaps I should say that I am ill and must go home. Am I home?

'Lilly!' Elaine says again, but now I am sitting in a chair in a small kitchen. I cannot remember how I got here or why. 'Drink this,' she says, placing a tall glass beaker in my hands.

The liquid is warm, and good vapours of herbs and spices clear my head as I drink. It tastes of honey and lemon and something I cannot name. 'Hold this on your face,' she says, handing me a cloth she has soaked in pale liquid. The coolness of it is soothing bliss. By the time I have finished the drink, the fog in my head has lifted and I am myself again.

'Thank you. That's so much better.'

The doorbell rings, and Elaine goes to answer it. I half-hear voices downstairs and then a familiar patter of feet. Ink hurtles into the kitchen, almost knocking me off my chair.

When Ink has calmed down and is lying with her head on my foot, Elaine opens a biscuit tin and hands me a mug of tea.

'Tell me how you got the bruises, Lilly. Every detail.'

I move the soothing cloth to the other side of my face and recount the incident in the woods. 'I thought I was concussed,' I say.

'You were. Magically concussed. Very hard to think straight when someone does that to you. Happened to me when I was a teenager. You know how mean girls can be.'

'But why would anyone want to do this to me? What's the point of it all?'

'The thing is, Lilly, you are an unclaimed witch, and others would like to get their wands on your power.'

'I don't feel very powerful.'

'Well, it's a tricky business becoming a midwitch. You think you know yourself, your body and what you're capable of, and then everything changes. It can be an uncomfortable time. One minute, you're on top of the world, and the next, you're drowning.'

Ink is happily snoozing, stretched out on a rag rug on Elaine's kitchen floor. 'How did she get here?'

'Grant. He told me he was concerned about you yesterday. I would have come sooner, but I was visiting my daughter.'

'Thank you.' I drink tea and watch the kitchen window open. A large black cat saunters in and sits on the window ledge, regarding me with large green eyes.

'Lilly, you're going to have to start asking questions or you're never going to get any answers,' Elaine says. I know she's right. I just don't know who to trust. 'You must be exhausted. Grant said he's fed your cat and stoked the fire. So why don't you stay here tonight? I'm sure I can find you a nightie. How about a soak in the bath?'

I am wary. Theo was the last person I trusted regarding magic, and look where that got me. But I need a magical friend right now. The cat jumps down and Ink lifts her head. The two black animals touch noses, the cat wanders off and

Ink lays down her head and sighs. Her comfort in Elaine's flat gives me confidence. 'That would be great. Thanks.'

When I'm bathed and wrapped in a long-sleeved, pink flannelette nightie and thick socks, I find her in the kitchen slicing a large pizza. 'So convenient living above a trattoria,' she says, handing me a plate. 'Not very good for the waistline, though.'

The pizza is excellent, and we savour it. Ink is asleep, and Elaine tells me she gave her some of Oscar's cat food.

'Thanks,' I say. 'I'm sure she thought it was a big treat.'

Wiping her fingers on a paper napkin, Elaine raises her eyebrows at me. 'Questions, Lilly. Ask me anything.'

'I have so many. I don't know where to start.'

'Let's start with today.'

'Today. Right. I was shocked to see Theo in the office after what happened. It's like no one believes me.'

'Lots of people believe you. But you know the saying "keep your friends close and your enemies closer"? That's the real reason Theodora Grimshaw is still a Coven member. Between you and me, this isn't the first problem we've had with her. Next question.'

'The others in my class were talking about their invitation – and their experiences. You know, seeing moving water-marks and things.'

'It's different for every witch.'

'I didn't see anything.'

'Have you got it with you?'

I fetch the envelope out of Big Bag. Elaine holds her hand

over it, then picks it up and takes out the slip of paper. 'That's because this is not the enchanted invite you were supposed to receive. Looks like Theodora, who is the administration's secretary, sent you the wrong one.'

'Made me think my magic wasn't working or something.'

'Seems like your old friend still bears a grudge. You're going to have to tread lightly.'

She clears our plates and stuffs the pizza box into the recycling bin. It's not the first one in there. Then she sits opposite, waiting for my next question.

'When Theo was staying at mine...'

'Pretending to be your friend...'

'Yes. Well, I saw she had a feather tattoo and so has Grant.'

'Oh, we've all got them. Every coven has its mark and all that.' She pulls up her sleeve and shows me a feather on the underside of her arm. Exactly like the one I've seen on Grant's arm, Theo's thigh and the sea glass Ink dug up from my ancestor's grave. The sight makes me cautious.

'You've heard the phrase "feather in your cap"? When magic and witchcraft were commonplace, witches displayed their coven's mark. A feather in your cap meant you had the prestige to belong to us. In those days, most witches had a bird familiar. Ravens being the most popular.' Elaine leans back in her chair and folds her arms. 'And "to go cap in hand" – that's another phrase with origins in witchcraft. Witches who wanted to belong to a coven would hold out their hats to its members, hoping for an introduction. These days, witches don't wear hats. Hence the tattoo. They are not actual tattoos. It's more a stamp. Quick and painless. You can choose where to have it.'

'When does this happen?'

'At the initiation ceremony – on the Spring Equinox. Nobody has told you anything, have they?'

'I don't think my mother thought I would become a witch.'

'What, you? A Blackwood! I think you're wrong. Blackwood witches are one of the oldest witch families. Check out your family tree when you get the chance. The women in your bloodline were some of the founding members of the Allingshire Coven.'

'Really?'

'You sound surprised?'

'I didn't think my mother was a member.'

'Of course she was. Nobody in their right mind would risk being a free witch. Things are bad enough now – well, you know that. Back then, a witch's life was more risky.' Elaine laughs and gets up. 'Your mum probably had her feather in a more private place. Lots of people do. Right, come on. Let's get you to bed. You must be exhausted. I haven't got a spare room, but I've made a nice nest for you and Ink on the sofa.'

Elaine's living room is crammed with furniture, books, pictures and ornaments, yet it doesn't feel cluttered, just homely. Streetlights illuminate the flowery curtains, and the sound of the city is strange. I lie there with Ink, listening to the traffic. Whatever Elaine thinks, my mother was not a Coven member. I cared for her when she was sick and knew her body like my own. She had no Coven mark. No feather.

I click my fingers, and a flurry of sparks flick out. Tiny beads of red and orange light float and fade. I click again. This time, the sparks are green. Bright like spring grass. They land on Ink's black head. She doesn't seem to mind. Big Bag is beside the sofa; I hold my hand over it, and my mother's wand slips into my palm. I have so many questions. So much she could have told me. All my life, I have lived without the knowledge of magic. Now I am a stranger in a strange land.

Chapter Five

In the morning, Elaine draws the curtains. She is already dressed in thick tights and a tweed skirt and jacket. Her neatly curled hair is a pale green. 'It's my day for Poorbrook House. Volunteering,' she says, hanging a lanyard around her neck. 'I've told Grant to collect you at eight thirty and drop you off on his way to work.'

'Oh, no need. I don't mind the walk.'

'Sorry, I forgot to tell you. Today's class is at Kelsted Castle. Now that you've all signed your Coven agreement letter, a more private place is needed to assess your magic. Grant will drive you. I told him to bring you some clothes from your place,' she says, pulling on a coat of green fake fur. I'm unsure what I think about Grant in my cottage rummaging through my clothes.

The doorbell rings. 'That'll be him now. I'll let him in as I go. Help yourself to anything.'

'Thanks so much!' I call to her departing back.

'No problem!'

The thought of Grant seeing me in Elaine's flannelette nightie fills me with horror, and I grab Big Bag and rush for the bathroom. I quickly shower and examine my poor face in the mirror. The bruising has gone. All that is left is a dark shadow, giving me an unwashed appearance. I was a zombie. Now I'm a grubby old woman. Is this an improvement?

Yesterday's clothes are on the floor where I left them. God, I'm worse than a teenager. I can't imagine what Grant has brought for me to wear. Probably something inappropriate like high heels and a summer frock. I shake out the dress I should have hung up and wish I had clean knickers and tights.

Grant coughs outside the door. I jump. Bang my head on the bathroom cabinet. 'Er Lilith, I got you some things from your place. I'll leave them here. Tea?'

Holding my throbbing head, I thank him. He goes into

the kitchen and closes the sliding door, and I drag in a large bag for life.

Everything I need is in there, all exactly right. The jeans that are currently my favourite – the ones that fit. Big comfy knickers. My toothbrush. A hair scrunchie. A warm check shirt and my big grey cardigan. The socks that are thick but not too thick they make my boots too tight. And, even more weird, my wrinkle cream and HRT.

In the kitchen doorway, I wrap the cardigan around myself. Grant is sitting with Ink's head on his knees. He's so busy whispering sweet nothings to my dog, it takes a few seconds for him to notice me.

'How did you know?'

'What?'

'Exactly what I needed.'

'I don't know. But North Star Cottage knows. Which is just as well.'

'Just as well?'

'That place of yours has serious intruder issues. It still won't let me in. I'm only allowed into the kitchen to stoke fires and feed familiars!'

The rose patterned bag for life in my hand, now containing yesterday's laundry, is my favourite. Was the cottage always this magical?

'I made you some tea,' he says, opening a cupboard and lifting out two bowls. I sit at the little Formica table while he gets cereal packets and milk from the fridge. He seems to know where everything is in Elaine's tiny kitchen.

'You don't look so bad today,' he says.

'Thanks.'

'Elaine makes a good potion for bruises.'

We eat cornflakes and drink tea. He scrolls his phone while he eats. Annoying. Then again, I don't particularly want to speak to him.

'Thanks for bringing my stuff and getting Ink last night,' I say, putting my dishes in the sink.

'No need. Auntie has a dishwasher.'

'Elaine's your aunt?'

'Auntie Elaine. Yep.' He slots them into the machine.

'So that's why she bosses you around,' I say.

'No.' He jabs the start button and the dishwasher chugs into life. 'That's because I'm a thrall of the Coven.'

I've obviously touched a nerve. 'Sorry you keep getting asked to do stuff for me.'

'I don't mind doing stuff for you, Lilith. That's not what I meant.'

Oscar, the cat, comes in and rubs against Grant's legs. 'You've already been fed,' he says, scratching the cat behind his ear. Normally, I would move on from the awkward moment by ignoring it, but something Elaine said last night has stuck with me. Questions.

'What does it mean to be a thrall?'

His dark eyes meet mine, and there's conflict in them. 'There's so much you don't know. Come on, or we'll be late.'

'That's why I'm asking you. I'm not trying to be rude or undermine you, but I see the way they treat you like... like...'

'Like I'm a servant.'

I nod and stoop to pet the cat to hide my reddening face.

'There's your answer. You've already worked it out.'

I go into the living room and fold the blankets and sheets into a neat pile.

'Ready?' he says from the doorway. He's put Ink's coat and lead on. The new red one I bought her for Christmas. 'Got your Coven agreement signed and ready?'

I pull it from Big Bag. There is something that bothers me about the whole thing. Signing this. My mother's warning.

I sit on the sofa with the booklet on my lap. 'I don't know what to do.'

'Why didn't you ask Elaine?'

Because I'm not sure I want to sign it. 'Slipped my mind.'

He sits at the other end of the sofa and Ink lies at his feet and lets out a long sigh. 'I think you have to tap your wand on it or something.'

'Is that what you do?'

'I don't have a wand.' He goes to the door. 'We'll be late.'

I stay where I am, staring at the booklet.

'What are you worried about? It's only a couple of weeks. Get your feather in your cap, and then you're done. Come on. Today might be fun.'

'What if I don't want to? You know... join the Coven.'

'You are joking?' He stomps back into the room and sits heavily, his gaze intense. 'You're not serious after all the shit you've been through? I don't know whether you're incredibly brave or bloody stupid.' He waves a hand at the window.

'Magic isn't about fairies and unicorns and glittery spells. There is some serious shit out there that can really fucking hurt you. Dark covens who practise malevolent magic. You think that bitch Theodora trying to steal your power and whatever that fucking thing is that lurks around North Star is it? Lilly, you don't even know how to make your magical mark. How the fuck do you think you're going to cope without the protection of the Coven?'

'So far, I don't feel very protected. "Persecuted" is the word that springs to mind. And anyway, aren't you fucking Theodora?'

He laughs mirthlessly and stands up. 'What, that evil bitch? I wouldn't fuck her if I was drawing my last breath and only she could save me.'

From the depths of Big Bag, I summon the little yew wand and smooth the paper on my lap with my free hand. 'Am I supposed to write with it?'

'Didn't you read any of those books Elaine recommended?'

'I tried.' But the information was so dull, and attending those awful classes is like being a kid stuck in a schoolroom on a sunny day. 'Maybe you can't teach an old woman new magic.'

'You can't concentrate?'

'I'm sorry. You've grown up with this stuff, but me? Honestly, I was happy without it.'

'Did you fall asleep in Imogen's lecture?'

'I did. But I was concussed...'

In two strides, Grant is across the room, kneeling before me. He takes my face in his hands and looks into my eyes. His closeness is disconcerting. I can smell mint toothpaste and his manly aftershave. His hands are firm and gentle and my heart pounds, which is ridiculous.

Just as quickly, he lets go and stands up. 'I think you've been shaded. It's subtle but it's there. How long have you felt – you know – not quite in control, a bit confused at times?'

'Most of my life.' I laugh but Grant does not. He's deadly serious.

'Think, Lilly. When could you last concentrate?'

'I don't know. Ages. It's probably the HRT.'

'After you fell in the woods?'

'Yeah. I guess. But I didn't see anything. It was more a sense that something was lurking, sifting through the trees.'

'High or low?'

'I don't know.'

'Think, Lilith. Did the threat come from above you or more at ground level?'

I close my eyes, trying to recreate the moment. All I can remember is the green-eyed fox. 'I don't know.'

'Come on. Get your coat. We need to see Ida.'

'What for? I'm not going near that woman.'

'You need someone strong enough to negate the spell cast upon you.'

'What about Elaine?'

'She won't break any rules. A negating spell is tricky. Some regard it as grand magic, and that's forbidden.'

'What about you? Can't you do it?'

Grant laughs and shakes his head. Ink stretches out on the rug and sighs. 'Lilly, do you know where you get your power from?'

'I didn't know I had to get it from anywhere. This isn't killing me, and I'm sure it can wait another day or two to get sorted. Let's go before I make you late for work.' I grab my warm coat from the back of the sofa and follow him down the stairs.

'That's the trouble. You're not thinking straight.' He locks the door with his own key. 'Witches need to replenish themselves, like recharging a battery. It's different for every witch. What makes you feel better?'

I am vaguely aware that I've read about or been told this. It's raining and cold outside. I put my hands in my coat pockets and sift through the things I habitually pick up. A stone from the beach, a small fir cone, a sprig of rosemary, a tiny snail shell striped in black and gold. Somehow, these objects have significance, and I lift them out. My mother was the same. She gathered things, turned them over in her hands and put them in her pocket. A habit I have inherited. Each item has a small vibration – like static electricity. 'I don't know. Nothing in particular.' My head throbs as I try to understand myself. 'I like moonlight. That makes me feel... calm. The sea. I feel better in myself if I go to the beach.' I hold out my found objects. 'Maybe these bits and pieces. Nothing much.'

Grant smiles. 'Looks like you've got your answer: nature.'

'I suppose,' I say, sniffing the rosemary.

'You'll have to tune in – see which works best. What makes you feel strong. Most people have a primary source and a secondary source.'

Ink sniffs the things in my hand and pees on a grassy verge. Grant is standing with his face turned to the sky.

'Rain,' I say. 'That's your thing.'

'Natural water, yes.' We walk together. Cars swish past in the wet. Ink trots between us, ears flat against her head. She hates the rain, poor dog.

'So what's the other? Snow? Hail? Sunshine?'

'Sex.'

I burst out laughing. 'Really? Sex renews your magical energy?'

We've stopped on the pavement, and I peer at him from under my hood. He doesn't seem to think this is funny at all. Suddenly, I can't stop laughing, which he ignores. By the time I've got control of myself, we have walked as far as County Hall. He must have parked his car near here.

'I'm not seeing Ida, if that's what you think,' I say walking past the huge oak doors. He catches me up. 'Lilith, you have to realise that you're not yourself. When this spell is negated, you'll realise how weird you've been feeling.'

'I always feel weird. It's called the menopause.' I start laughing again. Grant grabs my arm and turns me about.

'What's your problem? I'm trying to help.'

'I don't trust any of this. It's all so creepy!'

Grant sighs and leads me by the sleeve into a café

45

doorway so Ink and I are out of the rain. 'Ida's okay. She's a bit old-school. But compared to others in the High Coven, she's pleasant.'

'Pleasant! I think she's a condescending bitch. You seem to have forgotten that woman presided over a trial that nearly had me...' I don't know what it nearly had me, but it wasn't good. 'And you? You were fucking strange and not exactly on my side.'

'Lilith, I'm a thrall. I don't have a say, a voice or at times my own free will.'

'You fix me if it's so important.'

The rain on his face runs in little rivulets over his dark skin. 'I don't have the strength, even in this downpour. This time of year is tricky. In the summer, I can strip off... And it's been a long time since, well, you know.'

I can't imagine he has any trouble getting laid. How long, I wonder, is a long time for him between shags?

We move aside as a young couple dash into the café, shake off their umbrella and pick a table by the window. I could do with a bacon sandwich and a pot of tea. Ink gives herself a shake.

'Well, pop and see me when you've had a satisfactory fuck, and then you can iron my problem out.' He folds his arms and scowls. 'What are you saying, Grant? You can fix this if you fuck me!'

I've had enough of this magical nonsense and push past him and walk toward the bus stop.

He catches me up. 'No, no. It doesn't need to be so extreme...'

'A grope then?' I'm walking fast now. If I'm quick, I can get the bus to Kelsted.

'Lilith, will you stop a moment and listen.' He's grabbed me again, and I look pointedly at his hand on my arm until he lets go. A sharp tingling in my fingertips matches my rising anger. He lowers his voice and looks at the wet pavement. 'I could probably fix you with a kiss. That would help. Just a kiss.'

I laugh and tie the cords on my coat hood under my chin. 'I've heard that before!' All blokes think they can fix you with a kiss. What am I, a Disney Princess?

Ink harrumphs and trots to wait in the bus stop with drooping ears. Poor dog.

For a laugh, I grab his coat lapels and pull him toward me. Let's have a reckless kiss in the rain!

He steps back abruptly. 'You're wearing a wedding ring.'

'Yes,' I say, giving it a tug. 'It's stuck.'

'I can't kiss you. Not with that on.'

'I'm divorced!'

'I know! But these symbolic things have power for people like us.'

Bloody Mike or Mitch or whatever my ex is calling himself these days. I'm not sure who I am more angry with, Mike or Grant Bloody Rutherford for giving me the come-on then rejecting me because he's superstitious. I really have had enough of men and their constant double dealing.

'I have an idea.' He marches on, and Ink and I follow him into the park. The last time I saw him here, he was jogging in the rain in shorts. Ink normally likes to trot around and have a good sniff, but today she plods resolutely between us. Grant goes past the main open space of the park and into the gardens. In the downpour, there is nobody here. We follow the winding paths between the herbaceous borders to a pond. Ducks, hungry in the winter, swim over, quacking. Grant takes off his coat and then his jumper.

'Can't you take a shower or something? Find a swimming pool?'

'It's got to be natural water, Lilith.' His shoes and socks are off and he's unbuttoning his shirt. The ducks are getting out of the pond and waddling over. I suppress another giggling fit. 'Grant, it's cold. Can't this wait?'

I stand holding his clothes with the ducks quacking around my feet.

'I can't let you go to class shadowed,' he says, taking off his trousers and laying them over the pile in my arms. His designer boxer shorts are tight and navy. I don't know whether I'm relieved or disappointed when he keeps them on. His dark skin is swirled with tattoos, and I can't help noticing his very nice arse as he leaps into the pond.

A few ducks take flight. He doesn't swim. Grant rolls onto his back and floats in the murky water. The rain beats down on his face and chest. Just when I panic that he's dead or something, out he lurches. I'm about to utter some banality like 'you must be freezing' when he stands so close I am speechless. He's so fucking naked I don't know where to look —definitely not at the only garment he's wearing. I'm still holding the pile of clothes, which he takes off me and tosses under a nearby willow, where Ink is attempting to shelter from the rain.

'We haven't got long,' he says, sliding his hands inside my coat sleeves so he is holding my bare wrists. He's like ice. Goosebumps cover his dark flesh. His eyes are closed in concentration and his lips move as he casts his spell in a strange language. Kissing him is very much on my mind. As is running my hands over the swirling tattoos on his shoulders. I pull back, but he has me firmly in his grasp. He kneels, taking me down with him so our hands are in the wet grass. A thousand tiny ants scuttle through my veins and I don't want them to go. They are a part of me, my friends. He's calling them and they answer, flowing down my arms. I must not let them escape. I struggle to free myself but Grant is strong, and his big hands force mine flat onto the wet grass. The ants rush to my fingertips and flow away, and he lets go. I remain rooted to the spot while the last few scamper free.

I'm shivering, and Ink presses herself against me. Grant is getting dressed beneath the willow. Embarrassment engulfs us as we walk to his car. It's been such a weird experience we don't know what to say, so we say nothing. In the typical manner of women my age, I carry on and try to act normal.

When we arrive at Kelsted Castle ruins, he drops me off in the car park. Ink is fast asleep under a blanket on the back seat. 'Would you like me to take her with me? She'll be warm in the office. I'll pick you up.'

The rain does not seem like it will stop, so I nod. 'Thanks,' I say, and our eyes meet.

'It's best not to mention this.'

'I won't,' I say.

As I leave the car, I realise two things: my head is clear, and Grant has broken magical law to put me right.

Chapter Six

The ruins of Kelsted Castle cling to the top of a narrow hill. On a fine day, the views across Alling-shire County are spectacular. As I climb the worn steps in the fine rain, mist obscures the scene, and the tourists are absent. I wonder where everyone is, and for want of a better idea, I head for the visitor centre. In the empty café, I buy myself a tea.

'I was supposed to meet some other women here, but I'm really late,' I say, tapping my card on the machine. The young man removes one of his earbuds and frowns. 'Did you see some other women? A group? I'm supposed to meet them.'

He lifts the countertop, stands aside and points to a door at the back of a small kitchen. A path leads me through the ruins and down a flight of rickety steps. This part of the castle is not open to visitors, and I wish the weather was better so I could see more. Stone walls rise into the mist, and I stop to put my hand on the grey rock. A large black crow with beady eyes shelters above me, in an arch that once was a window. Without a doubt, this bird is someone's familiar. Its unfaltering gaze sends a shiver through me, and I continue my descent.

This new magical world is dangerous. Now my head is clear and my thoughts are sharp, not softened with a layer of confusion, I know I need protection. I need to belong. The Allingshire County Coven is like any institution – it contains good and bad people. I will just have to find the nice ones. At the bottom of the steps is a low door propped open with a stone, beyond which women are chatting.

'Ahh, at last we're all here.' Imogen is sitting on the ground with her class. 'Now we are thirteen, we can begin.'

Her voice is cheery, but the look she casts me across the windowless, candlelit cave is like a scratch. Quickly, I set down my things beside the wall where others have left their belongings. 'I have already explained how thirteen is a safe number for witches. There are many reasons, which I will teach next week. But let's get started. Please stand.' Same bright voice. Same scratchy look.

While everyone gets up, Imogen comes over. 'Did you bring your declaration?'

'It's in my bag.' I'm about to tell her I have not yet signed it when she waves her wand at the bags.

'No need to trouble yourself, Ms Blackwood.' The booklet wriggles free of Big Bag and floats to a smart leather satchel that hangs from a hook by the door. The flap opens, and the booklet folds itself and slips inside.

'Right! Let us make a circle and not waste any more time,' she says, walking purposefully and taking her place. I will tell her later I have not signed it. Best not to cause any more trouble. I slot in between two young girls.

Imogen touches the ground and stands with her arms raised. She mutters words I cannot understand, and then she looks around the circle. 'Today, we convene with these new witches to ascertain their power for the collective good of the Allingshire Coven,' she says, injecting a ceremonial tone into her voice. Slowly, she lowers her arms. 'Each of you will demonstrate your magical capability. Each of you will support your fellow witches with the acknowledgement that all magic has value. Every witch has a place in the circle.' Imogen sits and crosses her legs and everyone does the same, though it takes me a bit longer than the others. Sitting on the floor is not something I engage in often. My knees click loudly in protest as I try to get comfortable.

'Repeat after me,' says Imogen. I try not to fidget on the cold floor. 'All magic has value. Every witch has a place in the circle.'

When we have all said the words three times, Imogen waves a hand at the door, which closes with a thud. She brings forth a small, white, unlit candle and floats it to the middle of the circle, where it waits just above the ground. 'I invite you to light the candle and more,' she says. 'Who will go first?'

Nobody volunteers. Imogen smiles. 'Fine. Then let the candle decide.' She points around the circle to us all and, lastly, at the candle. The candle floats to Della Green. She cannot be more than fourteen. She reaches out, and the candle comes closer. Her gaze ignites it, causing the flame to rise high until a radiant column touches the ceiling. The flame flickers and changes colour – red then blue, pink, green and many shades at once, a shimmering rainbow flame. The colours divide and become fanciful birds that fly about the room before they fade away.

'Well done!' I exclaim, delighted.

Della grins at me. But Imogen has started the chant and we all join in: 'All magic has value. Every witch has a place in the circle.'

Ten witches light the candle and create a small spectacle. Horses of fire gallop across the cave walls, flowers blaze and drop petals of molten sun, clouds burst with scorching rain and the night sky is painted in a million dots of fire. Then it is my turn.

The candle waits before me, and I don't know what to do. Every witch has not so much as moved a muscle or uttered a word. I reach toward the candle. It floats further away. All eyes are on me. I should have thought of something while the others demonstrated their magical ability. Instead, the exhibition overwhelmed me. So I do the only thing I am sure of. I click my fingers and bring forth a spark. One small bead of light. The candle comes nearer, the light bead falls upon the wick and a tiny flame flickers. I snap my fingers again, wishing for coloured sparks. Nothing happens. My little flame goes out and the witches chant, 'All magic has value. Every witch has a place in the circle.'

Chapter Seven

Imogen announces that for today we are all finished and we may go. Among the happy chatter, as everyone retrieves their belongings and puts on their coats, I hear two witches talking about me.

'I thought she was supposed to be a midwitch?'

'*Hoped* she was more like.'

'Probably just a hedge witch and never noticed her weak magic until now.'

Imogen opens the door, and everyone rushes off to make the most of their free afternoon. As they climb the steps, I am left alone in the room, wishing I was in a friendship group. When they've gone, I pick up Big Bag and my tea. Outside, the sun is shining, and I find a spot past the café to sit and admire the view. While the sky clears, I cup my hands around my drink and slowly warm it up. This much I can do. I have a packet of biscuits in Big Bag, and I munch them and drink the tea. A hedge witch. Is that what I am? I try to remember any other magical incident – or anything that might have been magic that I overlooked. Nothing comes to mind. This is a shame because I'd be happy to be a hedge witch: a woman with simple magic that she can use for healing and kindness. What bothers me is that I am a midwitch whose magic is already fading. A witch who will amount to nothing. Then again, maybe that's just as well. This whole witch business is a bit late in the day.

I screw up the packet with a tinge of guilt. Another biscuit lunch. It's four hours until Grant is due to collect me, so I make my way into Kelsted village. My head is so much clearer, and whatever kind of witch I am, I'm sure there is nothing I can do about it. But I can do something about my wedding ring.

George Newell, Jeweller and Horologist is a small shop

that has been in the middle of Kelsted High Street for as long as I can remember. A little bell tinkles over the door as I go in. It's dark inside after the winter sun. Clocks tick as I peer at diamond rings and pearl necklaces. An old woman comes in, wiping her mouth with a tissue. I must have interrupted her lunch.

'Can I help?'

'I was wondering if you could cut my ring off. Or should I go to the doctor?'

'That depends. Is it very swollen?'

'No,' I say, showing her my hand, 'just stuck.'

'Ahh, yes. That won't be too much bother. Let me get George.'

She leaves, and I hear her shout, 'George!' There are muffled voices and a man comes in, all smiles. For some reason, I'd expected an old man. But this guy is my age. Must be her son.

'Stuck ring?'

He is wearing two pairs of glasses – one on his nose and another balanced on his bald head.

I show him, and he takes my hand in both of his. His touch is soft and warm as he turns my hand and looks at my wedding ring. 'When did you last take this off?'

'Never taken it off. Not in thirty years.'

'Mnnm,' he says, giving the ring a twist and a gentle tug. 'It's stuck over the knuckle. Be best to remove it. Don't want it causing trouble. But I'll have to cut it. Is that OK?'

'Yeah, that's fine.'

He ushers me to the back of the shop.

'Take a seat, Mrs?'

'Please, call me Lilly.'

He gets a small leather pouch from a cupboard, spreads a black velvet cloth on the table and sits opposite. In the pouch are various small cutting tools. He swaps his glasses for the ones on his head and takes my hand again. George is one of those men who got better with age. The lines on his face are appealing. His baldness makes him look virile, and a frisson of delight fizzes through me from his touch. He isn't wearing a ring. Just a very expensive watch that peeps under the cuff of his dark, tailored suit.

'I think the best thing is to make two cuts.' He selects a pair of cutters. 'Thirty years. Well done you. Putting a piece in to make the ring bigger is easy enough. That way, you'll still have the original – just with more gold!'

'Oh, there's no need...'

'Or have a new one. Nothing like an upgrade.'

'I'm divorced.'

'Ahh. Right then. Best get this off.' He slides the cutter under the wedding band and cuts the gold as easily as a bit of string. One more snip, and my wedding ring is in two. Seeing it lying on the black velvet cloth, my bare hand next to it, fills my eyes with tears. I rummage in my pocket for a tissue. By the time I've got myself together, he has put the ring in a little paper bag.

'Thank you,' I say, standing. 'How much?'

'There's no charge, Lilly,' he says and comes around the counter to open the door.

I expect him to shut the door on me, the hysterical woman. Instead, he steps out into the sunshine. 'Ahh, nothing like the smell of the air after the rain,' he says. I stand beside him, and we look at the high street, which is getting busy now the weather has improved. 'Always a difficult time, moving on... So many memories.'

I nod, not sure what to say. He straightens his already straight tie. God, he's smartly dressed. I look like a cowgirl in my scrappy jeans and check shirt. His phone trills, and he takes it out of his inside pocket. He smiles goodbye and returns to the shop, saying, 'Mrs Nacklehurst, how can I help...'

I check my phone. The crack is growing, a line halfway through the centre. There are messages from Cressida and Grant. He can't collect me as he's been 'called to London', whatever that means, but he has dropped Ink back at North Star Cottage. I'm disappointed I won't see him. Maybe he's embarrassed about this morning and the almost-kissing. Thoughts of wet, naked Grant fill my head. I look at my hand. Have I had my ring removed so I can move on or because I want him to kiss me? My stomach rumbles as I walk. Turns out biscuits were not enough for lunch. Who knew?

Cressida says Randy Landy was asking after me and asks when we can get together. For a laugh, I text back 'How about now?' and she's straight back with 'Yes,' because she's finished work early. Ten minutes later, she collects me in her little car and we head over to her place.

'How come you're off?' I say.

'Because that bloody classroom heater has broken. Again. So I told your old lover that there were three choices.' Cressida changes gear and the little car lurches. 'They could get some heating in that icebox of a studio right fucking now; the students could paint me with my clothes ON; or I could come back in the summer.' Cressida laughs her throaty laugh and pulls up abruptly outside a smart apartment block. She grabs a bag of groceries from the boot and we go in.

'Wow, I love your place.' Her flat is on the top floor with a view over the city. The open-plan kitchen and dining area is modern and colour-coordinated in shades of grey. 'It's like something out of a magazine.'

'Thanks. It's usually much tidier. Jane's on a business trip. Big clean-up Friday before she gets back. I swear I'd be a slob without that woman.'

'Looks okay to me.' There's not a cushion out of place.

'Trust me, by Jane's standards, this place is a tip,' she says, flinging the last of her shopping in the cupboard and slicing a big loaf of white bread.

'Did you eat?'

I help make sandwiches and tea. 'What does she do?'

'Jane? No idea. Something to do with computers. I don't think she really knows, to be honest.'

God, it's good to hear Cressida's laugh. I could do with a confiding chat. But witchcraft is a hard subject to broach.

Instead, we trade stories about Christmas and I share that my divorce is finally through. 'And look,' I say, holding up my hand. 'I had to get my wedding ring cut off at George Newell's.' My finger looks weird without my ring. There is a dent where it used to be.

'Extreme,' says Cressida.

'Yeah, it was a bit. But the jeweller was quite handsome, and he had to hold my hand while he did it, which was nice!'

'Did you sell the gold to Jeweller George?'

'No. I felt a bit upset. You know, end of an era and all that.' Lifetime of hope down the drain. Confirmation of sustained stupidity on my part.

I find the little paper bag and tip the broken ring onto the white granite. The two pieces spin. Cressida picks one up and examines it. 'Engraved. Sweet.'

'Is it?' I rummage in Big Bag for my reading glasses. 'First I've known about it.'

Cressida hands over the piece she holds with eyebrows raised. 'Why?'

'Never took it off. Superstitious I suppose, and he said something really romantic when we got married.' I give my glasses a quick wipe on my shirt. It wasn't all bad. He loved me once, I'm sure of it.

'No engagement ring then?'

'Pregnant. Married in a hurry. Middle-class sensibilities.'

'I can picture the scene: your father holding a shotgun; your mother weeping; you in white a dress, the picture of innocence.' Cressida is laughing, and I don't blame her. It all seems so bloody outdated.

'No. No shotgun. I never knew my father, and my mother didn't want me to marry him. I think the shotgun was in my own hand, if I'm honest.'

'So what did he say?'

'He said, 'Never take this off, Lilly. No matter what. Promise me.''

'And you promised.'

'I was nineteen. Of course I promised.'

With my reading glasses on, I put the two halves together. The writing is worn but when I tilt it to the light, I can make out the words: 'Mike and Theo Forever.'

I drop the broken ring as if it's on fire. The two halves clatter over the wooden floor. 'Bastard. Fucking bastard!' I find a grotty tissue in Big Bag. Oddly, I'm not weepy. I'm stunned. 'My whole life has been a lie,' I say quietly. Cressida waits for an explanation. 'Theodora Grimshaw was my mother's best friend's daughter. We spent most of our childhood together. That's what it says inside the ring. "Mike and Theo forever."'

'Did you know they were...?'

'This is the first I've heard about it. By the time we were young adults, we'd grown apart. She got posh. Went to a fancy school. Did business studies at university. She was always scathing about my *plumber*.'

'But she bonked him, the cow!'

'Mike was always a two-timing bastard. But you know

what really hurts?' Now I do feel like crying and gulp in a deep breath. 'What really hurts is that they must have been together...' A big sob takes me, and Cressida comes over and hugs me '...before we were married, and he loved her enough to buy her that. He must have wanted to marry *her*.' I'm properly crying now. Snot and tears all over the place. Cressida fetches a box of tissues and lets me cry. When I've got myself together again, she pats my shoulder.

'Mind if I borrow your loo?'

'Through there. First on the left.'

I have a wee and splash my cheeks with cold water. My face is like an overripe raspberry. Bruised and red. I take deep breaths, annoyed that even post-divorce Mike has the ability to hurt me.

The bathroom is stylish. White tiles with a green feature wall and lots of plants and pictures. One is a framed poem entitled, *You've Got to Look After Your Tits*. I read as I dry my hands, and I'm laughing so much by the end, I almost don't notice that the poem is by Cressida Marchant.

'That poem is brilliant.'

'Ahh, many a true word spoken in jest,' she says, pouring tea from a smart white pot. 'My mum died of breast cancer. Gotta watch out for those lumps.'

'I'm sorry.'

'It's okay. Rich pattern of life.'

'Do you write a lot of poetry?'

'If you can call it poetry. When I'm not stripped naked and being scrutinised by art students, I write verses for greeting cards. Been at it for years – turns out I'm excellent at sentimental clap trap. 'Anyway, I think you need two things,' she says, going to the fridge. 'Well, three things...' She puts an expensive-looking boxed chocolate cake on the table.

'Three things?'

'Yes, tea, chocolate gateau and...' – she cuts me a generous slice and pushes the plate over – '... a dating app.'

'A dating app!'

'Yes, child!'

'No way, the last thing I need right now—'

'The exact thing you need is a good old-fashioned, life-affirming shag! Either I send Randy Landy a message, or you hand over your phone.'

I give her my phone.

'What happened to this!' The crack on the screen has two new lines from the top corners.

'Dropped it.'

'Right,' she says, taking a swig of tea. 'Name: Lilly Black-wood. Age?'

I tell her and she nocks off a few years.

'Marital status? Divorced, thank god! Sexual orientation? Boring and straight. Occupation?'

'Unemployed.'

'Self-employed.'

'Doing what?'

'Bed and breakfast.'

'Doubtful I'll have any guests until the summer.' Or at all. The Coven forbids it.

'You'll have to revamp your website – North Star Cottage is the perfect winter retreat. Come and enjoy log fires, bracing woodland walks and local attractions.'

She's right, of course a few tweaks and my B&B could work. Maybe I could appeal to the coven. 'I'll have to get hold of Jason. No idea how that website works.'

'Interests?' Cressida will not be distracted from her mission.

Witchcraft. 'Err, gardening? Greyhounds?'

'Dogging in nature!'

'Ha. Be nice!'

'Reading, walking and horticulture.' Cressida takes my picture, messes about for a bit and then declares, 'Right, you're in. Time to start swiping.'

We sit on the sofa together and spend a happy hour mucking about with the app. It's fun, but I'm not convinced this is how I will meet somebody. Then I see George, the jeweller.

'Oh my god, that's him!' I say.

'Ahh, there you are, Gorgeous George, remover of errant wedding rings. He looks nice.'

He does. In his picture, he wears a dark grey suit and a nice pair of spectacles that suit him perfectly.

Cressida grabs the phone. 'Business owner. Widowed. Nine children.'

'Nine!'

'No. Four children.'

'That's still quite a lot.'

'Interests: shagging. Sorry! Cycling, keeping tropical fish and the theatre. Lovely. You can cycle to the theatre on his tandem. He'll ask you in to admire his fish, and boom!'

'Cressida, no!' I cry when I realise she's contacting him.

'Too late.'

'He'll think I was stalking him.'

'Actually, we could. Shall we see if he's on Facebook?'

Chapter Eight

I t's almost dark when I get back to North Star Cottage. I feel bad about leaving Ink all day without a walk. The kitchen door opens, and she gallops down the path and greets me with mad enthusiasm.

The kitchen is warm. Grant must have stoked the fires when

he dropped her off. I add more logs. He's kind, that man. Behind his slightly arrogant façade, he has a caring nature. My mind returns to this morning. So much has happened today. Almost kissing Grant... The whole naked thing and the expulsion of the whatever-the-fuck spell that had been cast on me... Failing my magic test. Getting my wedding ring chopped off. Crazy day.

I eat cereal in the kitchen. Maud perches on top of the dresser with her head under her wing, and Claudia and Ink lie by the range, sleeping off their dinner.

I prop my phone on the pepper mill. The cracks are spreading. I have never bothered with social media. Thanks to Cressida, I am now on a dating app, and my old Facebook account has been woken up. As she said, social media is an excellent way to check people out.

I put Grant Rutherford into the search. The estate agency comes up. A smart page with many glowing reports from happy customers. There are pictures of him and his team, but he doesn't have a personal profile. Shame.

It's a bad idea, but I put in Mike Turner. The Water Works – his plumbing and bathroom salesroom – comes up, and then I find his personal page. Looks like 'Mitch', as my ex calls himself these days, is active on social media. I scroll through pictures of him raising a glass at parties. He's taken up sport. There are selfies of him in a black wetsuit astride a jet ski. Another holding a bodyboard on the beach. I scroll down and down. I don't know what I'm looking for exactly. There are pictures of him next to women, but it's hard to tell if it's anything serious. One thing is for sure, though: newly divorced Mitch is having so much fun!

Ink gets up and goes outside, leaving the door open. I pull on my gardening coat and follow her into the moonlit garden. It's cold and crisp, and ice glints in the grass. With my face tipped toward the moon I stand with my eyes closed.

Everyone was so sure of their magic this morning, including Grant with his replenishing natural water. The moonlight invigorates me. But does it renew my magical energy? Should I feel more than a slight sense of wellbeing? A rush of power, perhaps, or the sensation that I could cast a grand magic spell? All I feel is pleasant. No, not pleasant – more like content.

Ink sniffs beneath the ancient yew tree that grows beside the garden gate. I amble down the path and put my hands on the knurled trunk. This also gives me something, but it's different from the moonlight. Long and slow and old. I press my forehead to the tree, and the old magic that resides within comes to me gently, peacefully. 'Is this it? Trees and moonlight? Is this the way to charge my magical self?' I ask. The tree, of course, says nothing, and I wander back to the warm kitchen.

The next day, I arrive on time at County Hall. Maybe the moonlight and the yew tree helped because I believe I could cast a small spell if they asked me. As I climb the stairs to the classroom, the young woman who shows witches the way is waiting at the top of the first flight.

'Ms Blackwood, would you step this way, please,' she says.

She is wearing soft, furry short boots that look suspiciously like slippers and a bright blue, very short jumper with a hood. Somehow, I know she is taking me to see Ida Carmichael-Grey. Did someone see Grant doing his naked-in-the-water shit yesterday? Is that why he was 'called to London'? Or is this because I was entirely incapable of performing any magic?

Ida sits behind her large desk when I am ushered into her office. The only item on the polished wood is the slim laptop.

'Lilly, I see you are still inviting guests to stay at North Star Cottage.' She turns the laptop around. The rooms on the website Jason made are charming. 'Perhaps we didn't make things clear enough. So I'm going to spell it out.'

A part of me wants to joke about the pun. One look at her face and any attempt at humour shrivels and dies. Ida comes around the desk and props her skinny arse on the edge, possibly in an attempt to be friendly.

'For most of us, keeping our magic under wraps is a way of life. We are used to living our lives in two parts. The magical and the non-magical. Now I know this is all quite new for you and that you are – how shall we say? – blasé about the dangers you could face, to say nothing of the dangers you inherently cause other witches...'

She flicks her hand, and the laptop floats and stops before me. 'Inviting strangers into your home – which surely you now realise is an ancient place of magical interest – is inadvisable.' Ida grasps the laptop, shuts the lid with a snap and tucks it under her arm like a clutch bag.

'The trouble is—' I begin.

'The trouble is you are not taking magic seriously. I was informed of your tardiness yesterday and how you refused to show your ability.'

'I didn't mean to be late. And I tried to make a spell but...'

Ida takes a small step closer and stares down at me. It takes all my resolve not to step back. My skin is crawling. I want to leave. Now.

She drops her voice to a whisper. 'Couldn't or wouldn't, I'm not sure what game you're playing, Ms Blackwood, but mark my words: this has got to stop, starting with cancelling the bed and breakfast nonsense.'

I swallow. 'I'm trying to get some money together. My pension is going to be crap, and I thought it would be a good way to make a bit of extra cash. Now that I'm divorced.'

She goes back behind her desk. 'Sit down, Lilly.'

I do. Was this chair here before? The laptop is open before me.

'Remove the bed and breakfast. Please.'

It takes me ages to resolve, and Ida glaring at me doesn't help. By the time I've rummaged in Big Bag for passwords, called Jason for them and found the various sites where he has listed the cottage, I'm almost in tears.

'Sit,' she says as I'm about to get up. 'As I see it, there are a few choices open to you. If you're short of money, the Coven would happily purchase North Star Cottage and its surrounding land. The money would easily provide you with a pension. And' – she holds up her hand so I cannot interrupt

– 'as neither of your children has demonstrated any magical abilities, it would be wise to hand over this ancient site to the magical community.'

'No.'

'No? Well, give it some thought. Your children – your non-magical children – will be inheriting a place of considerable danger. Have you thought of that? There is also the option of bequeathing the property to the ACC in your will.' She arches an eyebrow and stands.

I scrabble for Big Bag and dash to the door.

'In the meantime, you might think about getting a job. That's what most people do when they need money.'

Chapter Nine

I 'm late for class. Imogen does not acknowledge me as I take my seat at the back. Once again, she is teaching us about the benefits and history of the Allingshire County Coven. Even if I wasn't fuming after my encounter with Ida Carmichael-Grey, I wouldn't be able to concentrate on this boring stuff. Despite my newly cleared mind, I am unreceptive to Imogen's monotone. Under the desk, I search for a job on my phone. At lunch, alone in the classroom, I ring a clearing company. The woman sounds nice and invites me to 'pop in' the office this evening. I don't tell her I cannot drive – and as luck would have it, the 'Sparklatious' office is near County Hall.

At the end of the day, I am relieved the rest of our 'learning' will be online. Imogen hands out leaflets with the log-on information. We must complete the course and submit it – and she cannot stress this point enough – before the initiation ceremony on the Spring Equinox.

Outside, it is cold and almost dark as I walk to the Sparklatious office with the help of Google Maps. I find the door in a side street between a sandwich shop and a launderette and press the intercom. 'Oh, hi. I'm Lilly. I called earlier.'

The door buzzes, and I climb the filthy stairs. A woman about my age greets me at the top. 'Hello, love! Glad you made it. I'm Sheila. I thought by your voice you were older.'

Oh god, even my voice is getting old.

'I could do with somebody mature.' She laughs and coughs. 'Thing is, these young girls... They're delightful. But sometimes what's needed is someone who's actually cleaned a house!' She laughs and coughs some more. 'Now, what can I get you? Tea? Coffee? Which is ghastly, by the way.'

'Tea, please.'

We sit together and fill in the necessary forms, and she explains the situation. 'Mildred normally does the house-keeping for the posh clients. She's, you know, our age. She's having trouble with her knees. Finally got a slot for surgery next week. Cancellation. She's already had the left one done. Great success. I get the kids on the office cleaning – because they can't go wrong. Empty the bin, clean the loos, wipe the computer screens. Water the spider plant. Easy peasy. But these single gents and ladies in their posh flats. Well, they need a bit more care. Somebody with some initiative. It's not just cleaning that's required, it's homemaking – and that, as you and I know, is quite a different kettle of fish. I expect you have a reference that you can email me?' She suppresses another coughing fit.

'Yes,' I lie and wonder if I still have a copy of the reference I got from the job I had before working at Dunwickes Department Store. My only ID is my train pass, but Sheila is not fussy and makes a photocopy. Then she takes my picture and sets about making an ID for me. 'Mildred mostly did the high-end jobs. Our more discerning customers. They like to think they're living in a hotel.' She laughs. 'One asked if we could do a turning down service. I told her. "Mrs Trinket," I said, "if you require someone to fold your bedsheets down of a night, what you probably need is actual staff." They've all been watching too many dramas on TV, if you ask me. Got this idea they can pay a pittance and have a twenty-four-hour service – like upstairs bloody downstairs.' She snaps the newly minted ID together and attaches it to a purple and yellow lanyard. 'But if you can do some of that hotel stuff, they do like it. Fold the ends of the toilet rolls into a neat point. Give the cushions a quick karate chop. Can you do towel animals?'

'No, sorry.'

'Worth learning. They love a towel animal. Makes them feel special.' She hands me the lanyard.

Forty-five minutes later, I have the keys to four residences and a job sheet. And a purple tabard with a big front pocket. I can't believe my luck. I start tomorrow.

The following day, I am up early, tackling my own chores and walking Ink. Then I catch the bus at the end of Church Lane to Marswickham. 52 The Sidings is a short walk from the bus stop. It's a medium-sized townhouse in the middle of a row of the same. These are listed properties, and each has a front door painted in Marswickham blue. There was a big hoo-har in the local paper last year when someone tried to paint their door black and got told off by the Allingshire Preservation Society.

Inside, the house is quiet and still. There's a note on the draining board:

Mildred, could you put the washing on the airer and if you have time to deal with the balcony and the Christmas stuff, I'd be grateful. If you need to add another hour on to your time sheet, no prob. Many thanks, Rob.

P.S. Just put the tree and stuff back under the spare bed.

I walk around the small, smart house, judging what needs to be done. A small fake Christmas tree is in the lounge. Next to it are various boxes. A balcony that leads from the bedroom needs a good sweep and tidy, but the rest of the place only needs a regular clean. Even with the extra jobs, I don't think it will take me the four hours I am contracted to work here.

When I have organised the Christmas tree and shoved it under the bed for another year, I clean the house, carefully doing any jobs listed on my worksheet. Wash the kitchen floor. Iron five shirts. Change the bed. There are a few house-plants sadly dying in different rooms. I gather them into the kitchen sink for a refreshing drink and pull off old leaves, then group them on a low table in the lounge. Plants are like people – they never thrive when alone. I sweep the large balcony and arrange the table and chairs. There are plant pots full of dry soil pushed into a corner. They look dead, but I can feel dormant life within. Once watered, I arrange them so they can benefit from the winter sun. Then I reward myself with a mug of tea.

Before leaving, I walk through the house, ensuring every-thing is neat and clean. I check I have locked the balcony doors and notice green shoots of spring bulbs peeping through the soil. I knew those plant pots would like their new position. Strange to be in the home of someone you've never met. Walking to the bus stop, I muse on what I learned about 'Rob'. I know the size of his shirts (16 1/2) and that he reads thrillers. He's no gardener. He eats expensive ready meals (bin full of M&S packaging) and collects snuff boxes. He's nice and is suffering from a long and lingering grief (photos of a woman who I sense is dead).

I have opted to work this afternoon as well so that I can have a free day tomorrow. I take the bus into Market

Forringtcn and follow Google Maps to a block of new flats off the high street.

Instructions say I must enter by a side door off the street. I press the buzzer and wait. A doorman in a navy uniform opens it.

'Hi, I'm from Sparklatious. I've come to clean Penthouse Two,' I say, undoing my coat so he can see my purple tabard with its yellow Sparklatious logo.

'Ah yes, Sheila called. You must be Lilly. Pleased to meet you. I'm Ted. There isn't a lift for staff, but you can use the residents'. Everyone's out.'

I read the instructions on the worksheet as the lift whooshes me to the top floor. Mr Waterman has his penthouse serviced every two days. On each visit, I must change the bed linen and do laundry.

I leave Big Bag by the door and dump my winter coat next to it. This flat is ultra-modern. In the living room, there are white sofas, glass-topped tables, a soft pale grey carpet and a long low window overlooking the park. A massive TV screen fills one wall, and the whole place screams bachelor pad. I find a laundry basket behind the door in the big bedroom, which houses a huge TV and a king-size bed with a mirrored headboard. Kinky. I strip off the white silk sheets and can't help wondering how Mr Waterman gets anything 'done' on such a slippery surface. A pair of lacy red knickers flies into the air as I shake the duvet. I toss them into the washing basket and haul everything into the utility area. As I separate the lights from the darks, I am struck with the familiarity of his pants. I hold a pair of Y-fronts up. Then some jeans. No. Surely not. I pull out the worksheet from the kangaroo pocket on the front of my tabard: Mr Waterman — no mistake.

In the bedroom, I open the wardrobe door and look at the shoes. Maybe this Mr Waterman is just similar. In the bathroom cabinet, two wiglets perch on their little stands.

Mike.

Fucking Mike.

I have to clean my ex-husband's love pad while he takes me to court because he thinks I owe him half my fucking house. I put my head back and wail in anger and frustration. Finally, I've seen the light and got rid of him, and now fate makes me wash his underpants.

I'm the one with no money. Not him. I have nothing. A bit of cash left from my late mother that dwindles each month when I pay the bills. And Christmas hasn't helped. Everything here is new and expensive — from the modern artwork to the all-wool carpet. I'd like to squirt tomato puree over everything. I'd like to slash his fancy bed sheets and shred his white sofa with one of his Japanese knives.

But no.

I clean. Do the laundry. Make the bed. Wipe the smears (foot marks?) from the headboard mirror. Blow dust off the white, fake orchids. Iron his fucking shirts just the way he likes them. Fold the ends of the toilet roll into a point. Karate chop (almost killing) the many scatter cushions in the lounge. As per Sheila's instruction, I walk through the penthouse before leaving to make sure everything is as it should be. It's then that I think – towel animal!

From the cupboard in the utility, I select the biggest bath sheet. Since my screaming fit, my fingers tingle. My magic is on the surface. I throw the towel into the air and wish. The fabric twists, turns and folds itself, although I don't know which animal I want. When I see what my magic has produced, I laugh. I set the pig on the end of the bed and stuff the red knickers into its mouth.

Who says I'm just a hedge witch?

Chapter Ten

O n the bus home, I'm still seething. What annoys
me most is not the fact that Mike, aka Mr Waterman, lives in a fancy modern home. No, he's
welcome. What I hate is that it's as if me and the kids don't
exist. There is not one picture of us. Not one. I can under-

stand he wouldn't want a photo of me, but his children? His grandchildren? Truly, that man is a bastard.

I check my phone, hoping that Grant has left a message. Nothing. We almost kiss, he strips naked and frees me from some weird spell – and then silence. I'm tempted to ask if he is okay. Then the memory of him shrinking away from me with some drivel about wedding rings brings me to my senses. I am a divorcee with all the baggage. I'm sure a man like Grant – his naked, tattooed body springs vividly to mind – can have any woman he wishes. No doubt he's got a girl-friend, and she's not only baggage-free but much younger and slimmer than me. And his implications about how long it's been since he's had sex? Well, how long is a long time between shags for Grant Fucking Rutherford? Weeks? Days? Hours?

It'll probably be Christmas again before I have any hanky panky!

An old couple get on the bus and sit in front. Through the gap in the seats, I can see they're holding hands. I want to tap them on the shoulder and tell them how lucky they are to have an affectionate relationship as they head into old age. Instead, I draw a star in the steam on the window. God, I'm miserable. My phone makes a little beep and I take it out.

The dating app is flickering with hearts. When I fathom out how the stupid thing works, I find a message from Jeweller George. Would I like to meet him for coffee tomorrow morning? Coffee. That sounds perfect. Not as scary as dinner or the pub. Just a nice coffee. What could go wrong?

The next day, I take Ink for an early morning walk as far as the beach. I pick through the line of detritus the last storm left and gather any plastic into a bag. Then I sit on the shingle and watch the waves, turning a smooth stone in my hand and breathing in the cold, salty air. Alone, I can indulge myself, giving in to the many strange urges I have these days. I take off my boots and socks and stand where the tide just reaches. The sea sends cold surges of power up my legs. Eyes closed, I listen to the rhythm of the water and welcome the sea's icy lick. With arms outstretched toward the ocean and the breeze in my hair, I recognise that here, with my feet sinking into the sand, something within me revives. My magic strengthens with each breath of salty ozone.

It's only when I am putting on my socks and boots that I remember my mother doing this same thing. Even on days like today when the wind was chill and the sea gave your bare skin a bite. The memory is reassuring. She, too, must have gained strength from the beach. But do I feel stronger than after the moonlight? Is this it?

I'm not sure how I feel about meeting George for coffee. And a part of me thinks I should cancel. But I have made a resolution for this new year: no more huddling in my comfort zone. That I am nervous is a good thing. Also, I have heard nothing from Grant. Not one word. So I make another resolution: no more hanging around for men.

Hard to break the habit of a lifetime.

Chapter Eleven

I've brought Ink with me. If he hates dogs, best to find out early. Besides, she's a superb judge of character. In her best red fleecy jumper, she is petted by lots of people as we walk along Market Forrington high street toward Page's Bookshop Café. George is a natty dresser, and I have risen to the occasion. My hair is twisted and clipped into a lovely French pleat showing off the beautiful white streaks. Under my winter coat, I'm wearing a soft red jersey dress. It's old, of course. Absolutely no money for clothes. I bought it for Christmas years ago and I'm thrilled it fits. In fact, it fits loosely, and the colour suits me more now that my hair is grey. I've even got shoes on. Not boots or trainers: actual shoes. I feel like a proper lady.

George is waiting outside the coffee shop, wearing a long camel coat. I'm relieved I don't have to go in first or wait on the pavement. I'm also relieved he's turned up.

He smiles when he sees me and holds out his hand for Ink to sniff. 'Shall we get out of the cold?' he says.

I take off my coat as I follow him through the bookshop to the café. 'Ahh, two ladies in red!' he says, letting me enter the café area first. I choose a seat by the window, and he puts his coat on the back of his chair. He's in old jeans and a check shirt with a frayed collar. I'm curious. Has he dressed down to fit in with me, or is he only smart at work? I pull off Ink's fleece and put it on the ground for her to lie on while he goes to the counter to order.

'You are a beautiful creature,' he says when he sits down, and Ink gives him a proper sniff. He's brought her a dog biscuit, which she delicately accepts.

We trade small talk: the weather, Christmas and holiday plans for the new year. No plans for me, but he always takes his mother to Scotland at Easter. How sweet.

The tea arrives with scones and jam.

'So,' he says, adjusting his designer glasses. They are

round and tortoiseshell with a bit of gold, and they suit him. 'Are you recently divorced?'

'Yes and no. Mike and I were married young. We grew apart. Been living separate lives for the last ten years, I guess. All legal now. The divorce.' I can't help glancing at the dent my wedding ring left. 'How about you?'

'My wife died five years ago.' His hazel eyes glisten. 'It's been a lot, getting over her. I can't lie. But you know, I think I'm finally ready to move on. Hence that dating app.' He shakes his head and smiles. 'You been on it long? The dating app thing?'

'God, no. Friend made me do it.'

He laughs. 'My son got me on it in the autumn. You're the first person I've ever met up with. I've had a few, you know, chats back and forth. Maybe because I'd actually met you. And you seemed...'

He butters his scone and smiles.

'What?'

'Normal.'

I've spent the morning replenishing my witchy self in the cold sea. Yeah, I'm perfectly normal. I open a miniature jam pot and offer him some. He's easy to chat to. Ink settles herself for a nap with her head on my foot, and I'm happy until one of the staff opens a window and a blast of cold air surprises me. Not on my face. On my midriff.

I keep my eyes on his while my fingers discreetly explore. The whole side of my dress is open. No wonder it felt so loose and comfy. I haven't done up the stupid side zip!

With Big Bag over my shoulder in the hope it will cover my exposed flesh, I hasten to the loo. The only mirror is over the row of sinks – too high to be any help. I can't see what I am doing as I struggle with the confounded zip. 'For fuck's sake!' I curse, just as a woman comes out of the toilet. She washes her hands and dries them thoroughly under the blower, giving me a dirty look as she leaves. The next woman who comes in is more sympathetic. Then again, she hasn't heard me curse.

'Here, let me,' she says, propping her slim handbag on the edge of the sink. Together we try to get the zip to budge. She pulls it and I hold the material together – or try to.

'You're too fat.'

That's what she says as she goes into the cubicle. I stand there listening to her pee. She's right, of course, but what a horrid thing to say. She doesn't wash her hands. 'Dirty bitch,' I mumble under my breath as the door closes. I'm hot, but I wish I'd brought my coat with me so I could put it on and cover up the white, dimpled flesh spilling over my tights. All I have in Big Bag is a zoo-themed plastic poncho.

In a cubicle, I strip the dress off, do up the zip and attempt to get the bloody thing back on. I pull and tug and almost fall in the loo. Realising there is no way this frock is going back on done-up, I take it off. Several hair clips fall into the toilet as my hair makes a bid for freedom.

Other women are using the facilities. Toilets flush and the hand dryer whirs while I struggle on in silence. Now the zip won't open. I put the seat down and sit. Breathe deeply and summon the yew wand from Big Bag. I don't know a spell to fix a wayward dress, so I close my eyes and envisage the zip working and me in the dress with the zip done up while I move the wand up and down the fabric.

Real magic is not like the movies. The zip is still stuck, and I am naked while a bloke I hardly know waits for me in a café with my dog. He must think I'm having a massive shit! Big Bag provides a tiny pair of nail scissors and I cut the damn dress down the neckline. Because let's face it, this cursed garment is going straight in the bin when I get home. I get the dress back on, which is a massive struggle because I'm so bloody hot. Then I find a safety pin and do what I can to close the huge gap I have cut and retain some modesty in the boob area.

Finally, I leave the ladies' toilet. On my left, outside a door to the kitchen, is a long table stacked with trays of dirty dishes and teapots. I can't resist pinching an empty miniature jam jar as I contemplate making a dash for it. The thought is tempting, and I'm sure I could get Ink to find me. She managed it on a dark, rainy night miles from home, and she can slip her leash, no problem.

Three women budge past on their way to the loo. I'm like a rabbit in the headlights. I want to run – but cannot. George is a nice man, and I must get over my embarrassment. There's no point hurting someone's feelings just because I feel like a prat. I put a big smile on my face and concoct a story about how I bumped into an old friend and couldn't get away. In the café, our table is occupied by a mother and a toddler.

Have I been gone that long? He's done a runner – probably thinking I'd done a runner!

'Lilly!' George is in the bookshop, holding up Ink's collar and lead. He looks mortified. I weave between the crowds to get to him. Why is this place so busy?

'Your dog! She was quite happy, then she ran off. I think she went looking for you.'

She does that.

'I don't know if she went outside? I looked down the street and asked people...'

'Don't worry. I'll call her. I'm sure she hasn't gone far.'

'I thought you'd gone off. Then I thought, don't be silly, George, she wouldn't leave her beautiful dog.'

'Oh, sorry. Bumped into an old friend, got chatting.' I take my coat from him and put it on. 'I expect Ink's gone outside.' A bead of sweat trickles down my forehead. We can't get through the door because so many people are trying to come in. George stands politely to one side to let them pass, and I hear a familiar sound: Ink's happy growl. The one she reserves for those she really likes.

Crash! A display topples over, sending green paperbacks everywhere. I head toward the commotion, and sure enough, Ink is leaping about with joy because she's found Grant. I push through the people on their way to a meet-the-author event at the back of the bookshop. Grant, who is trying to calm Ink, spots me and smiles with relief.

Bystanders are trying to avoid the huge, growling greyhound in their midst. 'She's not nasty,' I say to a young couple clutching each other in terror. 'Look at her waggy tail.' Grant makes a grab for her. Not a chance. Ink is mischievous and slinks away between the book stacks.

When I spot who the author is, it's too late. Theo is sitting at a table signing her new book. Grant mutters something, which I assume is some magic directed at Ink. This usually works a treat, but not today. Ink is impervious to any command, magical or otherwise. Her head pops around a bookcase behind Theo. Grant and I are calling her. People are scattering. Ink leaps onto Theo's table with admirable agility and shreds the book she is signing. Torn paper flies like confetti and Theo, pen in hand, screams like a princess. The bitch. Cameras flash as I walk calmly over and put Ink's collar and lead on.

As we leave – Ink trotting beside me, book in mouth, tail in a happy hook – the crowd silently parts.

I'm glad of the cold blast of outside air, but Ink is not. I take her red fleece off George and turn to Grant, who has followed us onto the street. 'This is George Newell. George, this is...'

Grant steps forward, shakes hands and introduces himself. Then he sneezes loudly into a cotton handkerchief. The two men don't know what to say to each other. And Grant is glancing into the bookshop. He's clearly on some task for the Coven. Either that or he *is* seeing Theo. Lying bastard.

'Well. Nice to meet you,' says Grant, stifling another sneeze and wiping his nose. He nods and goes back into the bookshop. It's only then that I notice George is holding a copy of Theo's book. The cover is a photoshopped portrait of her with the title *Confessions of a Personal Assistant*.

George laughs. 'Must admit, had an ulterior motive for coming here today.' He waggles the book at me. 'Can't wait to get Ms Grimshaw's signature. Can you believe she lives round here?'

I'm left on the pavement with Ink, who is shaking the book vigorously to make sure it's dead.

Chapter Twelve

After the bookshop incident and the disappointing date with Jeweller George, I keep busy with the online witchcraft course. I hardly check my phone except to see if the kids are okay. No news is good news. Two days later, on the bus to work, I open the dating app.

Nobody else fancies me. No surprise there. Jeweller

George is giving me a wide berth, and who can blame him? And Grant Fucking Rutherford? Not a thing. But I do hear from Mike; he has left me a patronising voicemail informing me that 'we' must rectify the problem of selling the cottage. He doesn't want to take me to court even though his lawyer recommends this. We *need* to have a little chat and put things right. He has documents to prove he has joint ownership of North Star Cottage, and getting it on the market ASAP would be advisable. The message is clear, like he's reading it out. Good job I'm not cleaning his penthouse until this afternoon. Right now, I'd cut the sleeves off his suits like some psychopath ex-wife in a movie.

At Rob's house, a note on the draining board thanks Mildred for the new houseplants. I'd only watered and positioned them for growth. In the living room, the abundant plants look like replacements. Even the bulbs in the pots on the balcony are almost in bloom despite the cold. I don't notice any magic leaving me as I water them, but they're even bigger when the housework is finished. More proof that I have no control of my power.

When I arrive at the penthouse in my purple tabard, I'm still angry. Ted, the doorman, tells me I cannot use the lift because some residents are *at home*. The climb does not help my temper, and I fear I may do damage to Mike's belongings after all. I will tell Sheila the truth. It's the way forward. This is my ex-husband's apartment. I'm dangerously close to emptying the bin onto the white sofas and chopping the heads off his fake fucking orchids with his fancy Japanese knives.

The lock clicks and I stand in the quiet, dropping Big Bag to the floor. The hallway has no windows. Was it this gloomy before? I reach for the switch and stop. Strands of dark green smoke cling to the edges of the floor. I take a step, and they swirl from my movement. I bend down, trailing my fingers through the thin lines, and they disperse. There is nothing on my hand, yet I feel as if I have touched grease.

There is no smoke in the bedroom, but a murky smudge floats at the corners of the ceiling in the lounge. The large windows make it harder to see, but when I scrunch my eyes, there are tendrils on the sofa and beneath the glass-topped table. Somebody with magical powers has been in Mike's flat. I can't think of any other explanation.

Mike doesn't have a teapot. He has posh tea bags with tags and an expensive tin of biscuits. I carry the tin and the tall white mug and sit in the lounge. I need to think.

Moving about in the flat has dispersed the strange light. I know it's something to do with magic. But what exactly? I have completed two modules of the online witchcraft course. I was pleased with myself. Now, faced with something magical I don't understand, I'm sure of one thing: the Allingshire County Coven is teaching me absolutely nothing. If I want to learn – really learn – I must teach myself. The question is, how?

Grant is no use. I think he's on my side and he'd like to help, but he's tied to the Coven. That goes for Elaine as well.

She is too immersed in the establishment to believe something could be wrong, even if I explain that my needs as a new witch are not being met.

I've eaten all the biscuits. Hey ho. I put the mug in the dishwasher and the empty tin in the cupboard. He'll probably think one of his shagging partners got hungry. Bless.

I change the bedding. There's more underwear. Pink, lacy, crotchless knickers. They look scratchy; no wonder she left them behind. I put a wash on, clean the flat and iron his shirts. I'm starting up the fancy vacuum cleaner when I remember the old Grimoire in the library at County Hall. My familiars appeared on the cover – a hound, a magpie, a fox and a cat – as if the Grimoire knew me. I switch off the vacuum and stare into space. I read something in a section of the course entitled *Coven Requirements*: every witch must give a spell to the collective Grimoire. When I saw this, my worry was, what spell? I have no spells to donate. My magic is... what exactly? Instinctual? Organic? It only happens when I'm emotional. Every spell I've cast so far was another's. But the Grimoire knew me enough to show me my familiars – and nobody knows about the green-eyed fox. If it knew me, did it know my mother, and did she contribute a spell to it? Was she once a member of the Coven as Elaine says? A coven that she warned me against? If so, her magic will be in the book. Would the Grimoire show me her spell?

The posh vacuum has an automatic retractable cord. 'You could do with this for your dick, Mike,' I say.

Chapter Thirteen

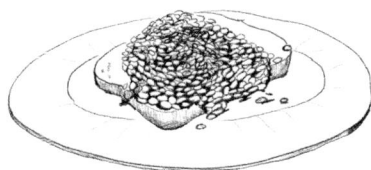

G etting my hands on the Allingshire County Coven Grimoire is my new obsession. Sparklatious does not require my skill set today, so I sit in the kitchen eating toast in my dressing gown. That day I wandered into the library at County Hall was definitely a fluke. If I want to get in there again, I'm going to have to think of something.

Ink woofs. Two police officers are coming up the path. I kneel next to Ink's bed and gently put my hand over her long snoot, remembering the nonsense in the bookshop. 'Shh, Ink. Don't make a sound.'

A knock on the door. Ink leaps up and barks.

'Mrs Turner!' says a policeman. 'We need to talk to you about your dog!'

Ink is barking, and I can't stop her. She's big, and from the other side of the door, she probably sounds dangerous. All I can do is pretend I'm out. Ink has other plans and goes to the door – which opens.

'Mrs Turner?'

I wish I wasn't wearing this old dressing gown. 'No. I was. Divorced now. I'm Lilly Blackwood.' Again.

'Ahh.' He makes a note on his clipboard. Is he old enough to be a policeman? Looks like he's in fancy dress to me. The other officer, a woman, is wandering around my garden.

'I understand you were recently at Page's Bookshop Café with your dog.'

I nod. No point denying it.

'And is this your dog, Ms, er, Blackwood?' He points at her with his pen. 'Your only dog?'

Ink has turned white.

Entirely white.

The cold air has sent her to her bed beside the range, and

with her head on her front paws, she thumps her tail in greeting.

'Yes.'

The young man squats and holds out his hand. Ink comes to say hello – and now she's old. She totters as if every bone in her body creaks. 'Oh, she's lovely. Is she a greyhound?'

'Yes.' Not just a greyhound.

'How old?'

'She's a rescue, so I'm not really sure.'

The policewoman, older than this lad, comes over, and they exchange a look. 'Is this your only pet?' she says.

'I have a cat.' And a magpie and possibly a green-eyed fox.

Old white Ink hobbles back to bed with a grunt.

'Has someone lost a dog?' I ask.

'No. There was an incident in the café. Big black dog ran amok. Tore up books, jumped on the table and almost bit a celebrity author. Did you see anything?'

'No. Looks like we missed all the fun.'

I offer them tea, but they can't stop, so I walk them down the path and watch them drive off. When they've gone, Ink ambles into the garden, stretches, shakes and changes into her normal, sleek black self.

I give her a dog biscuit from my dressing gown pocket. There's so much I don't know about what either of us can do. Ink is capable of more than I realise. My plans to get to the Grimoire should include her.

After a busy morning bossing the chores, I decide to go into Barrington and see if I can just walk into that library. I've even toyed with the idea of signing up for a tour of County Hall to get my bearings. But it's expensive, and I suspect they don't show the tourists where the Allingshire County Coven conducts its witchy business.

I'm making a cooked lunch for extra fortification when Ink woofs. A man in a suit is walking up my path. I take a moment to realise that it's Jeweller George.

'I hope you don't mind my coming over.' He stands well back from the door with a cyclamen wrapped in paper. Ink wags her tail as she wanders past him for a pee. 'It's just, I thought how rude I was – you know, going to get my book signed after all that business with your dog.'

He hands me the plant. 'I'm sorry…'

A man who says sorry!

'Come in out of the cold.' I quickly put the cyclamen on the dresser. Don't want it doing anything weird, like bursting into bloom in the next five minutes. 'Tea?'

'Please.'

I move a pile of laundry from a chair so he can sit with his back to the dresser, and I glare at Maud to keep her quiet.

'I was making some lunch. Would you like some? Nothing fancy. Beans on toast.'

'With cheese?'

'There could be cheese.'

'It's actually one of my favourite meals, beans on toast.'

I cut two more slices of bread, stir the beans and hope he doesn't notice I don't need to open another can. I'm greedy.

Anyway, who needs half a can of beans congealing in the fridge until they get thrown out two weeks later?

'No work today?' I ask.

'Half-day Wednesday.'

As we eat, he tells me the story of the jewellery shop his grandfather began. He has nice table manners and eats his lunch carefully, as if we're in a fancy restaurant. I make an effort to slow down and be ladylike.

'Did you get your book signed?'

'That's the awful thing.' He places his knife and fork together and puts the bit of kitchen roll I've given him for a napkin beside his plate like it's fine linen. 'I stood in the queue for ages, and the author wasn't there. I think she was a bit upset.' He glances at Ink sleeping like an angel in her bed. 'Once the staff had tidied up, she reappeared, and then that guy was there, the one you introduced me to. What was he called?'

'Grant, er, Rutherford.'

'Friend of yours?'

'He's an estate agent.'

'Ahh. Well, as soon as she spotted him, she went over and started shouting at him. Like it was all his fault.'

I'm all ears.

'You should have heard the language. Shocking. I think that fellow was shocked too. He just stood there while she hurled abuse at him.'

I must remember not to fucking swear in front of George. I take his plate and put it in the sink.

'Do you know what happened?' he says.

'Who knows what goes on in people's relationships?'

'I meant with your dog. What made her go crazy?'

Ink is on her feet. 'She's a rescue...'

'Ahh. Must have been a trigger for her. All those books. At least you know not to take her into a bookshop again.'

'Shall we walk? While the sun shines?'

We stick to Church Lane because of his expensive shoes. George doesn't strike me as outdoorsy. But he has his camel coat, which he fetches from his car.

We chat. He's pleasant company, and despite Ink's recent antics, he seems to like her. Even when she hauls a huge branch out of the ditch and smears his trousers with mud. I open the garden gate wide so she can drag the branch in. I expect George to leave, but he's in no hurry.

'What does she think she's doing?' He laughs, watching Ink take the branch past the cottage. She's taking it to the woodshed for kindling. I smile back and shrug.

'Lilly,' he says, his pretty hazel eyes crinkling. 'May I kiss you?'

I want to say, 'Hang on a minute, let me brush my teeth.' Too late. George has embraced me and is kissing me with a lot more expertise than expected. He slips his arm inside my coat and pulls me close so our bodies meet. Hello, George.

'Lilly,' he says, pulling back. He looks at my mouth. 'I'd like to make love to you, but...'

But what? He's kissing me again, and that's an impressive

erection I can feel, and he's certainly not shy about pressing it into me. He breaks away. 'Could we take a shower?'

My eyebrows raise, and I can't help grinning. This afternoon just got a lot more interesting. Breaking into a witch library will have to wait. Soap and water and gorgeous George naked. What's not to like?

Turns out George doesn't want to shag me senseless while I cling onto the taps. He meekly goes into the guest bathroom and locks the door when I give him a clean towel. Hey ho.

Because he's taking a shower, I feel I must. I get cleaned up in the family bathroom, opening the new body lotion Cressida gave me for Christmas. It smells divine and I rub it everywhere and hope it tastes nice. I'm excited, and my imagination is running wild. George is obviously a very intimate lover.

None of my underwear is fit for afternoon sex. The red kimono is... well, new, at least. I shrug it on. I look like I'm in an amateur production of Madam Butterfly. I take it off and opt for a towel artfully draped over my breasts.

I hear him drawing the curtains next door. Soon, he'll be in what was my marital bed. Strange to get in there with a different bloke. I almost giggle. Then I put my hand on the wall and have a silent word with my house. So far, the cottage has not locked him up or dropped a book on his head. Please, just let me have some afternoon delight with no funny business.

I go in. His clothes are folded on the chair. Trousers along the crease, shirt like it's come out of a packet. White under-pants and matching vest. This gives me the ick. Maybe he's on his best behaviour, I tell myself. I can hardly bottle out because I'm concerned he's too neat.

George is in bed, grinning. I drop the towel. He stares at my pubic hair, which needs trimming. Even naked, I'm not fashionable. Oh well. At least it's fluffed up after the shower. He scoots across and pulls back the duvet. Nice erection.

George. Lovely, clean George kisses me and kisses me. He has a little paunch but nothing awful. Some love handles on his hips. This makes me feel less fat. Kissing is his thing, and apart from grabbing a boob now and again, he keeps his hands to himself. George is a polite lover. When he asks, 'Lilly, may I enter you?', I giggle. Am I turned on or embar-rassed? Before I can decide, he hops out of bed, goes into the bathroom and closes the door. While he's gone, I grab a tube of KY jelly from the bedside drawers. Much like myself, it's old and a bit dried up. I have trouble getting the lid off. I'm using my teeth when George returns wearing a green knobbly condom.

'Would you like some of this, Lilly?' he says. I'm not sure if he means the KY or his bright green cock. He takes the tube, gets the lid off and squirts practically all of it into his hands. Plenty of lubrication. Good man, George. My legs part in anticipation. He sits astride me and massages my tits with vigour. His eyes are closed, and his green cock waggles up and down. I try to distract him. Pull him closer for a kiss.

Feeling like an ingredient in Bake Off, I grab his wrists. 'George!'

'I beg your pardon,' he says, smearing his sticky hands over the weird condom and wiping them carefully on the duvet cover. He gets between my legs and inserts himself into my vagina. It's then that I feel a powerful urge to fart. I clench. I don't think Mr Fastidious will be happy if I let the baked beans rip.

He finds his rhythm, and he's off. Bonkedy, bonkedy bonk. I clench all my internal muscles. What a world of good for my pelvic floor. I make my sex noises and grab his bum. I reach lower – tricky but doable – and grab his balls. They are smooth. Do men shave these days? I've never grasped a non-hairy bollock before. Nothing I do makes any difference. George is a fucking machine. Literally. 'George,' I whisper in his ear. I need a change of position, something to alleviate the tedium. Maybe I can pop to the bathroom for that fart.

Fucking George is lost in the moment. Good job one of us is. I hang on, not making a sound or moving, hoping he will realise I have lost all interest. Oblivious, George pounds away. I'm getting sore. 'George!' I say loudly.

'Alexa! One minute.'

'One minute, starting from now!' pipes Alexa from the bottom of the stairs.

Oh god.

Unperturbed by technology's rude interruption, George continues his mission. True to his word, just as the Alexa bot starts her rolling bleep, George brings himself to satisfaction with a manly grunt.

The bleep goes on, but at least George has ceased his relentless rutting.

'Alexa, stop!' I give George a shove and he extracts himself and the green condom and goes to the bathroom. Why do they bother putting knobbles on those things? I'm pretty sure no woman can feel them. Then again, it's probably for the man's pleasure. Most things are.

George is taking another shower. He'll be lucky. All the hot water has gone.

I fart as quietly as I can. Should I flap the duvet in case he comes back to bed for a cuddle? He's a cuddler for sure – so I flap.

As usual, I'm wrong. George gets dressed. Did he smell the fart or is he embarrassed about the Alexa thing? Who is she? His dead wife? His last girlfriend? He pads over to the bed, and I close my eyes, pretending to be asleep.

The kitchen door shuts, and I hear the bolts slide of their own accord. They do that. I watch him leave with his coat over his arm. It's almost dark and his headlights flash as he turns his car and drives away.

Chapter Fourteen

In the morning gloom, I make a mental list as I lie in bed. Call Sheila about my problem with Penthouse Two. Delete the dating app. No more one-night stands – or was it a one-afternoon stand? At least Mr Fastidious had a condom, so no fear of an STD. I don't think George would allow any germs to touch him. I end my list with going to County Hall and doing *something*.

Ink stands, stretches and flops beside me. I flick a blanket over her and watch the bare trees out the window. I should get up. Get busy. But crap sex, dark winter days and more nonsense from Mike about selling North Star Cottage has brought me low. I need to get a grip on my finances. Sparklatious pays low wages. I need another job or a better one.

Alexa beeps. 'You have *one* reminder. Meet-and-greet tonight at County Hall. 8pm for welcome drinks, buffet and dancing. Carriages 12.30am. Dress code: formal.'

I'd completely forgotten about this. Who has a bloody evening dress? Well, not me. I've a good mind to turn up in wellies and jeans. Why can't we meet and greet over tea and cake of an afternoon? It would be so much easier.

In my dressing gown, I open all the wardrobe doors in all four bedrooms and look through the rails of old clothes. I've barely got a summer dress, let alone an evening dress. I should've reminded myself a week early. Could have had a poke through the charity shops for something to wear. I sit on the bed, and Ink wanders in and puts her head on my knee. 'You're a magical dog. Can't you whip up a fabulous gown from these curtains?'

The house is freezing. George used all the hot water yesterday and the fires have gone out. It's another hour before I'm standing naked before the bathroom mirror. I'm orange. Not entirely orange. Oh, no, that would be simple. I'm streaked like I've been basted with barbecue sauce by a chef who didn't like his job.

I find my reading glasses on my bedside table and look at the cream Cressida gave me for Christmas: 'Tan 'n Glow'. That'll do it.

I shower, using everything at my disposal. Exfoliating gloves and gritty creams for problem feet. Silver shampoo for grey hair, which perks up my pubes but cannot neutralise my ginger skin. When the water is too cold to carry on, I dry myself and pull on warm clothes.

With a mug of hot tea in my (orange) hand, I speak to my spell book.

'How to fix a fake tan that has gone wrong,' I say clearly and open the front cover. Nothing happens. I attempt several more questions, and when it's clear that the spell book cannot help, I search for my phone – maybe Google has the answer. It's on the bed in the little room upstairs, and while I'm there I flick through the garments in the wardrobe in case I missed something. Sadly, an evening gown does not magically appear. Then I see that the door to the hiding place is open.

Inside, it is long and narrow. Both walls are hung with clothes. Mostly coats and a few tea dresses my grandmother wore. Ink joins me in the cramped space for a sniff. There are boxes and old suitcases. I have the feeling that everything was kept for a reason and, unlike much else in the cottage, should not be sorted out. I pick through shoes and boots toward the back. Soon, it is too dark to see, and I snap my fingers so I have flame between finger and thumb. My magic behaves when there is no one to witness it. Some dresses looped over a rail have potential. Sadly, my ancestor witches were slim. 'Looks like I'm the first chubby Blackwood witch,' I say to Ink, who is snuffling at a pile of blankets. The dust makes her sneeze dramatically, and I laugh. Silly dog.

I bring two cloth garment bags into the bedroom. The first contains a red beaded cocktail dress. Who was the cute skinny witch who wore this in the 1920s? Even if it was the right size, I'd need something to hide my marmalade skin.

The next bag has a man's dinner suit inside. Dark midnight blue. Double-breasted jacket. Velvet collar. Pink waistcoat with mother-of-pearl buttons and a white silk shirt. I can't decide how old it is as I hold it against me in the mirror. The next moment, I am trying it on, and it fits. 'Perfect solution for disguising tangerine streaks.' I tell Ink.

With heels, it looks fantastic. But I wouldn't be able to wear them even if I didn't need to get public transport. The suit smells musty, so I air it in the window. Another rummage in the cupboard turns up a box of old jewellery. Plastic pearls and coloured beads. Nothing worth money that I could sell to make ends meet. There is a pretty star-shaped diamanté brooch, though, which I like.

When I set off in the dark afternoon for the bus, I'm pleased with my outfit. With no shirt underneath the buttoned pink waistcoat, I'm showing a bit of 'evening cleavage'. I've fixed the star brooch to my lapel and fastened my hair into a French pleat. No need for a handbag. The jacket pockets contain the yew wand, my purse and lipstick. Best of all, my feet are comfortable.

Chapter Fifteen

The antique chandelier sparkles over the people milling about in the foyer at County Hall. Everybody is glamorous in long evening gowns and smart tuxedoes.

Music plays, and I'm so busy admiring the spectacle that

the doorman has to grab my elbow to get my attention. 'Tickets, please.'

I pat the pockets of my suit, even though I know I don't have a ticket. Imogen told us about the event. She clarified that attending was *encouraged*. That it was most important to 'show willingness to support the Coven from the outset'. She did not give us tickets, and nothing has come in the post.

'My name should be on the list,' I say.

'There is no list. Only tickets tonight,' says the enormous guy.

I look for someone I recognise. Everybody is a stranger, and my heart sinks. The doorman leads me by the elbow to another door, and just as I'm about to be ushered outside, a familiar voice says, 'That's alright, Dan. You may go.'

He loosens his grip.

'Thank you so much, Dan,' Elaine says, and he returns to his door. Was that witchcraft?

'I never got a ticket,' I begin, trying not to stare at Elaine, who's dyed her hair bright pink.

'Not now,' she says, smiling and walking me into the crowd.

'Lilly, do you know the Greens?' She introduces me to a couple. Their young daughter is in my class.

'Hello, Della,' I say, glad I remember her name. 'I loved your magical birds at Kelsted Castle. So pretty.'

'Thanks,' she mumbles.

Her parents exchange a worried look.

'We've driven from the north border,' says her father. 'Have you come far?'

'Foxbeck.'

'I don't think I know it,' he says.

'Well, Allingshire is the largest county in the UK,' I say.

Elaine interrupts and asks about Della's brother. As they chat, I watch people making their way up the stairs. At first, I am looking at their clothes. Then I see something else. Wisps of light, mostly from their feet. Puffs of smoke-like colour that fade as they pass. Some cling to the carpet, like the mist I saw in Mike's penthouse.

Elaine walks beside me when we take the stairs.

'Very established family, the Greens.'

'What is all this coloured vapour?' I point at the stairs, where purple and grey clouds blow from the people in front.

Elaine is wearing high wedges beneath her pink taffeta skirts, and progress is slow. The people behind us go past, and when we are alone, she speaks.

'Tell me what you can see.'

'There're colours everywhere. Like mist. Mostly on the floor, but some people've got it around them. And you. You've got it too. When you move—'

She holds up a hand, checks there's no one near and whispers. 'You're seeing orts. A manifestation of power.' She smiles briefly and pats my arm. 'You're a powerful witch, Lilly. Few can see the colours of magic.'

I'm excited, and I point to her feet as we move.

'Yours are pink.'

'Thank you,' she says. 'But remember, few can see it and it's bad manners to tell someone their colours. It's best you keep this to yourself.'

Doors at the top of the stairway open onto a ballroom. I stick with Elaine and try to join in the small talk as she leads me around the room. I'm not surprised friendly Elaine knows everyone. Ida Carmichael-Grey is with a tall, thin man. He does not have any orts that I can see. Ida has two colours – purple and white – that linger after she moves away.

The buffet looks delicious, and I pile my plate with ham and salads. Wearing a suit has the added bonus of a comfortable waistband hidden by the jacket. I reach for a crusty bread roll, keen to stuff myself with egg mayonnaise and coleslaw without worrying about looking bloated in a frock, when someone passes me the butter and I nearly drop my plate. Smart in an expensive dinner jacket and black bow tie, Grant looks at me with his dark eyes. Yes, he's handsome in his tuxedo but it's more than that - he has a glow about him. The only way to describe it is a gold shimmer. When he moves, he leaves a trail of swirling iridescent tendrils. It really is beautiful. I almost remark upon it. Then I remember Elaine's advice.

'Where are you sitting?' he asks. I nod at the table in the corner where Elaine is. He joins us, and I'm embarrassed that he has far less on his plate than me. Three old witches take up the spare seats. They are deep in conversation.

I almost take off my jacket. The pink waistcoat looks feminine, at least. Then I remember that I'm dressed like a bloke because I'm streaked like a badly painted sunset.

Elaine leans over to the other witches and begins talking to them, and Grant pokes his food with his fork.

'Thanks for what you did the other day. I feel much better now.'

'That's okay.' He glances at me. Is there something there? Something between us? Should I tell him about his gold shimmer, or does he already know? I'm about to speak when another witch comes to our table holding a plate. She says a few words to the others and looks pointedly at Grant, who stands and moves meekly away, disappearing into the crowd before I can follow.

I eat and observe the room. A band strikes up, dancing begins and my foot taps to the beat. Elaine, continuing her social networking, has gone. Now the lights are low, the orts are different. Those that were dim or non-existent show up in the darkness. Others do not show at all. There is so much I need to learn.

Ida Carmichael-Grey, tall and slim in a classic black gown, follows her partner onto the dance floor. She looks awkward, barely moving. Her orts have another strand in the dim light: a smudge of red.

Grant is also on the dance floor. Of course, he's got rhythm. He's dancing with someone. It's Theo. She's also in trousers. While I look faintly comical, short women never look sophisticated. Especially chubby ones. Theo's evening trousers, worn with killer heels and a sparkly backless top, are sexy and stylish. The music slows, and the singletons slink away. It's time for the couples to advertise their relationship status. Grant and Theo entwine, and he rocks her to the beat. His hand on her bare back, he mutters something into her neck, and she laughs. Bastard.

I can't watch. If I leave now, I could get the 11.30pm train. On the way out, I slip a few chocolate brownies into my pocket – and some cocktail sausages for Ink.

'Through the door at the end. It's on your left,' says a waitress as I leave. She thinks I'm looking for the loo. Probably a good idea. The train station toilets are scary at night.

I realise just in time that she has sent me to the men's toilet. I walk in the opposite direction until I find the ladies'. A full-length mirror makes me forgive her mistake. I'm a short bloke in a dodgy suit. No wonder Grant is posing with Theo on the dance floor.

I stand so long, feeling sorry for myself, that the automatic lights go out. I wave my hand to make them come on again. Darkness persists, so I snap my fingers for a spark. Nothing happens. My trial comes flooding back. My inadequacy and helplessness.

Within the walls of County Hall, magic is curtailed. Only Ida and the Truth-seeker had power. The library is different. I step into the shadowy corridor. It's quiet. The music has stopped, and Ida is speaking into a scratchy microphone.

Something about magical unity and a raffle. I had no money for a ticket, so there's no point going back.

On the floor, faded orts cling, including Ida's distinct strands of purple, white and red leading away from the ball-room. I know just where they will take me.

Chapter Sixteen

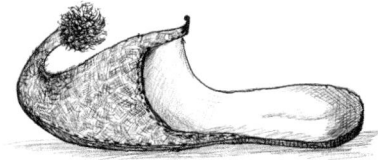

S ure enough, Ida's colours lead me to the library door.
I expect it to be locked. The door silently swings
open and closes behind me.

A low fire flickers in the grate, and the coloured orts of
many witches swirl around the tall bookcases and the wing-
backed chairs beside the hearth. On a table at the centre is the

Grimoire. My fingers tingle as I approach and place a hand on the cover. As before, the images etched into the leather move and morph until my familiars stand before me. Tonight, the fox is by far the biggest. Next is Ink. Maud the Magpie is small. Claudia is missing. No: she's crouched in the corner, small and faint. It seems the Grimoire is showing me who is the strongest. 'I'm sorry,' I whisper, touching my poor cat's tiny image. 'Theo took your magic, but I'll get it back. Just as soon as I find out how.'

In the quiet of the library, my breath quickens. A log in the fireplace crumbles, and I try to calm my anger toward Theo. Her betrayal cuts deep. My skin creeps with the sense of being watched. Everything is still. No one is here except me. I need to get a grip!

I place my hand on the ancient book and ask, 'Was my mother, Francesca Blackwood, a member of the Allingshire County Coven?'

I try to lift the cover. It remains resolutely shut.

'Show me Fanny Blackwood's spells.'

Nothing. Not even a flutter of pages. Either my mother was not a part of the Coven or this Grimoire does not behave like my own spell book. Some answers would be helpful.

I repair the fire with a fresh log. Force of habit. Then I meander, trailing my fingers over leather-bound spines and sensing the wisdom within. This library is so old. The books have been gathered from around the world. I read the spines: 'Rune Philosophy. Shadow magic. Ley Lines of Europe.' It's all beyond me. I wanted something more like *Magic for Witches*

Who Know Nothing on a bookshelf for beginners. Even if I find a helpful book, I wouldn't have time to read it here – and I'm sure that borrowing a book is forbidden.

Ida Carmichael-Grey's orts twist around a chair by the window. This must be where she likes to sit and read. I don't blame her. I'd do the same if I had a library like this at my disposal. Sitting in her chair gives me a thrill like sitting on the teacher's seat when she isn't looking. I almost expect it to do something. Spit me onto the floor or burn my bum. It's just a chair, though, and I sit and gaze at the bookcases. Is Ida to be trusted? I'm scared of her, but that doesn't mean she's bad. Probably it means I'm feeble. She certainly makes me feel inadequate.

I should go. If I'm quick, I could make the last train.

I mooch about and find myself inevitably back at the Grimoire. Maybe I should try again. Ask something it can answer – but what?

Voices in the corridor. I freeze. Straining to listen. Are they going past or coming in? I'm torn between standing my ground and hiding. There's laughter, and although I can't make out what they say, one voice is familiar. Theo's.

I duck behind the nearest bookcase.

The library door opens. More laughter. 'You go ahead. Got to pick up my notebook. Save me doing it in the morning. Meet you downstairs.'

Theo enters and waits until her rowdy friends have gone. I wish I could see her. There's nowhere for me to hide. All I can do is stand still, and hope she doesn't notice me.

Her killer heels click on the parquet floor. Is she going to ask something of the Grimoire?

'Mouse!' She raps her knuckles on the table. 'MOUSE!'

Ahead, a hidden door within the bookcase opens, and a small, thin man scuttles out in a red dressing gown and Turkish slippers.

'Do you have it?'

'You know it's forbidden in both worlds – making fake documents...'

'Spare me your righteous monologue.' Paper rustles and Theo says, 'Good.'

When the library door closes and Theo's stilettos have clicked out of earshot, I let out my held breath and wait. He must have seen me, but he returns to his door without a glance in my direction. 'Bitch,' he says as he goes in.

Well, that's something we agree on.

Clinging to the floor, Theo's orts are a pale yellow flecked with spots like frog skin. They're almost indiscernible. Interesting.

I tap on the bookshelf door.

'Mouse?' I say softly. 'Mr Mouse?'

Chapter Seventeen

The door opens. 'What?'

Mouse is small. Even I'm looking down on him. 'Are you the librarian?'

He stares beadily, his head cocked to one side. Of course he is.

'I can't find the book I need.'

He takes a large step and the door swings shut behind him and disappears. Must be magic.

'Sleep,' he says. 'I'd like to get some.'

'Sorry. Yes. I need a book about...' What do I need a need a book about?

Mouse raises his brows and folds his arms. His orts are pale grey, much like smoke, and are all around the library, particularly a chair at the fireside.

'What's the reason?' he says.

'Reason?'

'That I should help you, stranger. You don't bear the mark of the Coven.'

'No. That's because I'm new. I was attending the meet-and-greet.'

'Still need a reason.' He turns and takes a big step back to his hidden door.

'We both think Theodora Grimshaw is a bitch.'

He raises his shoulders. 'Have you moved to Allingshire then?'

'No.'

'You're a midwitch.' He faces me. Narrows his beady black eyes.

'Yes. Well, I think so.'

'You *think* so?' He looks around me and at the floor. What can he see?

'The thing is, I don't know anything about this witch stuff. Mum died, and I never even knew she was a witch until this...' I snap my fingers and send coloured sparks into the air like a cloud of glitter. My heart aches. 'God, I wish she was here. It's like...' I take a deep breath to quell the tears. 'It's like everyone is against me. Theo... I thought she was my friend.' I am crying now, which is annoying and pathetic. I pull out the neatly folded handkerchief from the top pocket of my jacket and blow my nose. 'A couple of months ago, I never believed in magic.'

'You should leave,' he says, glancing at the door. 'They've noticed you're missing.'

'Sorry.' More than his job's worth to help me. I head for the door.

'What do you want to learn?'

'Everything. Anything.'

'Come back tomorrow. In the afternoon. I can't give you any now. You can't walk out of here carrying magical books. Bring a big bag.'

I have one of those.

'Thanks.'

He nods.

'I'm Lilly. Lilly Blackwood.'

'I know who you are, midwitch,' he says, disappearing through his door.

Chapter Eighteen

I have no chance of making the last train and will need to get a taxi. An expense I could do without. I head into a ladies' loo to get myself together. I'm a mess. Streaked mascara and messy hair. I don't have Big Bag, so I wash my face with liquid hand soap and dry it with a paper towel. Unpleasant, yet necessary. Then I take down my hair. The pins are giving me a headache, anyway. I rake my fingers through the grey curls, sending them crazy. I look like a fucking witch. Pity I don't feel like one.

People are leaving the ballroom and I hang back, feeling unsociable. Della Green and her parents are the last out. They make their way down the stairs, and even though they speak in hushed tones, I hear every word.

'... she was one of your teachers?'

'No, Dad, I told you. She's a midwitch.'

'Are you sure?' asks her mother.

'That's what Imogen said. She's a bit odd. Doesn't do any magic.'

'But she remembered what you did. Silly girl,' her father says.

'Don't start. I had to do something.'

'We discussed this. Something simple was all that was required.'

'It was simple. And anyway, everyone did loads. Things have changed since you were initiated.'

'You'll be sorry when they make you pay,' he says.

The foyer is packed with people milling about saying goodbye. Della and her family blend into the crowd. The doors to the street are open, and there is a queue for taxis. And it's raining.

'Where did you get to?' Elaine asks me.

'Big queue for the ladies, so I went upstairs.'

It's not a complete lie.

'Grant's gone to get his car. He's going to drop me off and then you.'

I open my mouth to protest, but she continues, 'He won't mind. Never minds helping anyone.'

I'm trying to cook up a story about a taxi I booked when she grabs my arm. 'Come on, he's here.'

Rain. It's more like sleet. We dash to the car, and Elaine gets in the back seat. I want to sit with her, but Grant has already reached across and opened the passenger door. We drive smoothly away. He's taken off his jacket and rolled up his shirt sleeves. His bow tie hangs loose beneath his unbuttoned collar. In the confined space, his golden orts are rising like steam. Bloody hell, he's a handsome bastard.

'Well, that was fun,' says Elaine. She chats about different people and their news, and I try not to stare at Grant. His golden aura is annoyingly bright. Most people have a slight vapour. And why couldn't I see this before? I'll ask Mouse tomorrow. He must know a thing or two, living in a library.

When we pull up outside Elaine's flat, she leans through the middle of the seats and kisses Grant on the cheek. He tilts his head so she can reach. Bless. I'd like to slap him.

'Oh gosh. Nearly forgot. Where were you when they called the raffle?' She passes me a foil gift bag. I'm glad she doesn't wait for an answer. Grant makes sure she is safe inside before driving away.

The car is very quiet. He switches on the radio. Good.

Let's not talk about you fucking Theo. 'Love songs for dark winter nights,' says a husky-voiced female presenter. Great.

Soppy songs with repetitive lyrics play ceaselessly. I'm sure he's only doing this to please Elaine – no doubt he's going to rush back into Theo's arms as soon as he's completed his good deed – but at least I will be home soon. For that, I must be grateful. No need to pay a fortune for a taxi.

'Thanks for the lift,' I say when he pulls up outside my gate.

'No problem.'

'Let me give you some petrol money,' I say, getting my purse from my inside jacket pocket.

'There's no need.'

'Here,' I say, holding out my emergency fiver.

'It's an electric vehicle.'

He picks up the gift bag, which I've forgotten, and hands it over. I take it and close the door. I want him to drive away, but he's already out of the car. What? Does he expect me to ask him in for coffee?

'Lilith, I'm sorry about the nonsense at the pond. I should have been...' He looks up. The yew tree is shielding us from the sleet. '... careful. It was rash, and you were embarrassed. I just wanted you to be better.' He sneezes into a large paper hanky. Man-size. What else?

'It's fine. Thanks again.'

'It's not, though.' He comes close, and his gold orts swirl in the car headlights. 'Lilith, I want us to be friends. More than friends.' He's smiling, and I imagine kissing him right here under my yew tree. His manly arms keeping me warm. This is Mike all over again. Well, I've had enough of being strung along as an extra. I go through the gate, abruptly shutting it before he can follow.

'Tell me what's wrong. Is this because I wouldn't kiss you the other day?'

No, it's because you're another shit in a sea of shit. My face is getting hot. I'm not sure if it's anger, embarrassment or a hot flush. Probably all three.

'You're a liar.'

He flinches like I've slapped him. 'Your wedding ring. I see you've taken it off...'

God, he's coming closer all sad and hurt looking.

'You're fucking Theodora. You liar.'

'No.' He spreads his hands. 'You don't understand.' He sneezes. Wipes his nose politely. 'I'm not—'

'I saw you loved up on the dance floor. You think I'm going to let you touch me after what she did?'

'Lilith. I'm sorry. It's not what it seems.'

I'm so angry I'm gripping the top of the gate and red sparks are fizzing from my fingers.

'Looked like a tender moment to me. Shame she wasn't up for a diamond shag after all that dirty dancing.'

He puts his hands on mine. He's warm and his grip has an unexpected gentleness. I'd like a kiss. Even if he is streaming with a cold. A voice inside me screams, 'NO MORE SECOND BEST.'

I slide my hands free. Put them in my jacket pockets. I can still feel his touch on my skin.

'I don't even like Theo.'

'I think you have a lot of explaining to do. Starting with yourself.' I walk back to the cottage in the thickening sleet.

His voice reaches me before the kitchen door opens. 'My lips are sealed, Lilith. I can't explain.'

'Whatever.' I go in and give Ink her cocktail sausages.

Chapter Nineteen

The next day, I check my phone over morning tea. More cracks, I'm going to need a new one soon. My head pounds. I only had one glass of wine.

My son, Jason, says he is coming to stay, which is great news. I text Elaine and thank her for looking after me. Sheila from Sparklatious wants to know if I can cover for one of the office cleaning team who is off sick. It's the last thing I want to do, but I need the money, and I'm going into Barrington anyway to see Mouse at the library. After that, I can join the 'Office Sparklers' for the twilight shift. Can't wait.

There's another long voice message from Mike about the cottage. I don't bother listening to all of it. Something about him being the rightful owner of North Star Cottage and he has the deeds to prove it, which is absolute rubbish. Maybe I should get an early train and see my own solicitors. Mike had his 'let me help you understand' voice on. Prat.

I'm annoyed I lost my rag with Grant Fucking Rutherford. Why can't I be cool and dismissive? Every time I think of it, I cringe inside. I set about having a big tidy up for Jason's visit, pleased to have something to keep me occupied. I will put him in the big room and suddenly remember I need to change the sheets after my brief encounter with Gorgeous George.

Ink follows me as I strip the bed. She sniffs the pile of sheets. I'm sure that dog sneers. 'At least we can get these on the line,' I tell her. It's a nice, bright day.

In the ensuite, I clean the sink, shower and toilet and check the bin. It's empty, and I'm glad George had the good manners to dispose of his green condom. People who live in the city don't understand the vagaries of country plumbing and septic tanks, though. I feel around the U-bend of the loo in a rubber glove, making sure the bugger hasn't got stuck.

Is Jason bringing his boyfriend? I add another towel, just in case, and open the cabinet to give the empty shelves a quick wipe. There is a foil box – 'Dragon Condoms for pleasure'. On the back is a picture of eight different dragons. Each condom is displayed on an enormous erect penis. There are dragon heads and knobbles. One even has wings. I can't help looking inside the box. All present and correct. Only the green dragon is missing.

As I walk Ink over the fields, I call Cressida for a chat. She's delighted with my story about Gorgeous George. 'He obviously thinks he's coming back for more,' she says.

'I haven't heard from him.' I tell her about Alexa's timely interruption and sit on a tree stump while Cressida has a good laugh.

'Wait,' she gasps. 'I've got the condoms up online. Oh my god. Expensive. Fifty quid a box.'

'For novelty condoms?'

'Japanese, apparently. And...' She's laughing so much, Ink sniffs the phone and wags her tail. Even Ink thinks my sex life is hilarious. 'And you have to use them in order. I hope he used the green one first, or it's bad luck.'

'He did.' I should have put my kimono on.

'Good job, George. I like a man who reads the instructions. Next up...' – more guffaws – 'the dragon of purple passion.'

'Perhaps Alexa was Japanese,' I say.

Cressida can't take any more. 'Come over after the cleaning. I'll meet you from the station.'

Jason's impending visit spurs me on to wipe out the fridge. Two half-full jars of mincemeat lurk at the back. One is out of date – from last Christmas – and the other I decide not to waste and quickly make pastry.

After lunch, I set off for the bus with Big Bag over my shoulder. Ink follows me.

'I've got to go to work,' I tell her. 'You've have to stay here.' I turn her face toward the cottage. I'll miss the bus if I take her home and tuck her into bed. Ink wanders off, and my heart aches. I think she's lonely, but what can I do? Then I remember I'm going to meet Cressida after work.

'Oh, come on then,' I say, and she leaps alongside. Now I feel guilty because she hasn't got her coat on, and it will be even colder later on. The bus is approaching, but I turn back. 'We'll get the next one.'

Ink gives herself a shake – and now she's wearing a coat. As if that wasn't enough of a shock, it's a different one. Both her coats – a raincoat and a warm quilted jacket – are red. This one is a dark tartan, with black and green checks and a thick, fleecy lining.

'Hello, beautiful,' says Stan, the bus driver. Ink delicately accepts a dog biscuit from him. 'You are such a clever dog,' he says, patting her head.

Very clever.

Ink wags her skinny tail.

Stan gossips about Foxbeck and a new tea room that is opening as the bus lurches along. I can't concentrate. I'm fascinated by Ink's coat. I've never seen it before, and now, as she lies nibbling the dog biscuit between her front paws, orts rise like fine mist from her back.

On the train, I examine the coat. It's handmade. Tiny stitches and a perfect fit. Ink 'arrived' fully grown, and I have often wondered who she belonged to before. Did they know what type of creature she is? Or were they unaware of her abilities? Who made this coat for her?

We make a slight detour around the park when we get to Barrington. At County Hall, it's easy to blend in with the tourists and peel off to the library. Ink trots beside me and nudges her nose at the door, which opens. Winter sun filters through the windows, making the orts difficult to see. There is no one here and the fire is out. Ink stands by the secret door at the back of the room. She's been here before, then.

When Mouse comes out, they greet each other like old friends. 'You know my dog?'

'Grant Rutherford looked after her, didn't he?'

'Yes.' When I was locked in the loft. 'I brought you mince pies.' I put them on the table beside the Grimoire.

Mouse undoes the paper bag and takes one. 'Homemade?'

'This morning.'

'It's beautiful.' The star-topped pie is on his palm like it's precious. His black eyes glitter as he pops it into his mouth whole. When he's chewed and swallowed, he peers into the bag. 'Five more!' he says and takes them into his room.

The way to this librarian's heart is home baking.

He returns with an armful of books. 'Start with this one.' He taps a thin volume on the top as he balances the stack on the table. The Grimoire moves itself out of the way.

'It's a child's book,' I say, flicking through the illustrated pages.

'Magically, you are a child. Read these in order. Bring them back, and I'll give you more. Oh, and you'd better have this. You can keep this one.' It's a dictionary.

My magical education begins.

Chapter Twenty

The Office Sparklers don't mind Ink coming along. She's no trouble and mooches about and finds herself a spot for a nap until we pile into the van and go to the next office. We're a team of six and clean seven offices in two hours. It's hard work, but I don't mind. Two of them have the distinct glow of fake tan, so I blend in and have fun reviving all the pot plants when no one is looking.

At Cressida's, we drink too much wine and I stay over. The smart flat does not have a spare room, but Ink and I are okay on the couch. Cressida apologises about the cold. The heating goes off at night. Ink keeps me warm as I read about magic by torchlight.

The most helpful book is the *Illustrated Children's Dictionary of Magic*. I learn wands are handed down from mother to daughter. There are seven types of witch. Hedge witches are the most common, and sometimes women don't realise they are hedge witches. Midwitches are rare, and only a few become powerful. Unused magic can fade, and very few witches can see orts. I'd like to know more about orts but the children's books only provide basic information. Inside a book called *Let's Keep Magic a Secret* is a pamphlet: 'For New Coven Members'. It sets out the rules for magic tax. Every witch will give a measure of power – commensurate with each witch's ability – on initiation for the good of all. This magic will be stored, although it doesn't say how and only vaguely states that it will be used for protection and care. Whatever that means. Also, those with high and renewable energy will donate every year. This is the second time this has come to my attention. The first time, I put it aside. The magical world was new, and I understood so little. And I've been raised to pay tax like a good citizen. Why should magical tax be any different? After overhearing Della Green and her parents talking about it, though, I'm worried. I fold the pamphlet and replace it. Did Mouse put it there to make me think?

Sleep claims me.

In the morning, Cressida drops us off in Market Forrington. I have Mike's penthouse to clean. Annoying, but I need the money, and it's double time on a weekend. Mr Waterman wanted an extra 'do' while he's on a mini break. All Ink has eaten is a handful of dog biscuits from Big Bag, so I pop into a post-office general store on the end of his street and buy her some breakfast.

The doorman, Ted, lets me in the side door, and after he's gone back to his desk by the front door I double back to get Ink. We take the stairs, and Ink sniffs everything most thoroughly. Inside the penthouse, there are orts. Different this time. Faded yellow with light liver spots. They waft on the floor and lead into the bedroom.

Above the unmade bed floats a thin yellow cloud, and I walk in slowly so as not to disturb it. Ink slinks beside me. Mike is sleeping with a witch, and I know who. Theodora. Ink curls her lip, verifying my detection.

No use crying. It is what it is. Mike has probably been having an affair with her all along. While sweet, stupid little me was totally oblivious. Is Theo having an affair with Grant as well? The thought of Mike getting two-timed is amusing.

I feed Ink her breakfast in the most expensive dish I can find. Fill a crystal fruit bowl with water and set it on the floor, then make myself a posh tea and sit on the white sofa with Ink. Her paws are a bit dirty. Hey ho.

I read more witchy books and even take a few notes. I'm not an experienced witch, but even I know there is something odd about Theo's orts. The books don't have any in-depth information. Can Theo see orts? Will she know I was here? I hope not.

I can't face cleaning the penthouse. There's only so much an ex-wife can take. I get a bath sheet and two hand towels, carry them to the bedroom and fling them into the air over the unmade bed. They twist and turn and fold themselves into a huge cock and balls. A towel tribute for you, *Mitch*.

We take a bus to Barrington because I'm desperate for more reading. Mouse is not there, but on the floor beside his door are three books: *First Magic*, *Coven Histories* and *What Your Familiars Say About You*.

I take them, leaving the ones I've read and a packet of wine gums. Always feed friendly librarians. After that it's office sparklers and then home.

Chapter Twenty-One

When Ink and I get off the bus in Foxbeck, it feels like midnight. It's only 8.30pm. The little shops and the Fox Pub are shut. Not a soul is out on this dark winter night, and I feel an urgency to get home. I walk briskly around the edge of Fox Green. I never want to cut across the centre for some reason. Ink stays beside me. Normally, she likes to gallop ahead and find a stick or something for me to throw.

'We've had a busy couple of days,' I say, patting her neck.

Her muscles are tense under my hand. Moments before, she was loping along. Now, she is a coiled spring. Hackles prickled along her back. Lips curled to show long white fangs. She trots faster, and I jog to keep up. Behind us, all the cottages around the edge of Fox Green are dark, their curtains drawn tight against the night's chill. An icy breeze flaps my coat and trails cold fingers down my spine. I know what Ink's backward glance means: 'RUN.'

We sprint toward Church Lane.

Ink strides ahead and then turns. I run toward her, and as my feet hit the road, she runs past me. I spin around as she growls and leaps into the air.

Ink!

She's fighting something I cannot properly see. A dark shape that is neither man nor beast. I'm trying to scream. Trying to get to her.

'You're not safe here, witch,' a cruel voice whispers. I stagger, arms outstretched. Nothing is there, and Ink is still fighting the shadow in a whirling, snarling ball. I try to get my wand from Big Bag. The voice laughs and is gone, and Ink stands barking into the night.

Terrified, we run the length of Church Lane.

In the kitchen, I switch on the light, expecting my beautiful, brave dog to be injured and shaking with fear. Ink is nonchalant. She casts off the check coat and saunters to her water bowl and has a long drink. I pick the coat up. One side is ripped. Ink sniffs it, her brown eyes sad.

'I'll mend it,' I say, kneeling so I can hug her. I have a good cry, my face pressed into her neck. When I've got myself together and made a cup of tea, I call Elaine.

I imagine her at her kitchen table as I speak.

'Keep the dog close,' she says after I tell her what happened.

This much I already know. 'But what is it?'

'It's not good to talk about this stuff on the phone. But it's to do with your abilities. When they're new, they're easily stolen. Would you like me to send Grant over?'

'No. Definitely not. I'm fine. I just needed someone to talk to.'

'Call him anytime; he won't mind.'

'I will.' I don't even have his number.

'Anyway, I'm glad you rang. Ida got in touch. Said you'd had a bit of difficulty revealing your potential at Kelsted. Probably nerves. Not surprising. This is all so new to you. Nothing to worry about, but you'll need to do that bit again. At the castle. Just have a little practice beforehand. That's my advice.'

'I will.'

'Jolly good. I'll let you know when. Probably sometime next week.'

That evening, I sit in the kitchen in my dressing gown and mend the coat. The tear is jagged all the way through to the fleece lining. I'm amazed she wasn't injured, and I keep checking her. She's fine.

I sew as neatly as possible. The coat has been mended many times. Ink sleeps peacefully by the range, long legs poking out of the blanket I've draped over her. Now, more than ever, I realise she's my protector and my companion. Smoothing my handy work, I notice lumps in the seam. Small charms sewn into the fabric to keep her safe. My recent reading revealed that I can use my witch's eye to see hidden things. I take up the wand, hold the tip on my forehead, close my eyes and place my middle finger on each charm.

At first, I see only blackness. Then a bright image of each tiny gold charm appears in my mind's eye: a star, a four-leaf clover, a rooted tree, a lion and a frog.

After a soak in the bath to loosen the tan, I lie in bed listening to the rain. Ink sleeps pressed against me, her head draped over my legs. When she's near, I feel safe.

Whose magical creature was she before she was mine? I'm not the first witch to love this dog.

Chapter Twenty-Two

The next day is Sunday, and Jason arrives early by taxi. I'm glad of the company. He is full of stories and is enjoying his new job. But a mother knows when something is not quite right. We walk Ink to the beach. In the afternoon, Belinda calls in unexpectedly, and the two sit by the fire in the lounge chatting while I make chocolate muffins. Something is definitely up.

Belinda doesn't stay long – the twins need collecting from a party.

'Here, take some of these,' I say, filling a storage box that I know I'll never see again. I walk her to the car.

'I think he's splitting up with Jonathon,' she says.

In the evening, Jason goes to bed early. He looks tired. In the night, I hear him speaking on the phone. He seems happier in the morning, and Jonathon collects him, which is a good sign. But he doesn't come in to say hello, which is a bad sign.

After he's gone, I eat cake and read my witchy books. Little by little, I am piecing together this new world. I practise simple magic, which goes well. 'You know what, Ink, I could get the hang of this,' I say, pointing my wand at a candle and bringing forth a shower of glittering light that cascades like a fountain.

I have another go. This time, I imagine how it will look. When the sparks fly, they are waterlike and multicoloured. Fish and dolphins swim in shoals over the walls and then fade.

I can cast spells – I just needed a bit of help. The kids' books have taught me so much already. Who knows what I will learn when I start the adult stuff? At Kelsted Castle, I will prove that I'm a midwitch. I go to bed happy.

In the morning, I wake refreshed. A text from Jason says,

'Nice to see you and thanks for all the cake.' No mention of a bust-up with his boyfriend – so all good. Belinda has sent a picture of the twins and Brian eating the chocolate muffins. I'm not sure who looks happier, the kids or her husband. There is nothing from Dragon George, which irks me on a strange level. The sex was crap, and I don't want to see him again. At the same time, I don't want to be dropped without a word. That's why I'm useless with men. My ego is too complicated.

George and his dragons aside, I am cheerful. I'm singing as I feed the animals. Maud sits on my shoulder when I go to the woodshed. 'It's true what they say. You're only as happy as your most miserable child.' She gives my ear a friendly peck.

I'm desperate for more books. My cleaning jobs don't start until tomorrow, and I can't justify the expense of a journey to the library – not with my finances in such a mess. After the incident on Fox Green, I'm reluctant even to go for a walk. Instead, I strip out Jason's old room. I've been using it as a dumping ground for ages. When I mentioned changing it into my 'craft room', he didn't seem to mind. And he never sleeps in here when he stays. He's outgrown this space. It's just me that's hanging onto his childhood.

There are boxes of stuff that are not quite junk or the kind of bric-a-brac I could take to a charity shop. Much could be useful. A bag of fabric scraps. Another of wool. Jigsaws for rainy days. I find a shoe box full of knitted items. Belinda must have been about ten when she went through her knitting phase. There is a beehive tea cosy with a great many felt bees. A novelty hat with a stegosaurus on top. Lots of multi-coloured pompoms. One mitten and a set of Humpty Dumpty egg cosies the twins would like. Lastly, I pull out a bright yellow knitted bear.

For Christmas, I received one of those declutter-your-life books. Lots of pictures of a smart little woman smiling beside her achievements. A drawer of immaculately folded knickers. Colour-coordinated bookcases. Storage jars neatly labelled. To obtain true serenity, everything not directly useful must be sincerely thanked and then chucked out.

I try the hat on. Perfectly warm. I shall use it. Spare gloves are always useful, and a change of tea cosy would be lovely. I set the box aside, push Jason's single bed against the wall and arrange rugs and cushions to make it a sofa. Ink comes in to see what I'm up to. She sniffs about and takes the yellow knitted bear to the 'sofa' I've made. Glad she approves, I cover her with an unfinished blanket made from crochet squares. Ink doesn't mind the peculiar shape and garish colours.

Two charity bags later, I fill the empty shelves with all my witch stuff. I have an herb gathering hour and hang sprigs over the range to dry. Then I search the cottage for items useful for spellcraft. Pestle and mortar. Lots of candles. Crystal dishes. Jars of dried spices. Chopping board. And, of course, the spell book. Organised witch – that's me. I've even hung chintzy curtains and put my mother's old manual Singer sewing machine on the table to disguise the real purpose of my den.

I spend the rest of the day enjoying the new space I've made. Ink stays with me. She's tired. Did the shadow thing hurt her in a way I cannot see?

'Protection spell for dog familiars,' I say to my spell book and open the cover. A few pages flip to show a spell from the book's first author, Bethany Blackwood. I've got better at deciphering her spidery writing and transcribing the gist into a notebook. My room is so well stocked that I don't have to fetch anything. I grind herbs as a full moon rises over the treetops. The moonlight bathes my work table as I light a candle with a snap of my fingers and burn the herb mixture in a metal dish over a tripod. The scents fills the small room as I speak the spell words, bathe my hands in the smoke and smooth them over Ink's sleek black pelt. I do it again and again until the herbs have burnt away. Nothing is going to harm my girl. Exhausted, I get onto the sofa bed and pull the crochet blanket over us.

Ink is more her old self in the morning. I'm not sure if it was the spell or the rest. Either way, she has a spring in her step as she trots along the path to greet the arrival of the groceries. I get a big shop every two weeks to spread the delivery expense. Ed, the driver, always helps lug it up the path, and I give him a cuppa for his troubles and whatever snacks I have about the place.

'Tea?' I ask when the last crate is unpacked.

'No, love, can't stop today. Double busy. Malcolm's off sick again. Skiving more like. That's the trouble with the young. No staying power.' Ed rolls up his sleeves. The red, blotchy skin on his forearms matches his face. Poor bloke. I think he has an allergy, although I don't like to ask.

'Let me make you up a travel cup,' I say, rummaging in the cupboard for a paper mug. 'Cake?'

He's grinning. On a cooling rack are chocolate muffins I've made for Mouse. I hand one over. They're still warm. 'Ahhh.' He sniffs appreciatively. He's as bad as the dog. 'You ever make big cakes?'

'Sometimes. Used to when the kids were home. These days, I tend to make muffins or cupcakes because they freeze and I can get one when needed. A whole cake gets boring when it's just you.'

'The Mrs is forty-five next week. You ever sell 'em, the cakes?'

'I'll make you a cake, Ed. What do you want, chocolate?' I hand him his tea.

'I can pay. Can you decorate it? You know, "happy birth-day, Angela".'

I take down details and make a note on the kitchen calendar. We even agree on a price – god knows, any extra money will help.

I walk him to the gate and collect the post, and Ink and I wander around the garden in the winter sun. It's cold, but there are signs of new life even on this January day. A few bulbs peep through the soil, and there's a good smell in the air. Possibly optimism. My magic is behaving, and after the incident on Fox Green, I have stopped worrying about my mother's warning about the Coven. It seems ages since Ink found the sea glass with the etched feather and the warning 'beware'. She was right to warn me. Not everything is rosy within the Coven, that's for sure. When I join, I will be careful. As Elaine has said, it's like any institution. There are good and not-so-good aspects. And as for the magical tax... If that's the price for a safe life, then so be it. 'Nothing comes without cost,' I say to Ink. A few months ago, I had no magic, so giving a little away is no big deal.

That's what I'm telling myself, anyway.

When we get back to the kitchen, it's full of smoke. 'You're supposed to pop up!' I tell the toaster. Claudia stalks outside, affronted by my incompetence. I shake the burnt offering onto the lawn. Can I be trusted to bake a cake? I mark the calendar to ensure I make it the day before in case it goes wrong.

The post is mostly junk, which I stuff in the kindling bucket alongside the twigs. Two letters look official. A bank statement and another letter from Thorisson's Solicitors.

'Fucking Hell!'

Maud squawks on the dresser and flaps her wings. Ink lifts her head but stays under the blankets. It's chilly with the door open.

The bank statement is bad. I'm overdrawn. A huge amount. I can't understand. I was so careful at Christmas. Was my card stolen? I get my specs from Big Bag to have a proper look. Maybe there's some mistake.

'You absolute CUNT!' I yell.

From the doorway comes a polite cough. Dragon George

is standing on my doorstep star peering through the smoke billowing out of the kitchen.

'Something wrong?' he says. He looks like I've slapped him. Bad language can have that effect on some people. I almost laugh.

'My bastard ex-husband is charging me rent. Fucking rent to live in my own home!'

He takes a step back. I switch on the kettle. 'Come in out of the cold.'

George steps tentatively into the kitchen and closes the door with exaggerated calm.

'This is not his house. He's no bloody right to set up a standing order on my bank account. The shit.' I rip open the letter from his solicitor. I've missed a court hearing and will be fined. Evidence that I own the property is 'hearsay'. There is a copy of some deed stating Mike is the sole owner of North Star Cottage. I can't believe my eyes.

George places his camel coat neatly over a chair. 'I'm sure it's a misunderstanding. Please don't swear any more, Lilly. It doesn't suit you.'

'What?'

George comes nearer. He's smiling. 'Don't worry.' He tucks a lock of hair behind my ear. Does he think we're in a movie or some such crap?

'I'm here to make love to you. I'm going to take my time. Today, you will come more than once.'

His aftershave engulfs me in a wave of pine and citrus reminiscent of toilet cleaner. The cheap sort.

'Darling. This is our moment.'

'What?'

I glance where I shouldn't. He's already got a hard-on. What's worse is he sees me do it, and now he's pleased. 'I haven't stopped thinking about our afternoon,' he says.

I'm pressed up against the sink. George is edging nearer. Behind him, the chair tips his coat onto the floor. It lands in Claudia's uneaten cat food. He cups my face in his palm like I'm a tender virgin. 'Lilly...'

At least he's remembered my name.

'Let's go upstairs.'

'Fuck off!'

He flinches like I've poked him in the eye.

'Lilly, I know you're a sweet girl...'

George has some imaginary woman in his mind, and even faced with the truth, he cannot let go of the fairytale in his head. I know this because he's still got a boner. I put my hand over my eyes. I never want to see George or his dragon ever again.

'You need to leave.' My fingertips are fizzing, and I'm having trouble holding back an expulsion spell I didn't know I knew. The kitchen door opens. *Mrs Beeton's Cookery and Household Management* falls off the shelf with a bang.

Ink is on his coat. She's got herself comfy, long sleek greyhound body stretched out like she's running. He grasps a sleeve and shakes. Ink remains. Closes her eyes. He drags his coat and she wags her tail, enjoying the ride.

'Bad dog!' he shouts. Ink jumps up. Barks loudly and George stumbles out of the kitchen.

I retrieve the coat and hand it over. It's covered in dog hair, cat food and grot from my kitchen floor. George holds it at arm's length. 'I really thought we had something special. I'm sorry, but we're going to have to end it.'

Whatever.

Chapter Twenty-Three

L ater in the week, I take Ink with me to Barrington. The train is late and overcrowded, and we stand squashed in a corridor beside the toilets. It's not pleasant. When I get to Cranford, Holstein and Wigg, family solicitors, I already feel defeated.

Joan – the nice, even older than me woman on the desk –

is entirely unsurprised by my arrival. 'Go on up, Lilith,' she says, opening the door to the upstairs library.

'Ahh Lilith,' says Walter Cranford when we go in. 'Welcome, welcome.' He pats Ink on the head and I join him beside the fire. Ink knows when she's with magical people. She shakes off her coat and lies on the hearthrug with a sigh. 'Must say, I thought to see you sooner. Seems things have been hotting up in your neck of the woods.'

He pours me tea from a pot on the tray beside his chair. Is there always a spare mug ready?

Walter listens. About the overdraft, Mike's standing order for rent (Can he even do that?), my cleaning job, Mike's fucking penthouse in the name of Mr Waterman, Mike fucking Theo, the orts and the Coven saying I can't do bed and breakfast.

When I've finished ranting, he's motionless. Is the old man asleep?

'We can't interfere with Coven business, I'm afraid. But the law – that is quite another matter,' he says at last.

Walter assures me that Mike's solicitors are acting unlawfully. He should not be meddling with my bank account, and he most certainly does not have the deeds to North Star Cottage. 'It'll take a while, though, Lilith. To fix this. The mundane's legal system is slow. How do you think I got so old?' He chuckles. 'It will probably take a year to eighteen months to get a case together and a court date. But you leave it with me. Now we know he has a property in an assumed name – got to be tax evasion. It does give us leverage.' Walter hums to himself and stares into the fire.

'What can I do in the meantime? I have no money to pay you.' I feel very sorry for myself and swallow the lump in my throat. He pats my knee with an arthritic hand.

'It's a good job your mother was a seer. Fanny had the clearest of sight of any witch I've ever known. Don't worry, she paid me in advance for the troubles she foresaw. That reminds me...' Walter pushes himself up and hobbles to the other side of the room. He waves his walking cane over a bookcase and mutters. The leather-bound volumes shuffle and a small book floats from the top shelf into his waiting hand. 'I couldn't give you this before because you'd not come to terms with your abilities.' He hands me the book. Green leather locked with a brass clasp.

'Fanny was always convinced you'd be a midwitch. Even when they were trying to make her hand over the property because she had no magical heirs. She stood by her intuition. That was Fanny, through and through. Pleasantly stubborn.' He laughs, opens a writing bureau and rootles through a drawer. I think he's looking for the key. Instead, he finds a tin and prises off the lid with his thumbnail. Ink is there in an instant, sitting before him like she's about to receive a rosette at Crufts. 'You remembered,' he says, giving her a treat.

The tin reads, 'Cheesy Morsels for Clever Dogs'. I'm not sure she remembers anything, but she can smell cheese a mile off.

Walter selects a box file from a shelf and sits with it on his lap. Perhaps the key is in there. 'Ah ha. Knew I'd find it. You see, that's the beauty of actual physical paperwork. It doesn't get deleted or lost on your hard drive. Downstairs, they call me old-fashioned. Say what you like, but I can always get my hand on something when needed.' He pulls out a document and flaps it open. It's old and has a hand drawn map of North Star Cottage and the surrounding woods and fields. 'I'll get this to the young ones downstairs to find a solution for this mess. Your present finances are trickier. I think you could charge more for the field rental. It's not gone up since 1976, if I remember rightly. That should help. There's a bit in here that might see you through.' He hands me an envelope with a wad of cash inside. 'Shall I update the field rent?'

'Yes, please. Is there a key?' I say.

'For the book? No. Fanny said, "Give this to Lilly when she comes into her magic." She never provided a key.'

I feel better after my visit to the solicitors. 'Should have gone much sooner,' I tell Ink as we walk to County Hall.

Mouse is thrilled with his chocolate muffins and provides me with four more books. I'd like to chat with him. Once he's petted Ink, he takes his cakes into his secret room and doesn't return. For a man who lives among words, he's very taciturn.

Ink and I have a picnic on the bandstand. Even in the park, Ink keeps near. The danger, whatever it is, still lurks. No more wandering about in the dark. I book a taxi for when we get off the train later tonight. Hang the expense. The envelope of money has a thousand pounds in cash. I've never had that much money in my hand before, much less dragged it about in Big Bag. I stuff it into the bottom and put a few quid to pay the taxi in my purse.

I'm happy as I eat my sandwiches with Ink. Walter said not to worry. Mike's solicitors are acting unlawfully. But he's advised me to go into the bank and have a chat. See if I can fix it that way.

We are Office Sparklers until 8pm. I'm glad the pot plants are looking lush. I don't mind the work, and the young team I'm with are funny and friendly. But this is the wrong end of the day for me. I'm exhausted. When I get off the train, I'm glad I booked a taxi and don't have to get a bus and then walk, even though my travel expenses take half my earnings. The cash will help, but I'm going to need a job closer to home or one that's better paid. Not a lot of work in Foxbeck.

There is a light on in the cottage. I look at Ink for reassurance. She happily trots ahead, noses the door and goes in.

Jason is at the kitchen table, surrounded by suitcases and boxes.'You should lock the door, mum,' he says.

Then he bursts into tears.

Chapter Twenty-Four

Turns out my lovely boy has not only split up with his boyfriend. He's also lost his job. We sit up late talking it through. 'Have the big bedroom, it's all made up.' I say when we finally go upstairs. I had not realised, but Jason's job depended on his relationship with Jonathon, whose mother owns Kreate88, the graphic design company.

I'm up before light and try to work noiselessly so Jason can sleep in. Heartache is exhausting. I get the fires stoked. Move his stuff out of the kitchen to the bottom of the stairs. There is a large bag for life full of dirty laundry. I put a load in the machine. When the range is hot enough, I set about baking the chocolate birthday cake for Ed's wife. I'm popping it into the oven and telling Alexa to time it when Jason appears in sports kit. He rummages in his things and finds trainers. 'Off for a jog,' he says.

'Take Ink.' Since the incident on Fox Green, I'm not keen on leaving the garden. It's not something I can explain to my son. I can't say, 'I'm a witch, and there's a weird shadow thing after me, and I'd rather you stay indoors. If you must go, take my magical familiar.'

'Come on, Ink,' he says. 'Let's see you run.' Ink stays where she is on her blanket bed. 'Shall I put her on a lead?'

'No, she'll be fine. Probably best to keep to the lane. Woods are really muddy.'

'Will do,' he says, running down the path.

Ink remains by the range. Since I did the protection spell, she has a metallic shimmer around her in certain lights. 'I want you to look after him,' I whisper. She gets up, stretches and bounds after my son. Good dog.

The jogging is new, and they're not gone long. Jason is in good spirits. He's all talk about new beginnings. I make soup then drape the laundry on the airer while he looks for jobs online. In the afternoon, I go to work. When Ink and I get back, he's watching TV in the lounge with Claudia on his lap. It's nice to have someone about.

'How are you, love?' I say, picking my way around his stuff to hand him a cup of tea on the sofa. He's playing with his phone and watching TV with a laptop open beside him. That's the thing with the young. They can multitask on a level us oldies will never understand. I leave him to it.

The next morning, there's more rain. I'm icing Angela's cake when Jason appears in the kitchen and starts opening cupboard doors. He's in pale blue silk pyjamas. 'Got any muesli?'

'Cornflakes.'

'Might as well eat the box.'

'Toast?'

He makes toast.

Today is the day. I'm off to Kelsted Castle to redo the test. I'm ready. Last night, while Jason multitasked, I snuck into my 'craft room' and practised. The trouble before was that I didn't know what to expect. All the other witches knew what they would do, and I was overwhelmed. I've hardly seen any magic actually happening. I was unprepared, that's all.

'Does she like crusts?'

I'm so deep in thought as I pipe chocolate butter icing roses, I think he means Ink. Jason is holding out his arm, which he's covered with a tea towel, and is patting it like he's summoning a hawk. Maud sits on top of the dresser with her head cocked on one side, watching him.

'She likes raisins. She's never that bothered about bread.'

He finds her a raisin, and sure enough, Maud lands on his arm and takes it. 'Woah, hello! She's amazing, mum. Funny how you've got all these animals now Dad's gone.'

Dad's always been gone.

'Do you leave the window open for her?'

'Oh, she lets me know when she wants to go out,' I lie. Hard to explain that familiars open doors.

His eyebrows raise; luckily, his phone rings before he can ask any questions, and he goes into the lounge. He's still talking when I'm leaving half an hour later.

It's another damp day at Kelsted Castle ruins. A steady, fine drizzle falls from a grey sky. At least I've remembered to bring an umbrella. Ink keeps close as we make our way down the uneven steps to the cave. I'm confident. After all that business with Grant and the pond, no wonder I was disorientated last time. I push thoughts of naked, wet Grant and the almost-kiss away. Elaine said the next magical test session would be on this date, which makes me think there will be others there.

A single candle sits in the middle of the dark space, throwing flickering shadows over the ceiling and jagged walls. No one else is here. For once in my life, I'm early. Folding the umbrella, I prop it against the wall and hang Big Bag on a hook. Ink mooches about, sniffing. I snap my fingers a few times and am reassured by the spark. Today, all will be well. I am a confident witch.

Soon, there are voices, and Imogen comes in with eleven young women. I assume they are new witches like me.

'Excellent. You're here. Let's get started.' Then she sees Ink. 'Is this yours?'

She knows bloody well this is my dog. 'Yes.'

'You are not supposed to bring your familiar.' She glares at Ink, who is happily wagging her tail and letting the young women pet her. I'd like to say something about the fact that I was told to go nowhere without her. But I don't want to get Elaine into trouble. Imogen sighs theatrically and mutters something about old women. Then she hangs her smart bag and coat on a hook and sits in the middle of the room, as before. The girls sit in a circle. I go to join them, and Imogen points at Ink. 'Dog outside,' she says.

'It's raining.'

'It's a dog.'

'She's a greyhound. They dislike the wet.'

'And yet she's here on a rainy day when you were specifically instructed not to bring your familiar.'

Ink leans against my leg. I put my hand on her head, my fingers sliding down her long neck. There it is. The bristle of her hackle beneath the collar of her coat. She's got more sense than to curl her lip at Imogen. But this dog knows something is wrong. She steps backward – telling me to leave.

'Ms Blackwood. The dog. Put it outside and we can begin. Some of us have things to do.' Imogen folds her arms and waits like I'm a toddler behaving irrationally. She's half my age. I stare blankly. Her ort strands float around her, grey and green. Odd she has two. The young girls wait obediently with hands in their laps. Their orts are pastel-coloured mist.

'The choice is yours, Ms Blackwood. Dog outside and do the test or leave.'

'Why?' My face is red. Great.

'These are the rules. They're there for a reason.'

'That's not an answer.'

Imogen is on her feet. She takes me by the elbow and drags me to the doorway. Ink's growl resonates around the cave. 'I'm not prepared to be undermined by some old hedge witch with a mad dog.'

Her fingernails dig into my arm. Nasty bitch.

I look at my feet. I need to take this test.

'She can lie here,' I say, striving to keep my voice pleasant and putting my coat on the floor. Ink obediently sits on top.

'No.'

'She won't move.'

The girls are talking among themselves. Imogen leans close to whisper. 'I've dealt with your kind before. Just because you're old, you think you can change the rules to suit yourself. Well, you bloody well can't. So put the dog out. Or piss off!'

'Let me go first.'

'What?'

'I'll show you my magic and then I'll go.'

She smiles. 'We both know you cannot match the magic around you, Lilly Blackwood. So why don't you stop wasting everybody's time?'

The girls are quiet, trying to hear what we're saying.

Imogen minces back to them and sits, her face serene.

'We're going to wait while Ms Blackwood gets her things and her *dog* and leaves. Sarah, could you pop to the café and ask Melanie to join us so we can be thirteen.' When the girl, Sarah, has gone Imogen asks, 'Who can tell me why we need thirteen?' and flicks a hand, conjuring a barrier between them and me so I can no longer hear what they are saying.

A dark shape slides along the wall. Was it there before everyone arrived? Or has Imogen brought it? When I try to look at it, it moves, slinking into my peripheral vision. Ink stays close as I put on my coat and get Big Bag. The girls visibly laugh at something she has said, and Ink lowers her head. The shape is creeping over the stones toward us. She barks, and a shadow of herself leaps from her across the floor, shattering Imogen's barrier. The dark shape flees.

All face us. Nothing is stopping me now. I might as well cast the pretty spell I have practised. I summon the candle. It floats before me, and I say the spell words and send the magic from my fingertips. But I'm angry, hurt and indignant. Fire sparks fly and flames lick the walls. Ink's shadow self snarls and snaps at the fire. I'm vaguely aware that some girls are clinging to each other. I raise both arms and dark clouds form. Thunder crashes. Rain beats out the fire. The clouds pale and disappear, and a full moon shines silver light. All is calm.

One girl claps her hands with glee. Imogen scowls at her and stands, brandishing her wand. 'I'm not standing for this!'

'I am the midwitch.' The magic speaks. Just like the time I confronted Theo when she tried to steal my power.

All the girls are staring at the far wall, where Ink's

shadow-self prowls. Imogen points her wand at me with a shaking hand. Ink walks through the circle, rubs against the shadow, and the two become one.

'Put it away, witch bitch. Nobody got hurt,' I say.

Chapter Twenty-Five

The driver grumbles about Ink taking up space on the crowded bus to Barrington. I sit on a pull-down seat so she can stand in the luggage area. After my altercation with Imogen, I'm nauseous. The steamy, hot bus does not help. The cool air is a blessing when we finally get off, and I stand with my face turned up to the rain.

With Jason's arrival, I have not had time to read, so I avoid County Hall. I will call in tomorrow before office cleaning and bring a treat for Mouse. Today I have errands.

'We don't allow dogs,' says a young man at the bank wearing a blue polyester suit and pointy shoes. I am about to protest when he changes his mind and waves us into the queue. 'Sorry,' he says. 'Didn't realise.' I look at Ink, who now has a yellow tabard over her check coat with 'Therapy Dog in Training' in large black letters. Clever dog.

Another young man is keen to get anyone to use the vacant automated banking machines against the far wall. Everyone waits resolutely for a word with the only bank teller. Forty-five minutes later, I'm told I can speak to an advisor.

Eventually, a young woman steps out of a side door and ushers me behind a partition. 'Take a seat,' she says, straightening her shiny blue polyester skirt and hanging her matching jacket on the back of her chair. She taps the keyboard, peers at the screen and looks at me.

The partition wobbles violently. A pushchair wheel is stuck underneath. A toddler shrieks, and I lift one end up so the mother can get the pushchair out. Several people in the queue help balance the partition. The young mum smiles her thanks and gives her little boy a box of raisins.

'Sorry,' I say, taking my seat.

'We always get crowded on rainy days. I'm Abigail. How can I help?'

'Lilly. I'm recently divorced, and my husband – my *ex-*husband – has put a standing order on my account, and—'

'Name?' She taps the computer. Her nails are vast and painted with sunsets and palm trees.

I give her my details while rummaging in Big Bag for the relevant documents. My passport. Divorce papers. Bank statements. The partition shakes. Inches from where we sit, an elderly couple argue about how much to spend on their grandson's eighteenth.

'You seem to be overdrawn, Mrs Turner.'

'Blackwood. I'm divorced.'

She turns her screen and taps the display with a biro. 'Do you have funds elsewhere?'

A tall bloke rests his arms on the partition and reads about my dire financial straits.

'No. But that's what I've come to explain...'

'Our short-term loan plan is popular,' she says, fixing me with a smile.

'No. I don't need a loan.' I carefully describe what has happened. 'My solicitor has advised me that my ex has acted illegally. He shouldn't be able to access my account.'

She opens a drawer and lifts out a folder. 'These are the details of our popular flexible loan scheme.' She pushes it toward me.

'I'm not here to take out a loan. I'm trying to stop my ex-husband from getting into my bank account.' I tell her again about the standing order and that I had nothing to do with it and show her the statement. Again.

'Be with you in a moment,' she says to a man waiting by the side door. It's not even a customer unless he just happens to be wearing blue polyester.

'These are very popular with people your age. And if you turn to page 5, there is an option for releasing equity on your home.'

I start again. Because God loves a trier, or so I've heard. 'Could you tell me how my ex-husband accessed this account?'

She smiles at the lad by the door. 'Why don't you take this information pack and have a read, Mrs Turner? Pop back next week when you've had time to think.' She's standing and getting her jacket, a sweet smile on her pretty young face. 'Lovely to meet you.' She passes me the infernal folder. A happy middle-aged couple smile from the cover. I slap it on the desk.

'Sit down, Abigail.' Then I turn to the lad by the door. 'She's going to be twenty minutes. I suggest you go away and find something to do. And you' – I face the tall bloke leaning on the partition – 'would you mind minding your own fucking business!' He fucks off.

Abigail's mouth is a circle.

'Please look and see who can access this account' – I tap the number on my bank statement – 'apart from me.'

Her long fingernails flash over the keyboard. 'You're overdrawn.'

'Yes, darling, that's why I'm here – and no, I do not wish

to take out a loan or release equity on my property. My account has been *hacked.*' The people in the queue look over the partition with interest. I give them my best glare. The least they can do is listen politely from the other side without staring.

I lower my voice. 'If you can't listen to what I'm saying, fetch me someone who can.'

She looks at me properly for the first time. Now Abigail is focused, progress is made. I learn that all my accounts are 'linked' to Mr Turner.

'When? When were they linked?'

'After a divorce, these things happen. People forget to get everything separated.'

'That's as maybe, Abigail, but I have never had a joint account with my ex. It was always something he was keen to avoid.' Much easier to keep his 'extra marital' spending to himself.

'Are you sure?' She's peering at the computer. 'It seems like your saving and checking accounts are linked to your joint account.'

The boy reappears, sees my expression and goes away. She examines her nails.

'Could you check when these accounts became joined?'

She'd make a lousy detective, this kid. People shuffle behind the panel. Their feet squash raisins into the thin carpet. Ink has her head on her paws. Abigail clacks away on the keyboard, sunset nails on fire. I might be mistaken, but I think she's interested. There is a tiny frown on her smooth forehead.

'Two months. You're right. You've never had a joint account with anyone. Although this does still seem to be in your married name.'

'I changed it online when the divorce came through. It should be Lilly Blackwood.'

'There,' she says after more frantic typing. 'It's all in your maiden name.'

'If only I were a maiden.'

This is lost on Abigail.

'I don't know how this happened,' she says.

'He's always been a devious bastard. Have you unlinked my account and cancelled the standing order?'

'Yes, but I need to take it upstairs for verification.'

'That's fine. I'd like a print copy of what you discovered today.'

'We could send it in the post.'

'No, I'll wait.' Ink is stretched out. Her feet twitch to the rhythm of her dream.

'Could you fill this out while you wait?'

The leaflet says, 'How did we do?' Everybody wants feedback these days. Ironic when most service is rubbish.

She comes back eventually and hands me a folder. 'It will take two working days for this to show up on your online banking app,' she says brightly for the benefit of the listeners in the queue. I stuff the papers into Big Bag, and Ink gets up and stretches. She sees me to the door. Nice touch. 'How long have you been training therapy dogs?'

'Not long.' I hand her the leaflet. In the comments box, I've written, 'exceptional nails'.

Chapter Twenty-Six

The taxi drops us off outside the garden gate. I wince at the expense but I'm glad I don't have to walk because it's raining hard and I'm exhausted. Office cleaning was the last straw on top of an eventful day.

Light pours from every window of the cottage, welcoming us. Jason must have friends over. We run along the path. In the apple tree, there is a flash of white. I stop and tap my shoulder, and Maud flies down. We go through the kitchen door that Ink has opened.

Chaos.

Mugs and dishes fill the sink. Empty bottles and cans are all over the place. Some on the floor. There's a distinct smell of spilt alcohol, and Claudia has tucked herself behind the red geranium in the window.

Maud shakes her feathers, sending water droplets over my face. Bird on shoulder, I find Jason passed out on the easy chair in the living room with an empty gin bottle. There are wine glasses and plates, ashtrays and pizza boxes. The place stinks. Despite the cold, I open the windows, then build up the lounge fire and throw a blanket over my drunken son.

In the kitchen, Maud makes her crackling sound and flits onto the table to eat cake crumbs. The cake! The little shits have eaten the birthday cake. There's not one slice left in the cake tin.

'How was it?' I ask the bird. Delicious, by the way she's intently pecking up every morsel. Ink stands in the doorway with an expectant look on her face. She's taken off her coat, but she cannot feed herself.

I care for my faithful familiars. Feed Ink and change her water. Pour milk into a saucer on the draining board to coax Claudia out. Put proper bird food into a dish – because magpies shouldn't live on cake alone.

I'm still in my coat. Just as well. Log baskets are empty and out into the rain I go. Once I've fixed the range fire, I switch off all the bloody lights. The young are blissfully unaware of the cost of energy. I check Jason is alright and leave a glass of water near him. It's no good yelling. He's out cold.

My fatigue has more to do with the magic I used than the cleaning job. Regardless, I can't face the clearing up. I don't even have the energy to cry. All I can do is take a shower and go to bed. I lie with Ink beside me and listen to the rain. In the morning, I'll have to let Ed know there's no cake for his wife, which makes me feel really guilty. I hate disappointing anyone.

In the night, Ink wakes me. She doesn't normally fidget. She's digging at the blankets on the end of the bed, and I can see why. A strip of moonlight shines through the gap in the curtains. I draw them right back. Outside, the sky is clear. It might be a nice day tomorrow. Ink and I snuggle up in the moon bed. Bliss!

I wake very early, and I feel fine. The moon's light has replenished me. Perhaps that is the answer. Only I know it's not. All these things help: moonlight, sunlight, the sea, trees, nature. But there is nothing in particular that recharges me in a powerful way. This niggles me. I need to find out what really and truly is the source of my magic.

Jason is snoring in his bedroom. I heard him vomiting in the night. He's going to have a massive hangover. I gather dirty plates and glasses on my way to the kitchen. How many people were there?

Oh god, the cake. I put the kettle on and get my phone.

It's only seven, and Ed's not collecting the cake until eleven. Moving all the mess to one side, I wipe down an area and set about baking. Such a nice guy, Ed. Pity about his terrible skin. His face comes clearly to mind. Poor fellow.

I had a school friend with acne. Can't remember her name now. That's age for you. My mother made her biscuits. Told me to make sure I shared them with her. I didn't see her bake the biscuits, yet I remember the taste. Wellies on, Ink and I go into the garden to pick the herb I need. It takes some finding in the gloom, I persevere, I know it's here. Everything is.

By eleven, the cake is done. I've flapped it cool with a tray like a contestant in the Great British Bake Off. I've cheated with the decoration and put a spell on some chocolate to make butterflies.

Ed is thrilled and pays cash. More real money.

Jason, washed, dressed and smelling of lemony aftershave, comes into the kitchen as Ed is leaving. 'This is my son, Jason,' I say. Ink wags her tail and walks back and forth. Ed smiles, making his ravaged skin glisten. Helen. That was the girl's name.

'I'll pop the tin back.'

'No hurry,' I say.

'Let me get the gate for you,' says Jason.

'Who was that?' he asks when he comes back.

'Ed. Delivers the groceries. I had to make another cake for his wife's birthday.'

Jason is smiling at his phone. Fresh-faced and happy. No

hangover. Oh, to be young. Probably what he needed, a bender with his mates. What's a bit of mess? We'll soon clear it up together, and maybe I can get him to carry his stuff upstairs.

'Why don't you wear the new one?' he says, tugging on the ratty sleeve of my dressing gown.

Because I'm always doing messy jobs. 'I do, love. In the evening.' Yes, that's when I like to lounge about in my embroidered kimono. I stand aside so he can fill his water bottle. He drinks and fills the bottle again. Just as well – there are no clean glasses.

Ink woofs. A car pulls up in the lane and beeps. 'Got to go,' he says, grabbing a coat from the back of a chair. Two seconds later, he rushes back in. Kisses me on the cheek. 'Sorry about the mess. Love you.'

Bloody kids.

Chapter Twenty-Seven

S orter of gigantic mess. That's me. These days, it's even my profession. At least I don't need to be anywhere else. No, I have the whole day to tidy the cottage. I lug Jason's crap upstairs. Clean up from the party, including the vomit in both bathrooms. Drag a crate of bottles to the garden gate for recycling. Hang laundry out to dry.

Normally, I'd be off for a walk on a bright day like this. It's tricky when there's some weird thing trying to get me. I put thoughts of lurking danger aside and press on with the domestic chores.

I wash the kitchen floor. While it dries, I put on a pink crock and a wellington boot and waft about the garden, looking for flowers to cheer myself up. The animals come with me, Maud on my shoulder and Claudia and Ink wandering through the grass. Even on a bleak winter day, there is always something to pick if you look. I find a few snowdrops and hellebores and, at the edge of the wood, wild primroses.

I'm on my knees searching under the kitchen sink for a little glass vase when Ink woofs and canters out, leaving the door open. Must be a visitor we know well. I straighten up and fill the vase with water. For once, my house is immaculate. Usually, callers arrive when the place is a tip.

Grant Fucking Rutherford is standing outside examining his car keys with a scowl. Ink winds around his legs. Skinny tail whipping madly.

'What?' I ask.

'May I come in, Lilith?'

'Do come in,' I say with a mocking bow.

We both know there's no fucking way he'd be here unless he had to be.

He puts his keys in his pocket and touches the star with one hand as he comes in. Closes the door softly, hangs his coat on the back and tucks Ink into her bed. She lies there looking at him adoringly. Soppy dog.

'Tea?'

'Please.'

Of course, I remember how he likes it. Should I pretend I don't? I fill the kettle and look for a teaspoon. Probably need to organise this drawer. My sink is sparkling and empty of dishes. I set the flowers in the middle of my clean, clutter-free table. So nice he's seeing me at my best for once.

'Are you ill?' he asks.

'What? No.'

'Late night?' He looks at his expensive watch. God, he's irritating. 'You're in your dressing gown.'

Damn. He's right. And I've got odd socks on. I tighten the dressing gown cord. I'm not even wearing any underwear. Just a big purple t-shirt that barely covers my fat arse.

I glance at the kitchen clock as I turn to make the tea: 2pm. Brilliant. He thinks I'm a slob.

'My son is staying. You know how it is. Up late chatting. Leisurely breakfast.' I give him the tea and sugar. I've even chosen the mug he favoured when he stayed here.

I can't find a teaspoon. He carefully adds a modest amount of sugar with a dessert spoon and stirs. Then he pushes the mug away. How can you have a new mug of tea and not drink some? I know how that tea feels. Stirred and neglected.

'I came over last night. Your son was having a party.'

I don't get the chance to witter on about how nice it is for him to see his old mates.

'You'll need to have a word with him about his choice of friends. Jason was drunk when he answered the door. Very drunk.'

'Don't come here criticising my family, you dick.'

'I'm not criticising. I'm pointing out facts. Where were you?'

'None of your fucking business.'

'It is, actually—'

'Don't start with your Coven rules. I've had enough crap to deal with these last few days.'

He gets out a cotton hanky and sneezes politely into it. How can such a big bloke sneeze so quietly? He's not normal.

'May I use your toilet?' His voice is thick.

'Please do.' I've cleaned up the vomit.

I hear him blowing his nose. It's more manly than his sneeze. When he's back at the kitchen table, scowling at me with disapproval, I put my hand on his brow. 'You're not well.'

'I'm fine.'

His golden orts are less noticeable today. A slight shimmer.

'Have you had this since the pond?'

He grunts. Actually grunts.

From the fridge, I get lemons and go to the pots near the back step for herbs.

'There's no need.' He holds up a hand. I'm not the first witch to make him a cold cure.

'It was my fault, and it won't take long.' I chop and mix, put everything in a pan on the range with some moon-blessed water and give it a stir. The good lemon smell fills the kitchen. He has another quiet sneeze as I ladle some into a mug. I thought I'd be making a hangover cure this morning.

'Thank you,' he says, cupping his big hands around the mug and inhaling the fumes. I have an overwhelming urge to wrap him in a blanket. Instead, I wash up. That's the thing with Grant. One moment I'm furious with him, the next I want to... What exactly do I want to do with Grant? Hold him? Kiss him? Fuck him?

He drops the mug into the sink when he's finished. 'Much better. Thank you.'

'My mother made it when we got a chill.'

'Lilith I've got something to tell you.'

Here we go.

'At Kelsted with Imogen—'

'I was wondering when that was coming back to bite me.'

'Imogen wasn't happy.'

I was, though. I remember her face and nearly laugh.

'So now what? Are they going to put me in magical jail or some such shit?' I dry my hands on a tea towel and look up at him.

He takes a black envelope out of his back pocket and props it between a pot of cress and a shell in the window. 'She told Ida Carmichael-Grey what happened.'

'Her version of it.' Devious bitch.

He bites his lip. 'You can't join the Coven. They've banned you.'

'Hang on. They wanted to see proof of magic – which I certainly showed them – and now they *don't* want me.'

I turn back to the sink and the window. The garden used to feel safe. Now, there is something bad out there. 'I thought the Coven wanted to protect me?'

He follows my gaze. 'You need their protection, Lilith.'

'Looks like falling out with teacher has ended that.'

'I've had a chat with Elaine. She says you can still be initiated. She's willing to invoke strangers' rights for you.'

'I'll join another coven.'

'You can't. These things are territorial. Like it or not, Allingshire County is your Coven. None of the others would dare take you in when the ACC has rejected you.'

'And rejected me for what? Being disobedient in class? Grant, I'm a grown woman and Imogen is a bossy cow.'

'She's not saying you were disobedient. She's saying you were unable to do any magic.'

'That's a lie. There were girls there. They saw what happened.'

'Imogen's already made them make a statement.'

'She smoothed them?'

'That's illegal.'

'But lying – that's okay in your precious fucking Coven? I've had enough. You can stick your Coven up your arse. And your stranger rights, whatever that is.'

He turns me around to face him. 'Lilith, you're not safe. However you feel, you're going to have to mend this. Make your peace with Ida *and* Imogen.'

He glances over my head at the winter garden. I think he senses it too – the threat that lurks.

'I'll go to County Hall and show Ida that there's nothing wrong with my magic. It's here, and it's staying.' I snap my fingers and send a shower of coloured sparks into the air.

'You can't go into County Hall anymore.'

'I'm banned?'

He waves a hand through my sparks and almost smiles.

'So, what now?'

'Keep practising your magic. Keep learning and stay here.'

Big Bag is on a chair. I get the books out that I was going to return today. I guess that's over. 'You'd better take these.'

'You found Mouse.'

'Yes. The books have been a great help.'

'I'll bring you more.' He takes his coat from the hook on the door. His orts are brighter. He must be feeling better.

I follow him outside. There's a subtle vibration in the cold air.

'What the fuck is it, Grant? I need to know more about my enemy.'

'I'll bring some books,' is all he says. It's getting dark, and as we walk to his car, he holds my hand. His touch thrills me, but when we reach the garden gate, he squeezes and lets go. I watch him drive away. What was that about?

Does he fancy me? Or was that a platonic moment? Fuck knows.

Chapter Twenty-Eight

I go upstairs for a personal overhaul. There's nothing like shutting the door after the horse has bolted. Things are worse than I thought. Not only am I grubby and sweaty, four white hairs sprout from my chin. Four! And my lady 'tash is bountiful. A teenage boy would be delighted with my upper lip growth.

After a shower, shampoo and all-over session with my epilator, I review my HRT routine. I've remembered to take my pills every night this week. I re-fill the little box labelled with the days of the week. It's the only way I can keep organised. Then I look at the patch situation. Every three days is enough to confuse any woman. But yes, all the little boxes on the reminder sheet are ticked. I need a new patch today.

I get my reading glasses. No use trying to tackle the fiddly packet without them. When I have the sticky little fucker gripped with my fingernails, I survey my bum in the long mirror. Where to stick it? The instructions state it must be on a new site. My bum is a patchwork of little squares of leftover glue. No – they are actual patches. How can I forget to take the old ones off? Am I totally stupid? Apparently, I am. With my free hand, I peel away the old ones. Five. I have managed to leave five on. No wonder I feel slightly off – not ill, just not quite right. That's the trouble with the menopause. It's like the week before your period all month.

For Christmas, I received a lot of what used to be called 'smellies'. Do people still call gifts of cosmetics this? Probably not. I drag out from under the bed the large gift basket tied with cellophane and bows that Belinda gave me. I must have reached that age where I'm difficult to buy for. Or do they wish I'd make more effort with my appearance? Possibly both.

I get the monstrous basket onto the bed. It looks suspiciously like a raffle prize. I cut the cellophane with nail scissors and put it in my box of odds and ends, ready for another 'craft-a-noon' with the twins.

I'm wrong about the raffle. This is definitely for me. Silver shampoo and conditioner for long, grey hair. Body lotion for mature older skin. Yes, that's me. Wrinkle cream. Smoothing cream for dark eye circles and hand cream for tired hands. Me again. Thin lip plumping cream and a special serum for creased necks. Also me.

At the bottom is a small box of eyebrow tint. The picture shows two photographs of a woman. One with Father Christmas eyebrows and one with perfect brown brows. I read the instructions and have a go. I like the idea of 'trouble-free brows for six weeks'. What have I got to lose?

'Funny thing is,' I say to Ink when she comes in and nose bumps me in the bathroom, 'when I was young, the fashion was thin eyebrows. Plucked into a perfect arch.' I stroke her beautiful head and admire her whiskery face. Maybe we should all be more *dog*.

Ink goes into the bedroom and gets onto the bed with a harrumph. Using the mini spatula provided, I daube goo over my sparse eyebrows. Ironic that now big brows are in fashion, mine are patchy and grey.

'Alexa, five minutes.'

'Five minutes starting from now.'

Also in the basket is 'whitening gel for tea-stained teeth'. Might as well give it a go. I smear my teeth with blue gel.

In the kitchen, Big Bag is on the chair. The locked book Walter gave me is poking out. I push it in and take my phone. The cracks on the screen are spreading. They now look like a tree. I check for news of Jason. It's dark, and I haven't seen him since this morning. I have to remind myself that it's still the afternoon. He's a grown man, and just because he's staying here does not mean I have to track his every move. If he was in London, I wouldn't know what he was doing.

Despite my sensible pep talk, I'm still worried. That's the trouble with kids. As soon as they arrive on your doorstep, you sink back into mummy mode. Which everyone hates. Them and me.

Alexa beeps, and I refrain from messaging to ask if he'd like a jacket potato (subtext: 'Where the hell are you, and are you okay?'). Upstairs, I wipe an eyebrow with the removal cream. Not bad. Maybe this is the way forward. My phone rings and I race downstairs, hoping it's Jason.

It's Sheila from Sparklatious.

'Hi.' I can hardly speak with a mouthful of whitening gel.

'Lilly?'

'Mmmn.'

'Ahh. So glad I caught you. There's a spot of bother with Mr Waterman.'

You're telling me.

'He wasn't happy with his towel animal.' Her voice is raspy.

I bet.

'Also, his penthouse wasn't cleaned properly.' She sounds a bit miffed.

'Sheila, I'm so sorry.' Might as well be honest. 'I realised the place belonged to my ex-husband...'

'Ahh well, that explains it.' She has a thorough cough. I

expect she'll sack me when she gets her breath back. Can't blame her. 'Mildred is back. Knee op been a great success. So we need to have a rethink anyway.'

A wave of relief washes over me. No more Mike's flat. 'That's fine, don't worry,' I mumble.

'Also, the office cleaning... Well, I don't need you on that team anymore.'

Another wave of relief.

'However, I was looking at your information sheet, and I see you ticked light gardening. Was that by accident or...?'

'I don't mind gardening.' I can get anything to grow.

'This is a terrible line.' Short cough.

'Love gardening,' I say as clearly as I can.

'I don't normally deal with this side of the business, but I didn't want to let you down. Anyway, Steve. Steve is garden side. He says there's a gap for a spot of gardening in Foxbeck. You live there, don't you?'

'Yes.' No more travel expenses.

'Marvellous. It's at Fox Lodge. Do you know it?'

I do. She starts to tell me about the job. I make out sixteen hours a week and something about a key and a lion. Then her coughing grips her and she hangs up. I'm wondering if I should call her back when a text message comes through with enough information to 'get me started' and that Steve will be in touch with full details.

A gardening job in Foxbeck. I can't believe my luck and best of all, I can decide when to do the hours.

Upstairs, I wipe off the other eyebrow. Oh dear. My left

brow is darker than normal, but not too bad. The right? The right is like a huge black caterpillar – the ones you shouldn't touch because they cause a nasty rash. Hopefully, nothing weird has happened to my teeth. I brush and then examine them in the mirror. They look exactly the same. I have the slightly yellow gnashers of the middle-aged. The woman on the box has a gleaming smile. What would really improve my appearance? Photoshop.

In clean pyjamas and an old sweater – no point getting dressed now – I make scrambled eggs for tea. As I eat, I lift the locked book from Big Bag and lay it on the table.

The lock is a pretty brass clasp. The keyhole is tiny. I have already tried to prise it open with a metal nail file and pick the lock with a hairpin, and my opening spell won't work. After I've eaten and washed up – I'm feeling house proud – I search for the key. My mother left me this book. It must be here somewhere.

I tip out a dresser drawer of oddments that have no proper home: coins, pens, bits of chalk, stones, shells, paper-clips, Lego, broken crayons, a ping-pong ball, string and drawing pins. Endless bits of junk that aren't quite rubbish. There are three keys. One is small enough. None of them fit. I get my mother's old button tin and rake my fingers through the contents. Another key, long and thin with a skull-shaped bow. I know it's not the one, but I test it anyway.

My mother always said the best way to find anything was to have a tidy up. I set about the glass-fronted case in the lounge. It's full of old china, jugs, vases and glasses. I spend the evening dusting and rearranging with Classic FM on for company. I find two pearl hat pins in a toby jug, a big brown penny with King George V on it and four small witch bottles I carefully return to their hiding place. It's eleven o'clock. Still no key and still no Jason.

Fuck it. I call him.

'You alright, mum?'

Yes, I'm alright!! 'Yes, love.' If I drove, I could legitimately ask if he needed a lift home. 'Just letting you know I've left a key in the conch.'

There's laughter in the background, and he sounds slightly drunk.

'Great. Probs be back in the morning at some point.'

'Okay, love, I'll be at work.'

He's gone.

I put a spare key in a giant old conch shell and leave it on the doorstep. My mother did the same when I was young. I wish I'd asked where the shell came from. This gives me an idea. I check every shell for a hidden key. North Star Cottage has almost as many shells as it does things with a star motif. Even so, I go to bed keyless.

Chapter Twenty-Nine

The good thing about my new working arrangements is I can bring Ink without guilt. It's a beautiful sunny day on the first of February, and I remember to chant 'white rabbits' three times before saying anything else. Another superstition of my mother's. I hope it will bring me luck. Some key-shaped luck.

I stand in Church Lane outside my garden gate to assess the threat. Hard to believe there is any bad in the world on a bright morning. But I'm determined to use my instincts, such as they are. I put my hands onto the cold earth and close my eyes. I sense birds and new growth. All is well. Ink is with me, and we will be home long before dark. I look back at the cottage. I'm sure I've forgotten something, but nothing comes to mind.

Ink trots ahead. We both have our faithful old coats on. I'm in mum's gardening coat with the dinosaur hat Belinda knitted pulled down to cover my caterpillar eyebrow. Ink wears her check coat.

The walk takes forty minutes, but it's better than being on a bus.

Fox Lodge is at the end of Fox Lane. Must look good on the address. Fox Lodge, Fox Lane, Foxbeck. There is nothing else here. Only woods. No other property. We used to come blackberrying here as kids, even though my mother always forbade us to walk along Fox Lane. Ink waits by the huge iron gates, tail wagging. Obviously, this is where we're going. Clever dog.

The house is tall with a pointed roof and leadlight windows. The front garden is simple. Trimmed box hedges and a short lawn. Herbs edge the long gravel drive.

Sheila has given me a code for the electric gates, which I have written on the back of my hand. I tap it into the keypad and wait. The gate clicks and creaks open. As per Sheila's instructions, we go around the left side of the house, where there will be a key to the potting shed under a stone lion. The owners do not like to be disturbed. I follow the path, and Ink sniffs the ground and wags her tail. Who can she smell?

The back garden is beautiful. High brick walls mellowed with age enclose the space. There's a wooden greenhouse, vegetable beds, fruit trees and a pond. The shed is large and hidden behind a yew hedge. A wooden wheelbarrow is propped against the wall. Cold frames encircle a little court-yard where terracotta plant pots are neatly stacked. A stone lion – who looks like a dog in a wig – sits by the door. The key is under his foot.

This is so much more than a potting shed. Garden tools hang in rows on one side. On the other are shelves for storing produce. Potatoes, onions and four types of apples. I breathe the earthy, fruity smell. A window looks toward the house. There is a workbench and an old white sink. A kettle, a mug and a tin of tea bags. I've found my dream job.

Outside is a smaller shed – a toilet. Vintage, of course, with a pull chain.

Where is Ink? I hope she's not digging up a flower bed or something. She's trotting toward the kitchen door. She's no fool. It would be warmer inside. But I don't want her opening doors to someone else's house.

'Ink, come,' I call softly, finding a treat for her in my pocket. There's a question on her long, hound face: 'Aren't we going in?'

The house is quiet and still. There are no lights on. Maybe the owners are on holiday.

'Let's explore,' I say, coaxing her along the path with a dog biscuit.

Reluctantly, she joins me as we take a tour. From the kitchen garden a path under a long wisteria archway leads to the house's other side. Here is a circular lawn, rose bushes and perennials waking after their winter sleep. An oak tree stands sentinel over heavy wooden garden chairs and a table. A nice shady spot when the leaves grow.

The winter garden is speckled with snowdrops. Crocuses peek from the lawns. The shrubs are beginning to believe in spring. The garden has good bones – wide herbaceous borders, clipped hedges and established specimen trees.

I put my coat in a sunny spot on the path, and Ink settles on top. I set about pruning the wisteria. A calmness envelopes me as I work, and I'm aware of who toiled before me. Hands that pruned, dug, planted and shaped this space into a garden. I love it here. The well cared for tools with their worn wooden handles. The sound of a thrush raking through old leaves in the border. Ink snoring in the sun.

It's getting dark as Ink and I walk along Church Lane. No news from Jason all day, but the lights are on at North Star Cottage. He's home. What a relief. All is well, and I didn't let myself fall into anxious mother mode. Well, that's not exactly true. Of course I'm in anxious mother mode – my son is living with me. I'm pleased because I have not let him know I'm a gibbering wreck by sending him messages every hour.

In the kitchen, Claudia winds herself around my legs then goes back to the blanket bed by the range. Jason has kept the fire going, which is good. Maud ruffles her feathers from her nest on the dresser. Has she actually built a nest? I should get up there and give it a clean.

I expect to find Jason in the living room. The lights are on, of course, but he's not there. My imagination runs wild. Has he taken dangerous drugs and is lying in his own vomit upstairs? Is he in the grip of depression having lost his job and lover in one go? It's all my fault. I should have waited for him to come home. Made sure he was okay before going out. I'm a terrible mother. I check the downstairs toilet. Empty. I run upstairs. The big bedroom – his now – is empty and so is the family bathroom. I hear laughter and open the door to my craft room.

Jason is wearing headphones and smiling at his laptop. The room is now an office. He's sitting on a big swivel chair, and all my stuff is gone. I open my mouth to speak, and he waves me away. 'I agree to a certain extent, Clive. But let me do you a mock-up, and then we can go from there. Yeah, sure...'

I close the door quietly and creep away.

In Belinda's old room, which is now mine, all the things from my 'craft room' are in 'bags for life'.

Switching lights off as I go, I return to the kitchen. Jason does not appear until I am dishing up shepherd's pie.

'That smells fab,' he says, plonking himself at the table. I hand him his plate and the tomato sauce. He squirts a liberal amount and eats a few mouthfuls. 'Thought it'd make life easier if I set myself up in my old room,' he says.

Maud stretches her wings. A feather floats down, almost landing in his dinner. 'No room in here for a home office, not with all your pets, mum.' He laughs, flicking the feather onto the floor. 'I bagged your stuff up. Not sure where you wanted it.'

We eat. I'm starving after all the gardening. Nothing like outdoor work to give you an appetite.

'You remember Matthew?' he says.

'With the red hair? Did A Levels with you?'

'Yeah. Well, he came over the other night. Turns out he's gone freelance, and he's doing really well. So I thought, why not give it a go? He gave me loads of pointers. And!' He pauses dramatically and raises his mug of tea. 'I got my first client today. A guy starting a tree surgeon business wants a logo designed. Not exactly Coca-Cola but hey...'

'That's great, love. Well done. Not bad for day one!'

We clink mugs.

'Oh, and that tattooed bloke called by with some books. I put them on your chair.'

I clear the plates and switch on the kettle to make instant custard. Get the apple crumble out of the range. 'Bloody hell, mum! You're spoiling me!'

As we wash up together, Jason asks, 'Who is he?'

'Who, love?'

I know who he means.

'Mr Serious with the tattoos. He seemed pretty pissed you were out. Even more pissed that I didn't know where you were. He came round the other night as well.'

'I've got a gardening job in the village. Beautiful old garden.'

'Oi! Did you see that? Cheeky bird!'

'She's a crumb stealer,' I say, not looking.

'Crumb! She just took a teaspoon up to her nest. Absolute thief!'

Jason's phone rings, and he goes to chat with his friend. I finish wiping up, then climb onto a chair. It's about time I had a look at Maud's nest.

I have to laugh. 'Maud, really!' No wonder there are no teaspoons. They're all up here. There's a long-forgotten bread basket she's made into a nest. Her treasure surrounds it. Teaspoons. Plenty of those. Tinsel, a shiny bow, paper clips, five pence pieces and a tinfoil cupcake case... and those are just the things I can make out. Maud hops over and pokes her valuables with her beak. She's obviously very proud of her stash.

'You are a funny old bird,' I say, and give her back a gentle stroke. 'You can have it. I'm not going to disturb you. But we need the teaspoons back. Ooh, and the nail scissors.'

I pick out the spoons while Maud watches me with her beady eyes. There's not enough silver money to help with my financial crisis, so I leave it there, but I do find the top hat from the Monopoly set. I'm about to come down when I see a small brass key. I know without a doubt, this is it.

'Well done, Maud. You're a good, clever bird,' I say, pushing the key into my jeans pocket.

Chapter Thirty

Seconds later, Jason is putting on his coat. 'Off to Daniel's,' he says. I've never heard of Daniel, but he's already gone. I watch him wait by the gate and get into a car. No use worrying. He's a grown lad, living his own life.

I build up the fire in the lounge then soak my aching

muscles in the bath. I come downstairs in warm pyjamas and a jumper, and Claudia and Ink are stretched out on the hearthrug. I check my phone to be certain Jason isn't about to arrive, but his whereabouts are on a need-to-know basis, and I apparently do not need to know.

I take my mother's book from Big Bag and sit with it on my lap. The little key fits and anticipation fills me as I turn the lock. Two clicks, and the cover springs open.

Apart from the fire's crackle, the room is quiet. My mother was a witch and a seer. I know this now. Every memory of her has a new significance. Her superstitions have a deeper meaning, and as I gain confidence in my magical abilities, I understand how much she taught me without my ever realising. Every herb, plant and tree in the garden is familiar to me. Somehow, she passed on her knowledge of their properties. She sang songs to me in childhood that I now know to be magical chants for healing and protection. How hard it must have been to keep her true self secret from her only child.

'I'm ready, mum,' I say.

Every page is crammed with her neat, loopy writing. Her spells in the family shadow book are for every witch. This book is for me.

Darling Lilly,

If you hold this in your hands, you have at last come to your magical self. Prescience is a tricky gift. While there were many days that I longed to tell you what I believed the future would hold, fear held me back. Not everyone can follow the magical path. Many deny the abilities at their fingertips, preferring to live safely in the mundane than face the challenges of witchcraft. Their magic fades and is lost. So many midwitches lack the confidence to fulfil their potential. This is the reason I had Walter hold on to this, my Book of Truth, until you were comfortable with the fact that you are a Blackwood witch.

You must mark my words, Lilly. A midwitch is a powerful woman, and many will want to steal your ability. As I write, I hope that things have changed and that as you enter the last phase of your life, the modern world looks favourably upon those who call themselves witch and that the Allingshire Coven is free from corruption and evil. Trust your instincts.

Love Mum.

I sit in the old easy chair and read until the fire is low and a huge moon shines through the window. When I close the *Book of Truth*, I lock it again. My skin tingles with my newfound knowledge. The Coven has kept so much from me.

Standing on a kitchen chair, I return the key to Maud for safekeeping, placing it next to her breadbasket nest. She picks up the key in her beak, hops about on top of the dresser and secrets it beneath a collection of shiny sweet wrappers. She goes back to sleep with her head resting on her back. 'Clever bird, Maud.'

I take the book and hide it in the pocket of a long black cloak in the secret cupboard. The door slides shut and disappears, and I get dressed. There is more to be done this night.

Chapter Thirty-One

Outside, it is bitterly cold. Ink's breath is a puff of cloud as she trots ahead of me toward the woods. On my shoulder, Maud fluffs her feathers. The moonlight shines brightly through the bare tree branches. We wait beside the garden gate as per my mother's instructions:

If you have a familiar who lives in the forest, summon her. If she doesn't come, choose another night.

She didn't say how to summon the green-eyed fox. A fox is not a dog and cannot be called. I put my hands on the ground, close my eyes and wish. The undergrowth rustles, and the huge fox steps onto the path ahead.

Good. The sooner I get this done, the safer we will be.

The path is hardly discernible in the winter woods. The fox knows the way, and we follow. I stop at the place we usually go left and over the fields to the beach. Tonight we trail the green-eyed fox into the heart of Blackwood Forest. I have not come this way since I was a child tottering after my mother with Rufus, the lurcher, beside me. I was delighted because a large hare hopped along with us. Now I think about it, this hare often appeared in the woods.

The path we took on that night has long since disappeared. The green-eyed fox picks through the undergrowth. How the creature knows where I want to go or what I seek is a mystery. Yet here we are in a small circle of dark-barked trees. The blackwoods of my name, this place, and all the witches who came before me.

Pale figures walk around the circle of trees. Some raise a hand in greeting, others stare. I recognise my mother and grandma Gwen. Familiars walk with them: dogs, cats, birds, hares and frogs. The Blackwood witches have slipped through the veil of life and death to welcome me.

I step into the circle's centre with Maud, Ink and the

green-eyed fox. Claudia, her power stolen, has not joined us. There is a pang in my heart at the black cat's absence.

Around us, the ghost witches pick up the pace. With my hands raised to the moon shining through the dark branches, I ask for strength and make the chant my mother taught me when I was a child. From the black branches, dark leaves sprout and fall into my outstretched hands.

'Eat, eat,' the forest whispers. The small oval leaves are glossy and black and disappear on my tongue, insubstantial as dust. The power they imbue cannot be denied, seeping deep within me with warmth and strength. I am renewed. This is the secret power of the Blackwood Forest. The root magic of my ancestor witches who trod these woods before me.

When the last leaf is eaten, I snap my fingers. White light bursts forth in a flashing, sparkling beam, and I know that here and forever, I am a witch of Blackwood Forest. I need no other belonging.

After filling the pockets of the gardening coat with the little black leaves, I walk home. 'Thank you,' I say to the green-eyed fox and the forest when I close the garden gate. The fox, beautiful in the moonlight, slinks away on silent feet. Ink trots into the cottage, sheds her coat and stands by her food bowl. She's right. It's been a busy night. 'Snack time,' I say, delivering biscuits all around. Bone shapes for her and digestives with cheese and a mug of tea for me.

Three in the morning, and I'm not tired. There is too much whirring about in my head. New information I need to think through and a second task my mother told me to do as soon as possible. I set about making spell jars to keep North Star Cottage safe. For once, I am sure what to do and trust my instincts. Working outside on the stone bench, I light a heavy candle and put it in a glass lantern. I gather fresh herbs, salt and needles from the yew tree and add them in turn to four small jars. I invoke the protection of my ancestor witches and the Goddess with drops of moon-blessed water and leaves from the blackwood trees. Lastly, a few of Ink's short hairs, my long grey hairs and Maud's feathers. I seal each jar with black candle wax.

I somehow know where to put them in the cottage: on a hidden shelf in the cupboard under the stairs; beneath a floorboard by the old front door; in a nook in the loft; and in the cabinet in the lounge. In each place sit other jars and bottles from the generations of witches who have lived here. I lay mine down without disturbing the others. I hold my hands above each clutch, and there is a vibration in my palm. I know these witches – and now they know me.

Chapter Thirty-Two

Ink and I eventually fall asleep in the easy chair. I wake up cold to the sound of crying. In the dark winter morning, Jason is weeping over the kitchen sink while trying to stem a nosebleed. Ink stands near with drooping ears. 'Sorry, thought you were still in bed.'

'What happened?' I turn him about and take the cloth.

Not a nosebleed. He's been punched. I steer him to a chair, run a tea towel under the cold tap, hold it over his bruised face and cradle him to me. 'What happened, love?'

'Oh, you know. Got into a fight.' He takes the towel and looks at the blood, then replaces it.

He's lying. I'm sure. Not just because he's never been a boy to get into fights – Jason was always good at joking himself out of trouble – but because my hand is on the back of his head and the lie is like a dark stain in my mind.

I go to the kitchen cupboards and start putting together something for the bruising. And a tea. A tea for what? His confidence? That's it.

'Tell me what really happened.'

'You're up early, mum.'

I fell asleep in my jeans. 'Lots to do,' I say.

While he plays with his phone, I make a paste. Cooling mint leaves and a root of a nameless weed that sprouts at the edge of the path. I brew a tea using dried herbs and spices from the cupboard.

'So,' I say, smearing the soothing paste onto his face. 'Are you going to tell me?'

'Yeah, but don't make a fuss. It's just one of those things.'

I pour his tea and wait.

'We went to Archer's, that gay club in Barrington. It was fine, and the others left after about two o'clock, but I was chatting with this guy. Craig. When we left, there was a group of blokes outside, and they gave us a bit of hassle.' His hand shakes as he takes a sip of tea.

'You got mugged?' My mouth is dry.

'No, mum. They were gay bashers. They started on us. Calling us names. Craig got stroppy and started shouting back, and then they laid into us.'

'Was Craig hurt?'

'About the same as me. Black eye.'

'Did you report it?'

'To the police? God no, and anyway, what's the point?'

'Every point. If you don't say anything, they carry on waiting outside. You have to make a stand.'

'No, mum.' He gets up. Drops his mug into the sink with a clatter and heads upstairs.

'For fuck's sake!' I curse. I've been wafting about under magical trees in the moonlight and casting protection spells for my home and, all the while, my boy – my beautiful boy – is getting beaten up by thugs. I kneel beside Ink's bed and stroke her sleek black head. 'Am I losing my grip on reality?'

Her big brown eyes gaze into mine. Claudia brushes against me and gets into the blanket bed. I pet them both, one hand on each. A kind of double soothing for myself. Once I'm calm – well, no longer on the verge of tears or rage – I think more clearly. More importantly, I brush aside the ingrained feeling that I must not bother anyone. I get my phone and ring the police station in Barrington.

They are friendly and listen carefully to what I tell them. When I put the phone down, I'm reassured. I go upstairs and knock on Jason's bedroom door.

'You alright, love? How do you feel?'

No answer. 'Listen, love, I called the police station, and they were really nice. They want you to pop in and make a statement.'

The door flies open. 'I knew I shouldn't have told you. You always overreact. I'm not making a fucking statement. Just forget about it!'

He shuts the door in my face.

Kids. You try to help and end up becoming the enemy.

Maybe he'll change his mind.

I spend the morning faffing about. Jason stays in his room. Ed calls in to return the cake tin, and I hardly recognise him when he puts his head around the kitchen door. His skin is as soft as a newborn's bum. I'm good for something then.

'Fabulous cake, Lilly,' he says.

'Oh great.' I put the cake tin on the side.

'No, really. Never tasted anything like it.'

Witchcraft has a flavour, then.

'Tea?'

'No, can't stop.' He nods toward the lane where his delivery van waits. 'But a couple of the neighbours and my daughter-in-law were wondering if you could do cakes for them? I said I wasn't sure and I'd ask. They're happy to pay.'

This is unexpected. I give him my number and email address. At this point, any extra money is helpful.

He's only just gone when Belinda walks in. 'Where's Jason?' she says, but she doesn't wait for an answer. She throws her coat over a chair and goes upstairs. Ink gives up trying to greet her and wanders outside for a pee. I wonder

213

why she isn't at school, then remember it's Saturday. Another sign that I'm losing touch.

I make everyone sandwiches and set the table for lunch. Half an hour later, they are both in the kitchen. 'I'm taking him to the police station,' she says, putting on her coat and handing Jason his.

Good. There's no arguing with my teacher daughter. I cover the sandwiches. Maybe they'll eat them later.

Jason shoves a bundle into my arms as he leaves. 'You've ruined these,' he says. I've shrunk his pale blue silk pyjamas. I'm a mother who can do nothing right.

Gardening is the answer. At least the plants like me.

Belinda returns Jason. They had lunch in town but she takes some of the sandwiches with her and cakes. Jason goes to his room without a word. I walk Belinda to the gate.

'How did it go?'

'Fine. Really nice policewoman. I think it did him good to get it off his chest. Said he was glad he made a stand. I got the impression that it's not the first bit of trouble they've had outside Archer's.'

'Did they say they were going to do something?'

'Not exactly. But it was implied. "Monitoring the situation" was how they worded it.'

'Well, that's good.' I don't say that in my youth, there were police everywhere.

'Bullies have got to be stopped. The police were really nice. Well done, mum.'

Chapter Thirty-Three

J ason gets on with his new business. He's pretty grumpy and I'm relieved I've got a job to go to. I'm enjoying it. Starting a gardening project in the spring is perfect. The plants are waking up and I'm delighted with the fresh growth. The pay is better, and I'm doing okay with no travel expenses and the extra field rent money. I can afford my bills at least.

It still gets dark early, so I go to Fox Lodge in the mornings, work until after lunch then walk home. Never been so fit, which is an added bonus.

Fox Lodge is still empty. The owner must be away for the winter. As usual, Ink runs to the kitchen door and I call her back. 'You can't open doors to other people's houses,' I remind her. I get tools from the shed and the dog supplies I've carried here. I make Ink a hot water bottle and wrap her up on an old rug in a sunny patch where she can see me. I plan the work sunwise around the garden for both our benefit. No doubt I will do this backward to stay in the shade when summer comes. By the afternoon, I am pruning a Virginia Creeper that grows on the side of the house. Important to keep it in check so it doesn't encroach windows or start curling around the gutters.

The birds are singing, and new shoots are visible everywhere. The creeper, like the rest of the garden, has been well cared for by experienced hands. It does not take long for me to prune where I can reach. I take the cuttings to the compost heap and get a ladder. Like the wheelbarrow, it is wooden.

I should get going, don't want to get caught in the dark. Keen to finish my task, I move the ladder one last time, nearer a window. At first, I'm engrossed in my gardening, but I look in when the last sprig is cut. It's a lovely house. This window is near a sweeping staircase. Below, in the hall, is a grand piano. The landing has pictures. No, not pictures: paintings.

They're old and beautiful. Whoever lives here is even more wealthy than I realised.

Then I see a face. My face.

Hanging at the top of the stairs in pride of place is the nude portrait of myself with Ink. I'm so shocked I nearly fall off the fucking ladder! My mind races. I thought Mike bought and destroyed it. Whose house is this? How embarrassing. Will they realise it's me – their gardener? Will they still want the painting when they find out who it is? I don't think posh people have nudes of the staff on their walls. My cheeks burn.

I wipe my brow with my coat sleeve, and the secateurs fall from my hand. Spinning in the air, they bounce off the side of the ladder and crash through a downstairs window.

I cling to the ladder. One pane of the beautiful leadlight window is smashed. It probably has to be handmade by a craftsman or something and will cost a fortune to replace. Will they make me pay for the damage? Another bill is the last thing I need.

Well, I may be clumsy, but I'm honest. I try to call Spark-latious but there's no signal. Great. I can't leave the fallen glass inside the house. This window is in the hallway. For all I know, the owner could be old. Maybe they have small children. Or a dog.

'Come on,' I say to Ink. Reluctantly, she gets up from her warm blanket bed and follows me to the back door. I don't even have to ask her to open it. She trots right up, wags her skinny tail and goes inside.

'Hello?' I call as I step in, even though I know the house is empty. 'Hello?' The kitchen is new but old-fashioned. Oak cupboards, white granite. Lovely china in a glass-fronted case. Scrubbed flagstone floor. And it's toasty warm. Ink stretches out in front of the Aga. No wonder she wanted to come in. She could sense the heat.

I tiptoe into the hall. Not sure why I'm tiptoeing. Possibly guilt. I've smashed your ancient window and now I'm breaking into your house. And that picture you bought because you like greyhounds? Well, that's me. Fuck.

The antique glass is a million smithereens on an exquisite rug. My plan to dash in, pick up a few shards, put something over the hole, leave a note of apology and get the hell out is ruined. I need a vacuum cleaner or the tiny splinters of glass will get into the rug. I try my phone again. Nope. Better look for the broom cupboard.

A utility room off the kitchen has a fancy cordless vacuum. I set to work.

When the mess is cleared, I find a tea tray under the sink that will cover the hole. Ink is quite content, stretched out in the warmth. She's taken off her coat. I prop the tray over the hole with an orchid. A real one. I run my hands over the leaves for a moment and it bursts into flower. Pity my magical abilities do not extend to fixing broken windows. Can anyone do such a thing? How far does magic go?

The grand piano has a collection of silver frames. Dust-covered family photographs. Wedding pictures in black and white and group photos. There is a greyhound with a mottled brindle coat. Then another greyhound – a black one this time. Perhaps that's the reason they bought the painting.

Two boys hold a black puppy. There is something familiar about their faces. Fascinated, I go into the living room, where more dusty photographs are displayed in groups on spindly tables. The puppy grows up, and the boys become men.

It can't be.

'Ink?' I say. She comes in and flops onto a squashy sofa. 'You've been here before!'

Confused and angry, I climb the stairs with my phone held aloft. I find a signal in a back bedroom looking over fields. Furious, I google a number.

'Rutherford and Grey, Allingshire's premier estate agents. How may I help you?' says a pleasant girl.

'I'd like to speak to Mr um Rutherford, please.'

'May I say who's calling?'

'No!'

Moments later, his deep voice intones, 'Grant speaking. What can I do for you?' Smooth bastard.

'Why are there pictures of my dog in your house?'

'What? Lilith, is that you?'

'Yes, of course it's me, you prick. Why have you got pictures of Ink?'

'Where are you? Fox Lodge?'

'Yes fucking Fox Lodge.'

'What are you doing there?'

'I'm your new gardener.'

'Ink let herself in?' It's a statement more than a question.

From the bedroom, I can see the nude painting. I'm so embarrassed I hang up. I should have ignored the whole thing. But I'm freaking out. Why? Is Ink not really mine? I start to cry. Which is pathetic. My phone rings.

'It's me.' Arrogant fuck. 'Lilith, stay there. I'm coming over. Make yourself a cup of tea.'

Chapter Thirty-Four

M y first reaction is to head home. If I'm quick, I
will make it before dark.

No.

This is what I do when faced with problems. I turn away
and hope everything will be alright. Brush it under the carpet

and forget it ever happened. Well, not anymore. I need answers. And not just from Grant.

He's driving from his office in Barrington, so he's going to be an hour. I find blankets in the utility room and make Ink a bed beside the Aga. I ring Jason. Don't want him worrying about me being out in the dark.

'Hi, mum. What's up!' I'm impressed he's answered. The young don't do phone calls. I can hear voices in the background.

'You at the cottage?'

'No. I'm at Belinda's. Going to stop the night.'

'Okay, love.'

The twins are shrieking with delight.

'Got to go. Brian's here with fish and chips,' he says, and he's gone.

I make a mug of tea. There's no milk in the fridge. In fact, there is no food at all. Fox Lodge has the strange tidiness of an empty house. There are no orts. If there had been, they'd have settled like the dust. An old easy chair is pushed into the corner of the kitchen which I pull near the Aga and curl up in. After a busy day's gardening, I'm soon asleep.

When Grant arrives, it's dark. He switches on the kitchen light, switches it off again and whispers, 'Sorry.'

Ink is thrilled to see him. As they cavort, I look at my grubby gardening hands and pull a twig out of my hair.

He plonks a bag of shopping on the table. I planned to confront him as soon as he arrived. I want answers. Hard to get your act together in front of a man enveloped in golden orts.

'I'm sorry. I broke your window.' I pad through in my socks to show him the damage. He listens while I prattle on about Virginia creepers and secateurs. He looks from one of my eyebrows to the other. I feel explaining my caterpillar eyebrow will be information overload.

He removes his suit jacket and tie, drapes them over the banister and rolls up his sleeves as I follow him into the kitchen. 'Don't worry. I know a bloke who can fix it. It's only one pane. I thought you might be hungry?' He has a huge ready-made pizza. I am hungry. Hunger is a permanent state of the middle-aged woman. 'I know *you're* hungry,' he says to Ink as he opens a tin of dog food. She stands beside him, wagging her tail. Sweet he remembered to buy her some food. Then again, she is his dog, apparently.

He puts milk in the fridge and takes out a cold bottle of white wine and two crystal glasses from the cupboard.

'Grant, I'm not here to socialise. I don't want any wine. You owe me an explanation. How have you got pictures of Ink in your house? Why?'

'One black greyhound looks much like another,' he says, getting a corkscrew from a drawer and using the point to peel away the foil.

'She's wearing her check coat. And anyway, I know it's her.'

He winds in the screw, pulls out the cork with a pop and pours wine into the glasses. Why is it men don't listen to a word I say? My fingertips fizz with irritation. He puts a glass near me with a small smile, but he does not meet my eyes. I leave the wine untouched. He takes a good swig.

Ink has galumphed the food and is now licking the plastic bowl around the floor.

'How do you like the garden?' he says, opening the pizza box.

'Tell me the fucking truth!' I yell, picking up Ink's bowl and throwing it into the sink so hard it bounces back out. Grant catches it. Irritating shit.

There is sadness in his eyes. Like he can't speak. Beneath his golden glow, a veil covers his face, fine black threads over his mouth: a magical barrier between him and the world. I put my hand on his cheek and sense the obstruction. Beside me, one of the Blackwood witches emerges in a long dress and shawl.

He can't see my ancestor's ghost. She's small and thin, peering intently at his handsome face. She floats to my side, and cold lips whisper words I cannot hear. Holding the yew wand, I speak a counter spell which I hope will lift the hex, and she stands behind me, her hands over mine as I chant. Together we step around him once and then backward, retracing each movement, dragging the curse from him as we go. The smoke veil pleats and becomes a thread that we wind about the yew wand and toss outside. It rolls over the lawn and vanishes in a patch of moonlight.

'For fuck's sake, Lilith,' he says, pacing the kitchen and rubbing his face. You'd expect someone freed from a curse to be grateful. My ancestor witch stands with her arms folded, clearly unimpressed by Grant's antics. 'Thank you,' I say. She smiles and nods, steps back and is gone.

'Sister witches?' Grant asks.

'Something like that.'

'I need a shower.'

'No. No more fucking about. It's time to tell the truth. There is nothing to stop you now, and I need answers.'

'You might need answers, Lilith, but it's not as easy as lifting a hex. Magic has consequences.'

'You're worried about the Coven.'

'Of course I'm worried.'

I'm strangely calm. I push him into a chair and hand him his wine. I sort the pizza into the Aga and find a coke for myself in the fridge. I suspect alcohol and magic may not be a good mix.

'It's time to decide whose side you're on. Let's start with the hex and take it from there,' I say, raising my can.

He drinks his wine and tops up his glass. Runs a hand over his shaved head. 'I'm a thrall of the Coven,' he says at last.

I look at the ceiling. 'I've had enough of this bullshit.'

'I'm trying to explain. Anyone who is a part of the Coven but not considered worthy of the title "witch" becomes a thrall. A type of servant.'

'Sounds archaic to me.'

He shrugs. 'Witchcraft is archaic, Lilith. Things have been done the same for centuries. Anyway, as a thrall, you agree to serve the Coven, and in turn the Coven protects you.'

'Is it just men?'

'No. There are male witches. Not many, though. Witch-craft manifests in women mostly. A lot of men never develop their magic.' He smiles ruefully. 'Especially modern men. These days, guys are so out of touch with themselves.'

'Is that why you're a thrall?'

'Yes and no.' He looks at his hands.

'It's the sex thing.'

'Exactly that. Old superstitions die hard.'

Behind him, my ancestor witch emerges from the wall and stands behind him. Her arms are folded beneath her shawl, and she has an expression of utter contempt for Grant. Only the small lights under the wall cupboards are on. In the dimness, I can see her clearly and can't stop staring. She's short like me, and her hair is scooped into a bun. But it's her face I'm fascinated by. She's so young. 'You can't be more than twenty,' I blurt.

The ghost nods, and her smile is amazing. Heartfelt and beautiful. 'You're Bethany Blackwood.'

She holds up a finger. Then she sneers at Grant as if to say, 'What are you going to do about him?'

'Explain?' I say to Grant.

'Sometimes those who replenished their magic with inti-macy got into trouble because they abused their powers.'

'And have you ever abused your powers?'

'No. Fuck no.' He's on his feet. At the kitchen sink, he

splashes his face with cold water. 'No. Never. Just because that's the primary source of my strength does not mean I'd force myself on someone.'

I believe him, even though Bethany Blackwood is shaking her head. 'So they put a hex on you. Why?'

'It's not really a hex. It was a sealing spell. A silencing spell.'

Behind him, Bethany Blackwood looks at the ceiling.

'To stop you from telling me anything about the Coven.'

'You ever heard the expression "my lips are sealed"? That's where it originates from. Thralls, servants and associates are sealed so they can't share a coven's secrets. It's standard practice.'

'What happens if you do say something?'

'You can't. Even if you want to. Any open talk about the coven – it doesn't come out of your mouth.'

I check the pizza. It's done. He gets plates and a pizza cutter and tips a bag of ready-washed salad into a dish. We're both hungry and eat in silence. Bethany Blackwood is still scowling.

'It is Ink in the pictures,' he says.

I nod encouragingly.

'She was never my familiar. She was my mother's. But we adored her, my brother and I. After mum died, she stuck around. Usually they go off. It's one of those magical mysteries.' His voice is soft. He looks at the dog. 'She just mooched about. Like a normal dog. One day, some of the Coven came – routine check, they said. They asked if she was my mother's. I lied, of course. Said she was another black greyhound. Thralls aren't supposed to have familiars. Anyway, either she covered up her abilities or they thought she wasn't worth bothering about. They were happy, and that was it. Then something changed.' He pushes his plate away. 'She started to do things. Things she did when mum was alive.'

'Like what?'

'Opening doors. Playing tricks on me. You know the kind of thing.'

I'd like to hear about the tricks, but I don't want to stop his flow.

'She roamed. She went missing for three days once. It was then I realised another witch was nearby. I felt you that day in the department store. That's the weird thing about thralls. We may not have a lot of magical ability, but we can sense it in others from miles off.'

He's right about the weird part.

Behind him Bethany Blackwood silently claps her hands and I laugh. Grant looks over his shoulder. 'Can't you tell her to go away?'

'No.'

Bethany smiles and wanders about the kitchen.

'It was my duty to report finding you to the Coven. Because I live nearby, they set me to watch over you. The next time she went missing, I knew where she'd gone.'

I feel awful. Like I've stolen his dog. A dog he adores.

He clears the plates. As he passes me, he puts a hand on

my shoulder. 'She's a magical creature, Lilith. She's meant to be with a powerful witch. And they go where they will.'

'What did you call her?'

He stacks the dishwasher. 'Inka.'

'Inka?' I ask.

'Yes. You must have misheard her when her name popped into your mind.'

'Maybe she wanted a change.'

'Yeah, I guess.' We both admire her, sleeping on her back beside the Aga.

We chat about things that Ink can do. I tell him about her turning white and causing Mike's allergy. He tells me how she rescued his younger brother when he fell into a stream and how she liked to wear his mother's cashmere sweaters. We don't mention the bookshop incident or Theo.

'It's late. Why don't you stay over? There's plenty of room. Or I could run you back. Whatever you want.'

I look to see what Bethany thinks about this, but she's gone.

I'm exhausted. He leads the way upstairs, chattering about beds and towels and telling me to help myself. We both ignore the portrait. The nude elephant in the room. 'Here we go,' he says, opening a door. He switches on a bedside lamp and draws the curtains. 'Make yourself at home. If you need anything, shout.' Then he smiles. 'I promise my house won't lock you in or chuck things at you.'

I go in and close the door. Such a pretty room. Homely and chic. The bathroom has white towels and a white towelling dressing gown on the back of the door. There is even a little basket by the basin with a toothbrush in a packet, a tube of toothpaste and little bottles of shampoo and soap. Maybe he rents the place for Airbnb? Or does he have a lot of unexpected guests?

I take off my gardening clothes and shower. Brush my teeth and root about in Big Bag for face cream and my emergency HRT, which I keep in the miniature jam pot I pinched from the bookshop café.

In the bedroom, Ink is stretched out on the bed with a soft blanket on her, her tail thumping contentedly. He's left me a pile of clothes and a note: *Thought these might be useful. Help yourself to anything. See you in the morning. G. X*

My thoughtful host has turned down the bed and left me a mug of cocoa on the bedside table. The clothes pile has some big t-shirts, a soft grey jumper (cashmere?) and warm socks. I pull on a t-shirt and socks. It's cold up here, but the bed is warm. Of course, he has electric blankets. No wonder Ink has such a dopey expression of bliss on her long-hound face. I can't help looking at the note again before I turn out the light. What does 'X' mean exactly?

In the quiet house, I hear a shower running. Thoughts of Grant washing himself are very much in my mind. Made worse because I've seen him practically naked, and it doesn't take much imagination to add soap.

I turn off the electric blanket – don't want to cook myself alive. Younger me would have been greatly encouraged by 'X' and would be offering to wash Grant's back (and the rest).

Middle-aged me lets the warmth seep into her aching body. It's been a long and stressful day. I sleep.

In the night, I wake. Ink has gone, and Grant is talking downstairs. She probably heard him go to the kitchen for something and went to say hello. Soon, she is back beside me, and I cover her with the blanket, relieved she's not sleeping with him instead. I've got used to having a dog in my bed.

Like North Star Cottage, Fox Lodge is tucked away from roads and other houses. Only natural sounds reach me. An owl hoots. The wind blows. Ink breathes steadily. One benefit of the HRT is that it makes me sleep.

I wake again much later when the effect of the pills has worn off. I want to know the time. How long until morning? Should I try to go back to sleep or get up? On these dark winter mornings, it's hard to tell. It could be 7am and time to get going or the middle of the night. Ink harrumphs when I get out of bed to find my phone. It's 3.30am. I pull back the curtain and look out. There's not much to see in the dark night.

Now I'm out of bed, I'm acutely aware of Grant. Is he in pyjamas? Does he snore? Is he awake? After a bit of sleep, I must admit I'm randy.

Maybe I should find something to read? I'm sure I saw a bookcase on the landing. Curiosity killed the witch, I tell myself. Makes no difference. I creep out, shining the light from my phone on the paintings as I pass. An old woman in a red dress sits at a desk, a large book on her lap. There is something in her stern gaze that makes me move along. A vase of dahlias, loosely painted, petals softly falling on polished wood. Then me. Naked with Ink's head on my knee. It's here in pride of place at the top of the stairs. And what did he mean by 'X'?

I'm overthinking this like a schoolgirl. Grant was hexed. That's why he's been less helpful than he could have been. Basically, he's a nice bloke. A nice bloke I fancy. Quite a lot.

The bookcase is full of high-brow, leather-bound books. Not the beach read I was hoping for. A bedroom door is ajar. He's in there. I can hear him breathing. I peep inside. The room is large with a massive bed.

Grant, with his dark tattooed skin, is under that duvet.

Fuck it.

In I go. I close the door and pull off the big t-shirt. It's so dark I have to step across the room with my hands outstretched and feel my way around the edge of the bed. Pulling back the duvet, I slide in beside him. He's awake. I scoot nearer and he embraces me.

Dark love is a great idea. I'm not so self-conscious now he can't see middle-aged, slightly overweight me. He's much fitter than I am. Maybe I should work out. Take an exercise class. Have more sex.

He traces my back and strokes my bum. I put my hands around his neck and pull him against me. The kiss is languid. Almost like he was expecting me to slip naked into his bed. Cocky shit. I run my hands over his shaved head, which is bristly. Does he shave it every day?

His cock is not languid – it's most pleased to see me. With

one hand, I feel the length of him. Adequate, but smaller than I imagined. However, my sex-on-a-whim moment is coming back to bite me. There is no way that's going in without some lubrication. Why didn't I remember I am, in fact, an old, dried-up (if randy) hag? Not some moist twenty-year-old.

'Hold on,' I whisper. Out I get, making another blind walk to find the bathroom door. A dim light comes on automatically (this man lives in a hotel). In the cabinet, I find a tub of Vaseline. Perfect. I dab a sizeable glob where it needs to go and return to my lover.

He's sitting on the edge of the bed, and I bump into him and laugh.

'Hello,' he whispers.

In the dark, I'm empowered. I put my finger over his lips. 'Shh,' I say, pushing him onto the mattress. His skin is smooth and lovely, and he smells like an herb I know, though I can't think of its name. I kiss his lips as I sit astride him. His cock is so ready. I'd like to see him, to trace his tattoos with my lips. I almost reach for the bedside lamp. But I probably look a mess. No arty tattoos here, just my glue-marked, HRT-patched bum. And when did I last epilate my legs? Dark it is then.

As we kiss, his fingers find my clitoris. He gives it a light rub, which feels good. Wakes it up anyway. But Grant is much like any man in this department. A quick rub is all that's needed to send me over the edge – or so he thinks. And like most women, I perpetuate this myth and make a few guttural moans.

The next minute, he's guiding himself into me, and as I'm

on top, I have some control. We take the first couple of thrusts slowly. Not because he's so vast I can barely accommodate his impressive length? No. In fact, he's pretty average, and the Vaseline is doing a sterling job. No, slowly does it because my poor knees are unhappy with the arrangement. One of them audibly creaks, and I add a few well-timed moans so he doesn't think he's fucking a skeleton.

He's got me by the hips and is trying (I think) to get us moving together in a fluid, sexy motion. My knees are unable to comply. I slide off him and flop onto the mattress. He's soon on top of me. One hand grabs my tit and the other takes his weight. Classic fucking ensues, and it's much more comfortable for all concerned. I hang on with legs and arms until he gets the job done. There's a reason the missionary position is so popular. It's easy.

As we fuck, he finds a good angle, and I'm getting where I need to go. I'm moaning, but now I mean it. He stops. I move my hips, wanting a little more. Then I realise he's coming. He stays quite still then kisses my forehead, reaches for the tissues and gives me a wad. I expect him to go to the bathroom. Instead, he rolls onto his back and sleeps. Women must deal with the mess of sex. I sigh and feel my way to the bathroom. When I've cleaned up, I leave the door open a little so I can find the t-shirt. He's stretched out on the bed, one tissue-covered hand over his manhood. I can't believe he's fallen asleep in the cold without covers. I pick the duvet up from the floor as he lets go a massive, wet-sounding snore. A pause. Then he breathes out with a long 'phooow'. Is he ok? It sounded gurgly. I clutch the duvet in the dark, listening to the repetition of his plug-hole burble, long pause and 'phooow'. He's not dying, and I suppress a laugh and chuck the duvet over him, all thoughts of snuggling up for a cuddle gone.

Ink is not in my room. She often wanders at night. Alone, my fingers find myself. I was so close. But the moment has gone, and I can't be bothered. Instead, I think about getting up early and walking home as soon as it's light. I'm oddly disappointed with the sex. But that's the trouble when you anticipate shagging a bloke. Reality can never match up. He never had a weird, wet snore in my fantasies.

Chapter Thirty-Five

Morning dawns dark, with sleety rain hitting the windows. I check my phone. No news from the kids, so they must be okay. The cracked screen is most definitely a tree and is rather pretty. So long as it doesn't actually break I don't mind. It's late. Ten o'clock! I shower and dress in yesterday's jeans and underwear – not ideal – and another of his t-shirts, this time a blue one. I twist my hair up with a clip and do what I can to cheer up my face with the makeup from Big Bag. My eyebrows look bizarre but cutting a fringe is a bit extreme. I'm sure it's hardly noticeable. As I put the room to rights, make the bed and draw the curtains, I hear voices downstairs.

It's not only Grant talking to Ink. He's got visitors. I pause on the stairs and take a deep breath, then enter the kitchen. There is a lovely smell of eggs and bacon, and Grant is smiling from the end of the table. 'This is my brother, Barry.'

Barry salutes me with his mug. I pet Ink as she goes back to her bed beside the Aga.

'And this is Mrs Craggs.'

An old woman with a deeply wrinkled face sets down a huge plate of fried breakfast. 'Leave what you don't want. Mind. The plate's hot. Tea or coffee?'

'Tea, please.' Who is she? A relative? Member of staff?

She picks up the teapot. 'I'll do some fresh.'

'Oh, don't worry...'

'No, you can't have stewed tea for your first cup in the morning.'

'Thank you.'

'I hope Barry didn't wake you with his late arrival,' says Grant.

I pick up my knife and fork. 'Slept like a log,' I lie. The breakfast is amazing, and I could easily eat it all. I hate it when people tell you they've given you too much!

'Sorry. Thought the place was empty. Drove back from

London on a whim. Sometimes you have enough of the city.'
He doesn't look up from his paper when he speaks.

I smile at Grant, and he smiles back. Nice. It's hard to see
in the electric light whether his golden glow is brighter this
morning. He's all washed and shaved and is very handsome in
his black t-shirt and faded jeans. Barry wears a thick blue
dressing gown. Like me, he's slept in.

'Now boys,' says Mrs Craggs, setting a fresh pot of tea on
the table. 'What are you doing for lunch?'

'No need to bother,' says Grant. 'We'll go to the pub.'

'It's no bother.'

'No, don't trouble yourself. You've already done enough.'

'Right then. I'll just pop a duster round, since I'm here.'
She goes into the utility room. The men read the Sunday
papers, and I drag a section nearer. I have the distinct impression they'd be chatting if I wasn't here.

I pour tea, eat and pretend to read. But as they're not
looking at me, I can look at them. Barry is almost identical to
his brother. What does he do in London? Are they twins? Are
there any other siblings? He has orts, too – barely noticeable
in the bright kitchen light, but they're there. There's a dark
green shadow when he moves his hand. Quite different from
Grant's golden glow. I must find out what the different orts
mean as soon as I can.

Barry puts down the paper and reaches for the toast rack.
I pass the butter. They must be close. The same little boys in
the family pictures. With Ink. Does Barry realise Ink is Ink?
Maybe when Mrs Craggs is out of earshot, we'll start talking.

Mrs Craggs emerges from the utility in a different apron, armed with a bucket of cleaning stuff.

'Craggy, please don't trouble yourself,' says Barry. But there's no dissuading her.

'I don't know why you bothered her,' says Grant when she's gone. 'I'm sure we could have managed.'

Barry shrugs and takes another bite of toast. 'It's why we pay her a retainer. She's hardly rushed off her feet. Must be three months since anyone was here.' There is something familiar about his voice. I brush this thought aside deciding that he sounds like his brother.

I gather the plates and carry them to the dishwasher. Grant stacks. I go back to the table and collect the toast rack. It's made of china with hand-painted foxes. I rinse it under the tap and put it carefully on the granite draining board. Even I know you don't put antiques in the dishwasher. There's a strange atmosphere in the kitchen, so I leave the brothers to get whatever it is they need to get off their chests and head upstairs to brush my teeth. Mrs Craggs is remaking my bed.

'Oh, I was just here for the night,' I say, not wanting to put her to any trouble.

'Thank you. Nice to have a bit of information. Those two expect me to guess.' She strips the bed and bundles up the sheets and drops them in a heap by the door. I brush my teeth and redo my lipstick in the bathroom, and when I come out, she's struggling with a fitted sheet. I help, and we pull it on together and wrestle a fresh quilt cover over the duvet.

She looks at Big Bag on the floor. 'No luggage?'

'No. Unplanned visit. I'm actually the new gardener. Had an accident, and Grant insisted I stay over.'

'New gardener? Are you gardening today?'

'I might do a bit. Save me the walk tomorrow.'

'Well, you can give me a hand until the rain stops. Fetch some pillowcases for me, love.'

'Where from?'

'I keep them in the big room. Mr Grant's room. The tall cupboard by the little window.'

In Grant's room, there is a large ugly wardrobe but no tall cupboard. She pops her head around the door. 'Not this room. This is Mr Barry's room. The master bedroom. I'll show you.'

I look at the bed and green orts that cling to the edges of the room and reality dawns.

I've had sex with the wrong guy.

My heart is thumping in my chest, and I have a strong urge to run.

'Here we are,' says Mrs Craggs, flinging open the door. I follow her into a huge room with a four-poster bed.

A four-poster bed!

Who sleeps in a four-poster bed in this day and age? Who does he think he is, William Morris?

The walls are covered in hand-painted wallpaper, and there is a dressing table and stool, a small settee at the end of the bed and a fireplace with carved stone lions. She finds the pillowcases while I gape like a peasant.

'Henry Tudor slept in that bed. Well, the mattress is new. But you know what I mean. And Mick Jagger. But not together.' She laughs at her joke and hands me the pillowcases.

I've had sex with the wrong man.

'They knew how to make drapes in the old days. Never let any light in, not like the rubbish they call curtains nowadays. Seven generations of Rutherfords. All born in this bed.' She ties back the heavy curtains. Outside, the sleet is almost snow.

I might be sick. There is no other woman in this house, and even with my relatively low self-esteem, I don't think Barry would mistake me for Mrs Craggs. He knew. He fucking knew I thought he was Grant. And now what? We pretend it never happened. My mind is reeling between acute embarrassment and fury.

'Right. That'll do,' she says, straightening the covers on the historical bed. Henry Tudor and Mick Jagger – but not me.

I follow her into my room and help with the pillowcases.

'Not the boys, though,' she continues. 'They were born in hospital. Well, it's the modern way, isn't it, hospital? In my day, you birthed your kids at home. Had all three of mine in the kitchen.'

The bed's done, and we go into the master bedroom, where she collects a small tea tray from the nightstand. 'Mr Grant likes his morning tea. Always been an early bird. Same when he was a kiddy. Always up before the rest of the household. Some things never change. Grab the sheets, lovey.'

I gather the bundle of bed linen as instructed.

"Course, I used to live in when they were young. Where did you walk from then?'

'Sorry?'

'You said you walked here yesterday. Fox Green?' She glances at me with bright blue eyes as we go down the sweeping staircase.

'Nearby. Church Lane.'

'There's only one house on Church Lane,' she says. Then she stops. Turns fully about to look at me properly, her gaze like a knife.

'Blackwood witch!' The words come out in a whisper, and she drops the tea tray. It crashes down the stairs. I drop the laundry and reach out to steady the old woman, who looks like she's about to fall. Her mouth opens as I grasp her elbow and she screams. She is ridged, lips drawn back over yellow teeth, and the scream goes on and on. Bloodcurdling and unworldly.

Ink is at my side, barking.

The men rush up the stairs and grab her. Grant mutters something and she closes her mouth. In the silence, her eyes are wide with fear. She points at me. 'Blackwood witch,' she hisses.

Barry helps Mrs Craggs down the stairs. 'Now come on, Craggy. There are no Blackwood witches. They're all dead.' He glances at me, a question on his face. In the hallway, the dark green of his orts is clear.

Grant ushers me into the kitchen, where I lean on the table. Ink winds herself around my legs.

'Sorry,' says Grant. 'She's a screamer.'

My ears are ringing. 'What does she mean, Blackwood witch? Why is she afraid of me?'

'We need to talk, but not here.'

'I've given her a brandy and put her for a lie-down,' says Barry. He looks between us as if he is unsure who to speak to. He decides on his brother. 'Tell me Craggy is wrong!'

Grant is silent.

Chapter Thirty-Six

Confrontation is not my thing. I put on my coat, grab Big Bag and pull on the dinosaur hat to keep the rain off. Ink is already outside and we hurry down the long gravel drive

Older and wiser, I know I should have stood up for myself a lot more during my life. Said what I thought. Made my opinions known and argued my case. Hindsight is a wonderful thing. Recently I've been trying to be less passive. Basically, I'm hard-wired to please. Whether this is a generational thing or the core of my personality, it's hard to say.

In the last year, I have had more disagreements and temper flare-ups than in the rest of my life. Is magic or menopause at the root of this new argumentative self? Maybe it's just because I've reached a certain age of grumpiness. Today, however, is not the day for conflict. Today, I want to avoid any more unpleasantness.

'Where do you think you're going?' Barry strides across the drive and grabs my arm, digging in his fingers and swinging me around. I raise my hands and push the air in front of me. He falls backward on the gravel. He scrambles up and tries again, but I'm not having it. Back down he goes. I glare at him and walk on.

'Whore!' he shouts after me.

I stomp back. 'You fucking deceitful shit. You knew. You knew I thought you were him.'

He gets up and brushes leaves from his dressing gown. 'I never would have touched you if I'd known you were a Black-wood witch.' He spits on the ground, and his green orts are a dark shadow around him. The rain pours. He sneers as he looks me up and down, taking in my gardening coat, dinosaur hat and caterpillar eyebrow. 'No wonder you have to creep around in the dark to get a shag.'

Ink comes between us, displaying her hooked fangs.

There's a low, continuous growl in her throat. Just as well. Damned if I can think of something clever to say.

He points at Fox Lodge. 'Grant wouldn't have touched you. He'd rather die than fuck a Blackwood.' His arm swings around, and he points at the gate, which creaks and opens. 'Stay away from my family.'

Muttering some weird curse, he marches off.

It's a long walk back in the ceaseless rain. Ever the optimist, I hope Grant will pick me up in the car. But no. Men leave me out in the wet when I'm difficult.

The cottage is cold and damp. I light the fire in the range, get it stoked up and fetch more logs while I've got my coat on. Then I tackle the fire in the lounge. By the time I've fed bird, dog and cat, the place is warming up. I hang the wet coat to dry and take off my hat. It's all been a bit much for the knitted stegosaurs. He's lying on his side in a dejected manner. I know how he feels.

I put on a warm jumper and dry jeans and look at my reflection in the bedroom window. I've had a good think while walking home. I need a proper job. Perhaps I could take a course and train at something. Although at what exactly, I do not know. I have never secretly wanted to *be* anything. My only aspiration was to have a family. I'm part of a generation raised with the notion that keeping house and raising kids would leave me perfectly fulfilled. They never said that you have nothing when those kids have grown and your husband has traded you in for a newer, more exciting model. Less-than-perfect family life was never discussed – much like the menopause.

I lean on the window ledge, close my eyes and sigh. The magic, so new and so weird, courses through me. My hands fizz as I remember how easy it was to throw Barry onto his condescending arse. I'd laugh if I wasn't so embarrassed about last night. What a completely stupid thing to do. Unlucky in love. That's me. I have no judgement where men are concerned. I don't even want to think why they were so horrified that I am a Blackwood witch.

A flurry of rain pelts the window. In my overgrown garden, a willowy figure moves through the long grass. Bethany Blackwood turns her ghostly face to me and raises a hand. In greeting or farewell, it is hard to say. She drifts about. Rain is of no consequence for a ghost.

Ink comes and leans against me. 'I'm so fucking confused,' I say, putting a hand on her sleek black head. Her eyes are beautiful. 'Yes. I know what you're saying, Inky dog. This witch stuff is not going to go away. At least I have you.' I give her neck a good scratch. The face she pulls as I do this always cheers me up.

On the window ledge, beneath a jug of dried hydrangea heads, is the sea glass Ink dug up from Bethany Blackwood's grave. I hold it pressed between my palms. 'Show me,' I whisper, and the sea green glass reveals a feather etched upon the surface with the word 'beware'. The image fades as I put it down. Last time I needed moonlight and sparks to get the magic to work.

Now I need only ask, and it answers. Even a fool like me understands that this magic is getting stronger and... I search for the word as I go downstairs. Ink galumphs ahead. The fire is sluggish, probably because the wood is damp. As I pass, I cast a flurry of bright sparks at it, and flames rise. Instinctual. That is the word I'm looking for. Stronger and instinctual. That's it. Magic is becoming a reflex. I fill the kettle and smile at the memory of Barry on his arse in the gravel. That was pretty instinctual.

Jason returns in the afternoon. Seems like his sister has chivvied him out of his glum mood. He's all fired up about making a new portfolio and has a list of places that hire freelancers. When he's shared his news, he goes upstairs to 'his office', leaving a bag of laundry behind him. I put aside my spell books, get the laundry on and cook spaghetti Bolognese from frozen mince. It's a massively annoying task getting the meat to submit. It wants to stay frozen, but I persevere, hacking it into ever smaller lumps while the tomato sauce bubbles around it. Pity my magic doesn't fix the laundry, defrost the mince or do the dishes.

I could do with a big shop, but I don't want to spend the money. When the sauce is bubbling away, I check my email on my old laptop and look for a job. I'm surprised that I have four requests for birthday cakes. Well, three. One is from a Mr Richards who'd like me to make a cake in the shape of his cock. He's attached a picture. There's always a pervert lurking. I press delete.

After some online sleuthing, I email everyone back charging a bit more for the cakes to make it worth my while.

Over the spag-bol, I tell Jason about my cake venture. He's on it straight away. 'I'll change your website, mum. The one I did for the bed and breakfast. I want some example websites for my portfolio. Wish you'd taken a picture of the chocolate cake you made for Ed, the delivery guy.'

The one I made after he ate the first. 'I was thinking about putting some leaflets up locally. Fox Tearoom. Maybe one in the post office?'

'Sounds like a plan. What you going to call it? This cake business?'

'You decide, love.'

Jason stays in his 'office' for the next few days. He seems happy, which is the main thing. All three people have agreed to my ridiculously high prices, so I'm busy baking and putting a quick spell on the icing to make them look amazing and worth the money.

I'm happy cooking, but I'm not convinced there will be enough people wanting cakes to make up for losing my gardening job. I do maths on the back of an envelope. At these prices, I'd need to make two cakes seven days a week, which would almost give me enough to live on. I make a list of what I could offer. Boxes of cookies. Wedding cakes and fruit cakes. Maybe I could do iced biscuits? I try to work out appropriate prices and root about in the kitchen cupboards for cake tins and biscuit cutters. It's not exactly a business plan, but it's a start.

Jason enthusiastically takes pictures of my creations before people collect them and puts them on the website. I'm testing a chocolate cake with a skewer when Ink woofs to let me know someone is coming.

'Open the door,' I tell her. Martin, the postman, is holding a handful of letters and a small box. We have two postmen, both called Martin. One is quiet and leaves the stuff in the box by the gate. Chatty Martin comes to the door. Secretly, we call them Martin the Mouth and Shush Martin.

'Something smells good,' he says as I slide the almost-done cake back into the range cooker and carefully add another log.

'Alexa, five minutes,' I say.

'Five minutes starting from now.'

'Ooh you've got one of those robot thingummies. Does it interrupt you?'

'Only if you say her name. How are you?'

'Mustn't grumble.' But he does. He tells me all about his mother-in-law, who says she's sprained her ankle but it's definitely gout if you ask him. The wife's still got the old trouble, and there's no telling when that might end. Ink potters down to the gate with him when he leaves, her ears twitching as he chats on.

The letters are mostly bills, but there is a scribbled note from Walter Cranford. I have to fetch my reading glasses to make sense of his scrawl. Apparently, Mr Waterman, aka Mike, has many tax dodges in that name. Walter is confident he can use this as leverage to stop the impending court case. I slide the letter next to my divorce papers among the cookbooks on the dresser. A filing system would be a good idea. I'm sure Walter is right and he can persuade Mike to back the fuck off. Then I remember the orts in the penthouse. Someone else was there apart from Theo. I picture the green orts and the penny drops – Barry Rutherford! I shudder to think I had sex with that awful man. The Coven is behind it all. They want North Star Cottage and Blackwood Forest. And they're willing to go to any lengths to get it. I'm safe for now. But they'll think of something else.

The box is addressed to me. Curious, I wash my hands and open it. Inside is a set of leaflets Jason has designed.

'Jason!' I call up the stairs. I'm crying when he comes in. 'These are amazing. You're so bloody clever.' I hug him.

He's called my cake-making venture 'Fox Bake' and he's designed a cute logo of a fox with a cupcake on its head. 'It's brilliant.' I prop one in the kitchen window. The fox has green eyes, which feels like a good omen.

A few minutes later, he's dragged his old push bike out of the shed and is pumping up the tyres. 'Wish one of us could drive,' he says, wobbling around the lawn. Ink sits beside me on the doorstep star like she's seen it all before. I put my hand on her head and wonder how old she is.

'Where are you off to? It's freezing out here.'

'I'm going to distribute some of these,' he says, waving the leaflets.

I stop myself from saying, 'Make sure you're back before dark.' It's hard work trying not to be a nagging mother.

He is back before dark, and I put all my troubles aside for the next few days. The café on Fox Green has asked for scones, fruit and cheese, twelve each week. I have five birthday cakes to make next week and two anniversary cakes to make for the weekend. Jason bought me nice cardboard cake boxes online. Happy and busy, with fewer money worries, thoughts of witchcraft are far from my mind – apart from the spells I put on the icing. Somehow, having a lot to do makes me get more done. The cottage is up together and I'm cooking proper food for Jason and me every day. It's great having him around, and for the first time in so long, I feel useful and in control. I've even asked Elaine over for tea and cake.

Maybe Fox Bake is the way forward.

Chapter Thirty-Seven

I'm mixing a coffee sponge for an anniversary cake when Ink woofs, stretches, touches her nose to the door and goes outside. Mike is standing on the doorstep.

I'm so surprised I almost tip over the bowl. Mike strides in and calls up the stairs. 'Jason, come on!' He sits and waits. Maud walks up and down the dresser, making her clattering sound. Claudia gets up from the kitchen table, where she was napping on a tea towel, and struts out.

How dare he just walk in here? I feel the familiar tingle in my fingertips. Irritation and magic are a potent mix. I carry on beating the cake with a wooden spoon to stop myself from yelling at him about hacking my bank account and *Mr Waterman's* penthouse. I've never liked arguing in front of the kids. Once again, I draw a veil over Mike's less pleasant side. I know Barry Rutherford is involved but I doubt Mike needed much persuading.

He's looking at a Fox Bake leaflet. 'Should you be selling cakes from a kitchen full of dirty animals?' he says mildly.

I turn, and a blob of cake mix plonks on the floor. Ink saunters over to clear it up.

'Aren't you supposed to have a food hygiene certificate or something?'

'Why are you here, Mike?'

'Jason asked me to come and get him.'

God, he looks smug.

The sound of a suitcase bumping down the stairs stops all conversation. I want to shout, 'Don't bump! It makes dust.' But 'nice' mummy must grit her teeth and smile.

Mrs Beeton's Cookery and Household Management flies off the dresser and delivers Mike a glancing blow on the back of his head. He's on his feet and cursing as nervous hands check his wiglet thing. I beat the cake and try not to laugh. Don't worry, mate, it still looks like shit.

Jason wheels in a suitcase. 'I'll put this in the motor,' says Mike. Big smile. Lots of bonhomie. Perfect father figure.

'Mum, have you seen my walking boots?' Jason is in the under-stairs cupboard, and he finds them before I can tell him I know nothing about any boots. I fetch a plastic bag to put them in while he drags in another large hold-all and a smaller suitcase. Not a weekend trip, then. I want to ask where he's going and for how long, but he's waving his mobile at me.

'I sent a group chat thing to your phone – you've got to accept it, though.' Jason kisses my cheek and lugs his stuff down the cobbled path. I wave as the sports car rumbles away.

I could cope if I'd had a heads-up. The suddenness of the situation is the problem. One minute, I'm all happy, baking cakes, stew slow cooking for dinner, and the next I'm alone.

I sit on the floor with Ink and warm my back on the range. It's a great place to have a good cry. I'm still there with Claudia on my lap, Ink resting her head on my shoulder and Maud perched on my foot when the kitchen door flies open.

It's Elaine. I'd completely forgotten she was coming.

'May I come in?'

Still snivelling, I wave her into the kitchen and extract myself from my familiars. I'm hardly up before she's got me in a hug. Bless her.

'What's happened?' she says. I tell her about Mike's sudden arrival and Jason's sudden departure. It all sounds pathetic. She pulls off a piece of kitchen roll and hands it to me. I sit and blow my nose while she puts on the kettle.

'You can't get it back, love,' she says. 'Family life. When it's gone, it's gone, and we women must make do with snippets of a life we once had.'

That sets me off again, and I have another big sob. I'm useless.

'Two things,' she says when I've got myself together. She pushes a leaflet over. There's a cartoon of a smiling, grey-haired woman tearing up L plates with the caption 'You're never too old to learn to drive!'

'I'm going to take my test. I think you should, too.' She stirs the teapot and puts on the beehive cosy. It could do with a wash.

'That's great. But I can't afford it. Certainly couldn't afford a car.' And I'm terrified.

'Mmm,' she says, putting a drop of milk into two flowery mugs. 'And the other thing. The Coven heard about your altercation with the Rutherford brothers.'

I don't get to say anything because Ink woofs and opens the door. A young woman stands on the doorstep. 'Hello. I've come to collect a chocolate teapot cake.'

I jump up. 'For your Gran?'

'Yes. She'll be 89.'

I fetch the cake and lift the box lid.

'That's perfect. She's going to love it. Thank you so much,' she says, handing me cash. Ink and I walk her to the gate.

'Freezing out there. Wouldn't be surprised if it snowed,' I say, shutting the door and wrapping up Ink beside the range.

'You're selling cakes?'

'Just a few...'

'Don't you need a hygiene certificate for that?'

'Probably.'

Elaine pours the tea. 'So, the long and the short of it is that Barry Rutherford put in a complaint about you. Said you used malicious magic against him. But the good news is that the Coven has decided you should be initiated. I mean, if you can use magic against Barry –he's a powerful witch himself – then obviously there's no chance your magic is fading. If anything, it's getting stronger?'

I nod and sip my tea. Elaine adds sugar and stirs. Her hair is pale blue today, and she is wearing her Poorbrook House lanyard: 'Elaine Waters, volunteer historian'. In the photograph her hair is red.

'I suppose the next thing you're going to tell me is that the Coven wants to reprimand me.' I'm trying to keep the irritation out of my voice. After all, Elaine is just the messenger.

'No, no. The complaint was withdrawn.' She raises her eyebrows as she takes a sip of tea.

'What?'

'I've known those two boys all their lives. It's not like Barry to back down. There's only one person who could make him do it.'

Grant's name hangs in the air between us.

I give my nose a good blow. Never easy on kitchen roll; it's too thick.

'Elaine, you've been very kind to me, but I feel I'm still

being kept in the dark. There's so much witch stuff that no one's telling me. And as much as I'd like to put aside magic and get on with my life, it's not going away. My magic is here to stay.' I pick my tea up and put it down again. 'One minute, the Coven says it wants me and the next, it doesn't. And let's be honest, they seem to put a lot of obstacles in my way and then...'

My mouth goes dry as I remember Mrs Craggs and that awful scream. I drink my tea. Elaine's orts don't float around her; they waft on the floor near her feet. As far as I can tell, she is not the victim of a silencing spell. I think good old-fashioned loyalty keeps Elaine from telling me the whole story.

'What is it about Blackwood witches that makes everyone so worried?'

Elaine traces a finger over a knot in the table's woodgrain that looks like a face. This must be hard. I'm aware she's been told to keep me in check. She's just trying to be nice and friendly about it.

'I took a hex off Grant yesterday so he could speak freely.'

Elaine's eyes widen. There's also a faint smile on her lips. 'Ida won't be happy about that.'

'She did that to him?'

'She does a lot of things.' It's the first glimmer of defiance.

'It's prehistoric, doing something like that to a person. And Grant... He can be annoying, but basically, I think he's a person who would try to do the right thing.'

Elaine smiles. 'He is. You're right, but...'

'I know about the sex thing.'

'He's never abused it. He's not like that.'

Grant in that bloody four-poster bed flits through my imagination. I change the subject.

'Do you put a spell on your hair?'

Elaine scowls.

'It's always such a lovely colour,' I add, realising I've offended her.

'I forget that you haven't grown up with all this. We never speak about the spells we put on our hair. It's not the done thing.'

To hide my smile, I fetch a tin of scones. They're supposed to be for the tearoom, but I can make more. I put the tin, knives, plates, butter and jam on the table. 'I've run out of cream.'

We busy ourselves with the scones. I think we both need a pick-me-up.

'These are terrific.'

'Thanks. Old recipe of mum's.'

The mention of my mother brings us back to the conversation at hand.

Elaine finishes her scone and takes a deep breath. 'The rift between the Blackwood witches and the Rutherfords began long ago. There was a marriage way back. I'm talking medieval Britain. The Ruffheads, as they were known then, were the big landowners around here, and the eldest son, Ulric, married a peasant girl against his family's wishes.'

'Bethany Blackwood?' I say.

'Yes. Bethany was young and beautiful and also a witch.

The family was furious about the association. The son was promised in marriage to another Lord's daughter. They married in secret. The father disinherited them. He hoped his son, when faced with poverty, would leave his new bride, return to the family and marry the high-born daughter. But Bethany, although not rich by the Ruffhead's standards owned Blackwood Forest and the surrounding pasture. They built North Star Cottage, and the two lived a simple but happy life.'

I top up our tea from the pot. We both cup the mugs in our hands to make it hotter.

'Medieval life was hard and disease was rife. The son got sick, and not even Bethany, with all her gifts of healing, could cure him. He died.'

'And they blamed her.'

'Exactly. They had a daughter, and the Ruffheads wanted to take the child. But Bethany refused to give them custody. The Ruffheads tried to chase her off the land - claiming it was theirs.'

'But they didn't manage it...'

'No. She had legal proof the land was hers.'

I think of the hand drawn map Walter showed me.

'The Ruffheads were not the type of people who take no for an answer. They accused Bethany of witchcraft and said she'd used dark magic on their son.'

An icy chill crawls up my spine.

'They burnt her at the stake on Fox Green.'

I think of the ghost I know and her young face. Outrage pours through me, followed by a deep sadness.

'What happened to the little girl?'

'The Ruffheads say Baby Bethany died.'

'There's a grave. She lived until she was old,' I say, realising the first author of the family spell book was the daughter of the girl who was burnt on Fox Green.

'Which is why it's more likely she was raised by one of Bethany's sisters.'

'She had sisters?'

'Three.'

'They were witches?'

'Oh yes. They moved into North Star Cottage. That's when bad things started to happen to the Ruffheads. Some say it was fate. Others say they hexed them. For years, the family suffered.'

'In what way?'

'You name it. Failed crops. House fires. Stillborn babies. Illness. Financial ruin.' In the end, the family made a bargain with the three sisters to lift the curse in exchange for land and money.'

'And the Ruffheads lived at Fox Lodge?'

Elaine laughs. 'No, that was a little hunting lodge. The forest was bigger then. The Ruffheads lived at Poorbrook House. Their estate stretched across half of Allingshire. Your mother never told you any of this?'

'No. This is all news to me. She must have thought it was all in the past. Or perhaps she didn't know.'

Elaine shakes her head slowly. 'She knew.'

'I can see how they feel they've fallen on hard times if they used to live at Poorbrook House. But that's all ancient history, surely?'

'The Ruffheads believed the curse was never lifted. It's one of the reasons they changed their name to Rutherford.'

Ink gets up and has a stretch. The door opens, letting in a blast of cold air, and she goes into the garden. Maud flies once around the kitchen and joins her. I close the door.

'Seems like there are a lot of old grudges,' I say.

'That's only half the story. Do you want to hear about the new grudges?'

We both take another scone.

Chapter Thirty-Eight

The Rutherfords, as you know, are in real estate. But they have a lot of interest in local industry, which they've been involved with since Victorian times. Bertram Rutherford had a woollen mill in Market Forrington, and it did so well he wanted to build a railway to transport his goods cheaply to London. The quickest route would have been through Blackwood Forest.'

'Oh dear.'

'Oh dear indeed. There was a lot of legal wrangling. The rich were used to getting their way, and the Blackwoods were not budging. At the time, there were three generations living at North Star Cottage. There was a scandal about unholy proceedings.'

'They were accused of witchcraft again?'

'Exactly. The scandal was so bad, local people tried to chase the Blackwood women off the land.'

'What I don't understand is why they keep accusing my family of witchcraft when they're witches themselves.'

'Well, they weren't. Not until the railway business. They decided the Blackwoods always won the altercations because of their unnatural powers. That's when Bertram decided to fight like with like. He and his brother married the Thornbury sisters: witch twins from Scotland.

'He thought they'd give him an edge, but these young girls were no match for the Blackwoods. And, of course, he never realised that most witches draw strength from their birthplace.'

Everything about this place gives me strength, not just the strange blackwood trees. Elaine picks up Claudia, who has wandered in, and stands her on her lap.

'What happened?' I ask.

Elaine sighs. 'In Victorian times, childbirth was dangerous. Both the girls died birthing their first child.'

She scratches Claudia at the base of her tail.

'And...?'

'I'm trying to tell this without upsetting you.'

'Just tell me.'

'The brothers were distraught. The younger one went mad and threw himself over the cliff at Horseshoe Cove. He was broken-hearted. Bertram did something else.'

I wait.

'He got the Thornbury witches in Scotland to curse all the women in your family to never have lasting love.'

I laugh. 'I am unlucky in love.' Like sleeping with the wrong bloke.

The door flies open, and Ink trots in. Outside, heavy rain is falling, and it's already almost dark. 'Why don't you stay for something to eat? I've got a bit of stew in the oven,' I say, clearing away the tea things. The mixing bowl is still on the counter, and a magpie feather is floating on the mixture. I may not have a food hygiene certificate, but even I know this is not acceptable. I scrape it into the bin. I'll start again tomorrow. Elaine goes to use the bathroom and I run hot water into the sink for a quick wash up.

The whole story, although intriguing, is crazy. Far-fetched, like something from a book. Then I think of my long marriage with a constantly absent husband. I don't know who my father was, and my mother never had a man about. Never. And grandma Gwen? Same story.

Fucking hell, I'm cursed.

Elaine and I busy ourselves in the kitchen. She peels

potatoes and I set the table. We wash up. I stoke the fires and feed the animals. We talk about banalities while we eat: the weather; how time flies; the early Easter.

As soon as we're both fortified, I have more questions.

'I'm sure lots of old families have stories about grudges and wrongdoing that happened years ago,' I say light-heartedly. 'Surely, it's all in the past. And the past can't be changed. So we ought to move on.'

Elaine raises her eyebrows. 'It's not all in the past.'

Here we go.

'Your mother... Well, it's only a rumour, but they say your mother...'

'Tell me. At this point, I'd rather know.' Anyway, I can't believe my sweet-tempered mother would ever do anything wrong.

'They say she stirred the curse.'

'What?'

'Well, after many years, hexes and such lose their strength if unattended.'

'And?'

'Barry's wife died in childbirth.'

'Oh, come on. Why would my mother do such a thing?' I drop my plate into the sink, sending a tidal wave of old washing-up water over myself. 'She never had a bad word to say about anyone. She certainly wouldn't want anyone dead.' I wipe the wet floor and throw the cloth into the washing machine. The stories of the past were fascinating, but now everything is getting too close to home. 'You can't blame every bad thing on some ancient curse. I'm sorry his wife died. That's awful. But he – they – can't believe it had anything to do with my mother stirring up a curse. It's ridiculous.'

'Tell that to the Rutherfords.'

Chapter Thirty-Nine

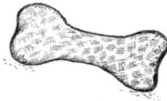

When Elaine's taxi comes, I walk her to the gate with a torch.

'Don't know how you manage out here in the middle of nowhere. Do you ever get scared? It's so dark,' she says as we wait under the yew tree. Elaine is a city witch.

The moon and the stars glint through the tangled branches. I breathe in the frosty air and say, 'No street lamps here.' An owl hoots and the trees rattle in the breeze. The taxi comes slowly, bouncing over the humps and potholes. 'Thanks for coming over. Lovely to see you.'

'Thanks for the stew and the cake,' she says, settling a cake tin on her lap while she fastens her seat belt.

The taxi leaves and I drink in the peace. Switch off the torch so I can properly admire the night sky. I'd like to amble along the lane in the moonlight, but Ink has gone through the garden gate and is waiting for me on the path, clearly indicating it's not safe. I can't feel anything, but the dog's senses are more attuned than mine.

We go indoors and I bolt the door. It's not late, but the dark and the emotions of the day have left me drained. I head up to bed.

Once I'm tucked up with a spell book and Ink is snuggled next to me, I check my (tree) cracked phone and join the family group Jason has set up. He's called it 'Turner Family Chatteroo', which makes me smile. When opened I'm met with loads of pictures. I scroll through, sending heart emojis and banal comments like 'Wow, have fun' and 'Great stuff'.

I feel betrayed.

Mike has taken Jason, Belinda, Brian and the twins skiing. If the pictures are anything to go by, they are having an absolute blast. The twins are scooting down the Italian slopes like they were born to it. There are lots of photos of Jason,

Belinda and Mike falling over and laughing. There are no pictures of Brian. Like me, he's the quiet one holding the camera.

They are staying in an idyllic, snowy lodge. The food looks good too.

When you're all alone, it's easy to have a good weep. Once I start, I can't stop, and I have to get loo paper from the bathroom. It's scratchy and cheap. I sit on the edge of the bath and cry. Snot and tears and plenty of gasps. By the time I've got myself together, I'm red and blotchy. I splash my face with cold water and apply more wrinkle cream.

In the morning, I feel better. Letting go is impossible when anyone is around. After the good cry, I slept surprisingly well.

I wash my hair. Do the tasks that stop me from looking like an ogre. Epilate my hairy face, legs and arms and pencil over my eyebrow to make it resemble the caterpillar living on the other side of my face. Find some jeans that fit – never an easy task. Put on a nice warm shirt and jumper and a bit of makeup to cheer myself. Getting washed and dressed before even a cup of tea gives me a sense of achievement. I press on. Feed my familiars, get the logs in and stoke the fires. I even have a tidy-up and strip Jason's bed.

When I do sit down to tea and toast, my phone is blinking. It's not the 'Turner Family Chatteroo' – good, I don't think I could take any more of that. There are two messages. One from Elaine informing me of the date of my initiation in March. Not long to go, and I'm still unsure. The other is from

Cressida, who says she could come over for coffee if I'm free. I message back 'YES'. A dose of Cressida is exactly what I need.

While I wait, I bake scones – because we ate my tea shop order yesterday – and start the coffee sponge I had to throw away. Then I experiment with a cookie recipe I vaguely remember my mother making. I'm taking them out of the oven when Ink opens the door. Cressida is sailing up the path in a full-length orange coat, her hair tied in a pink scarf.

'You look amazing,'

Cressida chortles.

'Hello, beautiful,' she says to Ink, holding the dog's face. 'I have something for you.' She comes in, throws the bright coat on the hook on the back of the door and roots about in a flowery rucksack.

'Here we are, you magnificent, black, long-faced beast!' Cressida brings forth a paper bag. Ink's skinny tail is a wagging blur. 'Ah ha!' she says, lifting out a huge bone-shaped biscuit. 'A bow tie bicky, just for you!'

Ink gently takes her treat and puts it carefully in the corner of the kitchen. She digs an imaginary hole. Not a deep one. Moves the biscuit into it and then, using her nose, covers it with imaginary soil. This takes some time, and Cressida and I watch. 'Saving it for later,' I say when, at last, she is satisfied and returns to her bed with a sigh.

'Do all dogs do that?'

'Oh, I've no idea. Ink's a funny dog.' She can do magical stuff and daft things like pretend to bury a biscuit.

I make tea and we try the cookies, which are still warm. Some are cherry and almond. The others are hazelnut and chocolate.

'Bloody hell, you could sell these, Lilly!'

I push over a leaflet and tell her about Fox Bake. She's wildly enthusiastic and takes some to put up at the University.

'How is the life modelling?'

'At this time of year, chilly.' She laughs. 'Did you hear that Randy Landy was dragged in front of the board of governors?'

'One of the students caught him shagging?'

'Worse. He got caught shagging one of the students.'

'How awful.'

'To be fair, it was one of the mature students. She is thirty-two.'

'Still, massive age gap.'

'Huge. See what he has to do to find the same level of friskiness after you!'

'Don't.' I'm blushing. I put another log in the range. The dog biscuit has gone. I poke the corner with my foot as I put the scones into a box. Sure enough, I can feel it under my toes. When I look, it's not there. What else has she hidden?

'So, are you going to tell me why you've been crying?'

I groan.

'Come on, out with it. You hardly drink, so those blood-shot eyes are unlikely to be the demon alcohol. Let me guess, your bastard ex-husband has...' Cressida laughs.

'Actually, can't think of anything that shit hasn't already done.'

I tell her about the ski trip and show her the photos. 'It's not that I don't want them all to have fun. And god knows Belinda could do with a holiday. Teaching is a killer. It's just all those times I tried to get him to come on holiday, he was always adamant that we couldn't afford it.'

'Because he was spending all his spare cash on his love life.'

'I guess. You know we've never had a family holiday. Not one.'

'You must have been away with him before the kids.'

'Pregnant at nineteen doesn't leave much *before the kids*.'

Cressida pours more tea.

'Do you know I've never stayed in a hotel?' I say. 'There was a youth hostel trip in the last year of school to Cornwall, if that counts.'

'No, it bloody doesn't.'

I laugh. 'Sorry. Don't mean to be so self-absorbed.'

'It's okay to be angry with him, Lil. He's an absolute cunt. No two ways about it.'

'Thanks. I know this. I just need someone to tell me.'

'Happy to oblige.'

'Fancy a walk?'

'What, not sit here and eat all your baked goods? Go on, then. Beautiful day.'

Cressida is wearing sequinned pumps. I find her wellies and an old coat, and we set off.

'What's your news?' I say.

'Funny you should ask. You know I write a few poems. Well, in a crazy moment of madness, I've decided to self-publish, and—'

'Oh my god, that's great!'

'And I've entered *Poems to Make Your Fanny Laugh* into the Allingshire Literary Festival.'

'That's brilliant. Well done, you.'

'I think Jane's sick of me scribbling away in the closet. She commissioned a book cover for me.'

'That's so nice!'

'Nice. The woman's a nightmare.' But she laughs affectionately.

'Is it out now?'

'No, the editor is weeping over it. Hopefully I'll get it out in a month or two.'

We've walked as far as Horseshoe Cove. The view is breathtaking from the cliff. Ink is already on the beach. We leave our coats at the top because we're both boiling hot, and conversation stops while we concentrate on the steep steps. A pang of sadness bumps my heart when I think about the Ruffhead brother who killed himself when his wife died. And Barry. Another dead wife.

Cressida soon pulls me from my melancholy.

'I love the beach!' she says, standing in the surf in her wellies. I join her, and we watch the waves, feel the sand suck our boots and listen to the cry of the gulls.

'Simple pleasures,' she says, stretching her arms toward

the horizon. 'Talking of simple pleasures, how is your sex life? See any more of Gorgeous George and his dragon cock?'

'No, but there is a bloke I fancy.'

'Go on.'

We sit on the shingle.

'I accidentally shagged his brother!'

'Fucking hell, Lilly! I bet that didn't go down too well.' She's laughing her head off. And telling her helps me see the funny side. A bit.

When she's stopped laughing – it takes a while – I tell her the gist about our two families and the curse. Of course, I don't mention my own witchcraft and magic. I don't want to freak her out. But I do speak about the history of magic in my family. Cressida is a good listener, and talking about some of this stuff really makes me feel better.

The tide is coming in. We jump up before we get soaked and climb the steps. A cold wind whips around us when we reach the top, and we're glad of our coats as we walk back in the gloaming.

Cressida doesn't say a word until we see North Star Cottage. It looks so cosy and peaceful, nestled in my unruly garden with smoke rising from the chimneys. Hard to believe there has been so much heartache associated with it.

'Well, if you ask me,' says Cressida as we lever off our wellington boots on the doorstep, 'it's about money.'

'Money?'

'You've got something that the Rutherford's want. I bet when you dig right down into it – put aside all the chat about

witches, curses and deep family feuds – it will be money.'
Cressida stands at the kitchen window. 'There'll be something
in the woods they want. You've got to find it first.'

I think about the blackwood trees. Do they know about
them? Is that what they want?

The witch ball spins slowly in the kitchen window, and
misty clouds fly across the surface.

Chapter Forty

F cx Bake occupies me for the next few days, but Elaine's story keeps popping into my mind. The whole thing feels ridiculous – and horribly true. Not the bit about my mother stirring up an old curse. She'd never have hurt anyone. But the rift between our two families is real. Lately, I've been remembering her telling me about herbs and their uses, and now I recall her constant admonishments about not going along Fox Lane. Then there are Cressida's wise words that its probably about money. Only in this case, it's not about money, it's about power. Magical power. There's no doubt that the Rutherfords and the coven are after the blackwood trees.

I walk to Foxbeck with Ink, a basket of scones and a Bakewell tart for the tearoom. It's a freezing cold, sunny day, and I'm wrapped in a big coat and the dinosaur hat. As we come to Fox Green at the end of Church Lane, I stop. Another memory – so embedded I have never thought or questioned it until now – emerges. My mother would never walk across the green or let me. I skirt the edge. Now I know why: that's where they burnt Bethany Blackwood at the stake. There is nothing to see in the middle of the space: a couple walking their labradoodle; a few crows striding about; a seagull stamping for worms.

I drop my baking into the tearoom. They offer me a coffee, which is kind, but I say I've got loads on my to-do list. Really, I'm not in a chatty mood. They pay me cash, which is good because now I can pop into the little shop. Ink hangs her head as I clip on her lead and tie her outside. 'No escaping. Wait here. I won't be a minute,' I whisper, giving her a dog biscuit from my pocket.

It's early, and the shop is not busy. I grab a few essentials and the caster sugar I need for this afternoon's cooking. The basket is heavy, and I wish I'd come on Jason's old bike so I could hang it over the handlebars. When I go outside, Ink has gone. Drat. I untie her lead and collar.

'Ink!' I call, looking everywhere. The labradoodle couple is still there. The woman is picking up the dog poo. Why is it that men never poo-pick?

I can't see Ink, and now I'm panicky. I put my fingers to my lips and whistle, loud and shrill. The crow flies off, the seagull doesn't care and the labradoodle gallops toward me like a ball of wool on legs. Ink trots out of the post office, ears pricked. Woolly dog sees her and barks. Ink looks behind her and Grant appears, coming out of the post office carrying a large box. Unfortunately, his expression doesn't match the smile on the Amazon parcel.

My knee-jerk response is to walk away. Ink ignores the barking dog, returns to Grant in a tail-wagging wiggle, and, delighted, goes back and forth between us. Idiot dog. The labradoodle is furious and is barking itself into a frenzy. Its owners rush across the green, calling, 'Joy! Joy!'

The inappropriately named dog dashes nearer in a snarling frenzy. Ink barks. Once. 'WOOF!' Everybody stops. The labradoodle. Its owners. The tap-dancing seagull.

'You should keep your dog under control!' the woman squeaks, scooping up the ball of wool and glaring at me. I'd like to tell her to fuck off. I hold my tongue. She strides back to her husband, who is standing well back. They go off, muttering to each other.

In the kerfuffle, she's dropped her poo bag. I pick it up

and take it to the bin. Grant watches me drop it in with a big scowl on his face.

'Shit happens,' I say, turning to go.

He catches up. 'I'm sorry about...' he trails off. Neither of us know what to say. 'Let me give you a lift home.' He takes my basket, puts it over his arm and balances his box on top. His big, expensive car is parked at the edge of the green.

'That's okay. I'm happy walking.' I reach to take back the basket, but he moves so I can't. We walk in step with Ink between us. When we get to Church Lane, I stop, expecting him to give me my shopping and go.

'You look, erm well,' he says.

'You look like shit,' I say. It's true, but when a bloke like Grant looks like shit, it's in a rugged, manly way. When I look like shit – well, I look like shit.

'New hat?' he says. The dinosaur has flopped over.

'No. Its Prehistoric.'

He puts down the basket. 'Lilith...'

Oh god, here we go.

'About the other night...'

You don't know the half of it, mate.

Then he grabs my coat, pulls me near and kisses me. No messing about. Full on, holding me tight to his body, mouth open, tongues, the lot. When he lets me go, he holds my face in his hands. Is he going to say something romantic? My heart is beating fast. He looks from one of my eyebrows to the other and frowns. I stop clinging to him like a rescued heroine. We walk on and I straighten my hat trying to regain my composure. Not easy when you're shocked to the core.

'Don't you think kisses are like hot cups of tea?' he says. 'They taste better outside on a cold day.'

'I'm not sure,' I say, pulling him closer so we can kiss again. We bang noses but get it together. When we stop, my lips burn and I'm pretty randy. We walk on, both smiling away.

Then I remember the Barry incident and stop. There's no way I'm doing anything until I've told him. Barry is the sort of bloke who'd use our liaison against me.

'I accidentally shagged your brother.'

'My brother's a bastard.'

'Totally.'

We walk on. He knows then.

'Lilith,' he says, stopping halfway along the lane. 'Other things – more than tea and kisses – are better outside.' He lifts one eyebrow and I laugh.

We walk off the road and climb a fence into a field. I follow him until we are far from the lane. The grass is deep and green, and Irk runs in search of rabbits.

Grant takes off his coat and lays it on the grass in a sunny spot. He's wearing jeans and a red cable-knit sweater. I look around the field.

'Nobody can see us here,' he says.

'I'm checking in case there's a bull.' I take off my hat.

'No, leave it on.' He's laughing now and unbuttons my coat – slowly. This is a profound moment for him from the way he's staring into my eyes. Less so for me. Without my reading glasses, he's a blur. He casts my coat to the ground. I'm wearing a big green sack dress, thick tights and green wellies.

The best plan is to leave on the dress – it's bloody cold – and ditch the tights, comfy knickers and wellies. On the lane, I was full of lust. Now I've got the giggles. Then again, maybe he just wants to lie on his coat and make out. Yes, of course – sensible, slightly serious and often grumpy Grant just wants a bit of outdoor canoodling. As usual, I'm jumping to conclusions. I take off my wellies and lie on the red coat lining. I really do hope there isn't a bull.

Grant lies beside me, propped on one elbow like he's on a knitting pattern. Knit one, purl one – yes, please.

He's kissing me, and his hand travels up my woolly leg. It goes all the way. Past my waistline, under my vest... The next moment, my bra is unclipped. Smooth bastard. I wonder if he practised when he was a teenager. Grabbing my bare boob, he sighs. Rubs his thumb over my nipple. My need to touch him is urgent, and I find the edge of his jumper. No vest. I run my hands over his back, and reason gives way to lust.

He must feel the same, because he sits back and hauls off the sweater. His dark skin and swirling tattoos have me on my knees touching him. Kissing his neck, breathing in his manly scent. I stand and get rid of my undergarments; I don't want my huge knickers and panty liner putting him off. And nobody looks good in winter tights. He can now reach the parts of me he needs. Then – fuck it – I haul the baggy dress, bra and vest over my head. I'm naked in a field!

The cold air on my skin is a shock. He stands with his back to me, kicks off his shoes and takes down his jeans and pants. The swirling tattoos curl down his back and over his tight arse. He faces me, and more tattoos swirl around his big cock. Another shock.

There's no time to think. We have our arms around each other. He's a fabulous kisser. My nipples, hard from a combination of cold and arousal, are touching his bare chest. Middle-aged, middle-class me would feel less exposed lying down. It's like he reads my thoughts and we lie on the coat. Red satin lining soft as sin against my bare back. A shiver runs over me. 'Let's warm you up, Lilith,' he says, parting my legs with his knee.

Big Bag is on the kitchen table. I only put my purse in the basket. Impromptu outdoor sex was not on my to-do list. Now I'm about to get pummelled without any lubrication. Grant nibbles my neck and moves to my nipples. Cold and hard, they are very responsive, and desire crashes through me. His cock is pressed against my thigh. Then he puts his other knee between my legs. Here we go. I'm going to be sore for days. Maybe I should call this off. Annoying because I want him. Badly.

Turns out Grant is not going for penetration. He's going down. Kissing my skin, he spreads my thighs with his hands until he's blowing hot breath onto my pussy. With one hand, he parts me, and he licks me all the way up. His tongue finds my clitoris, and all I can do is hold onto the grass and look at the sky. This man has had more sex than me. I'm completely at his mercy, and faking will not be an option. He slides two fingers inside me, heightening the feeling, and when I come, I have to wiggle away because I can't take any more.

He laughs. Wipes his mouth on the coat lining. Before I know it, he's inside me. Hard and long. Definitely the biggest fellow I've accommodated.

He fucks me in an unusual way. On his knees. Not on top of me. I reach out, wanting to hold him. I need to feel his skin. But no. He pumps away, slowly – and then he finds the sweet spot and I cry out. Fuck, that's good. He grins as he holds my legs and hits the spot again and again. I'm undone. Howling at the sky like the wanton witch I am. He keeps at it until I'm quiet, my orgasm a silent, breathless thing. Then he finds his own rhythm – slightly faster, deeper – and I watch him as he climaxes. Golden orts shimmering. Eyes closed, head back. A manly grunt. I clench my fanny to prolong his pleasure. He's the most beautiful man I've ever seen. And his tattooed cock.

He lies back, pulling me near to rest my head on his chest, and flicks my coat over us both. Ink lies next to me in her check coat. There we stay, under the blue winter sky. High above, birds circle effortlessly on currents of air.

I know how they feel.

Chapter Forty-One

I t really is too cold to lie outside with no clothes on, especially at our age. We get dressed. I watch him from the corner of my eye. He is a fine-looking man, and I'd like to trace my fingers over all those tattoos. In fact, let's be honest, I have a lot of questions about his body art. Do many blokes get their dicks inked? I blush. Turn away and concentrate on my clothes, pulling on my dress and sitting on his coat – avoiding the cum stain – to grapple with my tights.

When I'm ready, wearing my wellies and my daft hat, he rolls up his coat, stuffs it over the top of the basket.

He walks me home. Ink trots ahead, keen to get inside. He takes his parcel and carries the basket to the doorstep star. 'I'm going to get my car,' he says.

The fires are on their last embers, but I soon get them going. I put away my shopping, pop upstairs and freshen up. Make us both a cup of tea.

An hour later, I pour his tea down the sink. He hasn't come back. He didn't say he was – but somehow, it was implied. Or am I acting like a teenager? Reading too much into everything. Then again... Why are men such shits all the fucking time? I have a sandwich. Check my phone. Nothing from Grant, but there are more pictures of Jason, Belinda and Mike having *so much* fun skiing. Great.

I have a cake to bake. A sponge with pink icing and a unicorn theme. Might as well press on. No idea what a unicorn-themed cake is – but Google soon plugs my knowledge gap. By the time I'm icing unicorn eyelashes, it's dark outside. I'm so engrossed in my creation that I think the thumping is the radio. Then I realise it's Ink's skinny tail hitting her blankets. She gets up, stretches and opens the door.

Grant is there with a bouquet and a silly grin. All is forgiven. The flowers are gorgeous – they're not from the supermarket. No, these look properly expensive from that smart florist in Market Forrington. A massive hand-tied creation that is already in a fancy bag of water. I'm glad I don't have to arrange them. I carry them into the lounge. They go with the room – all faded pinks and soft greens.

'These are fabulous, thank you.'

'It's a bit corny,' he says.

'No problem. Be as corny as you like.'

'I've booked us a table at the pub,' he says and grabs me as I go past. We kiss and happiness wells up inside me.

I dash upstairs, shower quickly and put on a nice dress for a change. When I come back into the kitchen, he's looking at my unicorn cake. 'This for your grandchildren?'

'No, it's an order.' I hand him one of the flyers that Jason made.

'You've got some talent.'

I'm pleased with the cake, especially as I haven't used any magic on this one. I'm getting quite good at icing. 'I'll put the edible glitter on it tomorrow before it's collected.'

'Edible glitter. Is that a thing?'

'Very much so. And metallic sprays.'

'Come on, Inky girl, get your coat on. We're off to the pub,' he says. Ink obliges. Gives herself a shake, and there she is – dressed.

Although it's not far, it's bitterly cold, so we drive to the pub on Fox Green. I haven't been here for years and years. Happily, it has not changed, and we sit at the back near the fire. Grant takes off Ink's coat so she doesn't make it disappear and settles her near the hearth on a thick rug he's brought from the car. She gives him an adoring look. The feeling's mutual.

A waitress lights a candle on our table and hands us a menu.

'I'm assuming you don't mind a bit of pub grub,' he says.

'Lovely.' I was going to have a tin of soup, don't worry.

We both order fish and chips. There is something cosy about eating the same thing. He has a beer and I have a shandy. It's like we're a couple, especially as we sit there without speaking. I have so much to ask him, I don't know where to start. Also, I don't want to break the mood. We've had great sex. He's bought me flowers and now here we are in the pub. Asking him about family curses, witchcraft, why his brother was in Mike's penthouse and how old my dog actually is would only spoil the moment.

'Tell me about your grandchildren,' he says.

I do and show him a recent video of Sophie and Amy skiing without ski poles, like they've been doing it all their lives. 'That's the thing when you're young. Everything is so easily learnt.'

'They're not at school?'

'Half term. Easter is early this year. Got any kids?' At our age, there is always history. Marriages. Divorce.

'No. Would have liked some. But no.'

I'm wondering why. Please don't let there be another dead wife. The fish and chips arrive. Huge portions. 'Bloody hell. They've battered Moby Dick,' I say.

'I've never been married, Lilith. Had a long-term partner for many years. But we split up. She wanted to go and live in Italy.'

'But you couldn't because you're a thrall of the Coven.' I say this for a joke.

'Yes. Exactly that.'

'Fuck.'

He laughs.

'It's serious stuff, this thrall business,' I say.

'You've no idea.' He's smiling, but we eat in silence for a while. The waitress brings Ink a bone-shaped dog biscuit – or bow tie, as I now call them.

'Oh, isn't she lovely,' cooes the waitress as Ink gently accepts her treat.

Now we're eating, it's hot by the fire. Grant throws off his jumper and I my cardigan. He's in a short-sleeved shirt, and I can't stop staring at the feather tattoo because it looks so different. It's still a feather, but when I saw it the first time, it was pristine. Now it's ragged, like an old feather that's been left in the rain.

'Why has that changed?' I'm pointing at his arm, and I'm annoyed with myself for blurting out the question.

He sighs and pulls back his sleeve so I can have a proper look. 'The feather reflects the fact that I am less than perfect.'

'There's so much about this stuff that I don't know.'

'It's simple enough. If I break the rules, the Coven's mark changes.'

'It's because I took that hex off you!' I whisper, not

wanting to be overheard. The pub is busy, gentle chatter filling the air, and usually, I'm glad they are not playing loud pop music.

'Among other things,' he says, taking a swig of his beer. He moves his plate and comes to sit next to me on the bench. Now we are both looking across the busy pub. His leg is touching mine, and a frisson of excitement flicks up my thigh. Is he feeling it too? There is a slight smile on his lips.

'Eat your chips, Lilith. You're going to need your energy.' He pushes his leg closer.

I blush. Get it together, woman. This isn't your first rodeo!

'What *other* things?'

'Well, you met my brother...'

My face is bright red now.

'Barry is...' He picks up a beer mat and examines it.

I should ask why Barry was in Mike's penthouse. But the truth is I don't want to get all confrontational.

'He's a rare male witch. Most guys with magic have so little we are insignificant. But Barry always had power even when we were kids.'

Not in bed, he doesn't. And your cock's bigger. Should I tell him this?

'He's a leading member not only of the Allingshire County Coven but also of the Alliance of Witches. This is a group of the main seven covens of the British Isles.'

'How many covens are there?'

'Hard to say because there are lots of small ones. There are about twenty major covens.'

'I never thought there'd be so many.'

'Witchcraft is more prevalent than you think. And nowadays, although it's a bit taboo, it's no longer illegal, so people are more comfortable with their magical abilities.'

'Except for me.' I laugh.

'You are certainly proving to be a nuisance.'

I give him a shove, and he chuckles.

'You haven't noticed any abilities in your children?'

'No. But I've only just become aware of my own. As far as I know, they seem...' I don't want to say 'normal'.

'Non-magical,' he says.

'Yeah. Will Belinda be a midwitch?'

'Hard to say. Will you warn her?'

'Yes. I think so. Eventually, definitely, before I die. My mum was a seer, but I don't have any of that.'

He puts the beer mat down.

'What can you do?' he asks.

I eat another chip to avoid answering but they're cold now. The waitress takes our plates. 'You were telling me about your brother?'

'Ahh yes. Sorry about the other morning. He gets annoyed.'

'Elaine told me about the ancient family feud.'

'Thought she might. Basically, Barry blames the death of his wife on your mother. He believes she stirred the curse up against us. And' – I'm about to interrupt, but he raises a hand to stop me – 'present company excepted, the Blackwood witches are renowned for...'

My fingers are tingling with irritation and I'm only a breath away from defending my mother and Bethany. Burnt at the stake.

'...being difficult.'

'Difficult!' I spit the word out, and several people at the bar turn to look at me. I don't give a shit. 'My mother would *never* hurt anyone,' I hiss.

The waitress comes over with the puddings written on a slate, which she props on the table. 'Interest you in something sweet?'

I want to leave.

'Yes,' says Grant. 'We could do with sweetening up. We'll have the chocolate brownie and two spoons.' He waits for her to leave. 'This is what happened. Your mum, Fanny, had trouble when the Coven modernised to combat dark forces that arose.'

'So she was a member?'

'Then she left.'

'She didn't have that tattoo,' I say, waving my hand toward the feather on his arm. It looks even more faded now.

'Are you sure? It's a magical skin mark. It's not actually a tattoo.' He brushes his hand over it.

'Do all covens have these marks?'

'Not all.'

I stroke a finger over the feather expecting to sense the

magic. Nothing. Not a hint. 'It must seem strange to you, all this,' he says, resting his hand on mine.

'That's putting it mildly. I'm still not keen on receiving this mark. Can they control you with it?'

He shakes his head. 'No, it's just for protection. There had been a lot of threats and attacks on witches of all abilities, and the ACC got together to do something about it. They wanted to perform grand magic to create a shield, but this required a lot of power – so much so that they would levy a magical tax on all members and those that paid the tax would receive this protective mark.'

'But my mother disagreed.'

'She did. It was a huge scandal in the magical world. My parents were always going on about it – how Fanny couldn't see the greater good of joining forces. My brother was newly-wed. He was ambitious and a powerful witch, and he'd recently been voted onto the board of the ACC.'

'Is it always about power, who is on the board?'

'Not supposed to be. But isn't everything about power and money in the end?'

I nod.

'He and Fanny had a massive argument. In the end she left the ACC.

'Then his poor wife died.'

'Yes.'

'I'm sorry, but whatever you think, she wouldn't stir a curse. No matter what.'

'Lilith, I've heard these stories all my life. I don't know

who is right or who is wrong. But one thing is for sure: we've got to make an end. Hate never did anyone any good.'

The pudding comes, and he squeezes my leg.

He's right. We share the pudding, which is delicious. I can't think of the last time I did such an intimate thing. In fact, I don't think I ever have.

Mike was not a sharing kind of guy.

Chapter Forty-Two

He drops Ink and I home in his car. I'm unsure whether I should ask him in for a 'coffee'. But the truth is, I'm knackered. I play it cool, leaning over the passenger seat, and kiss him goodnight.

My lips burn as I walk to the kitchen door. God, that man knows how to kiss.

After such an exciting day, I expect sleep to claim me until morning. Instead, I listen to Ink snoring and worry about ancient curses. There is something about the night that amplifies any problem. I sit on the edge of the bed and hold my head in my hands. That poor young girl was burnt at the stake in the middle of Fox Green, and people walk there unaware of the horror that took place. In my old warm dressing gown, I go downstairs and make tea. Decaf. I'm not totally mad.

I stoke the fire in the range and sit with my hand on the spellbook. 'How to lift the curse on the Rutherford family?' I ask, then open the cover.

The book does not answer, the pages remain closed.

A pale face at the window startles me. Bethany Blackwood gazes into the kitchen.

I open the door for her. Which is ridiculous. A ghost can go anywhere, surely? She stands on the doorstep star. Ink arrives, stretches and walks around the witch. She can see her, then.

I switch off the kitchen light. In the darkness, Bethany's features are clearer. Such a delicate young face. 'I'm sorry for what happened to you.'

She doesn't move, just stares into the kitchen.

'I want to speak to my mother.'

She nods her head and wanders away.

I pull on wellington boots and a coat over my dressing gown and follow her into the woods. She leads me along a path to stand beneath a blackwood tree. Just one. Not the wide circle from before. I put my hand on the trunk, feeling the rough bark and the solidness. Reassuring myself that it is not an illusion. More witches emerge, but my mother and grandmother aren't among their wispy forms. Ink sniffs at the base of the tree.

The forest is oddly still. The witches are silent as they mill about. I need answers. 'I want to know,' I begin, and the ghosts surge nearer in a group. Their forms are so intermingled I cannot tell one from the other. 'Did my mother, Fanny Blackwood, stir the old curse on the Rutherfords?'

The ghosts part, and there she is. My mother is balancing a small bulbous jar on her palm. The glass is etched with a star. The north star. The contents swirl as she circles it in the air. Her lips mutter a spell I cannot hear. I lay a hand on Ink's head to keep myself steady as the bitter truth sinks in. My mother, with her sweet temper and calm ways, stirred the curse.

She and the other ghosts don't wait for my judgement. They disappear before I can ask them why. I watch the place where they were until Ink sighs, returning me to the here and now.

It's the middle of the night, I'm in my pyjamas, an overcoat and wellies, and I have no idea where I am. 'Take us home, Inky dog,' I say, patting her back. I snap my finger for a flame to see by and follow her out of the woods.

I eat a few blackwood leaves as I close the garden gate. My inner magic is strengthened. My heart, not so much. Nobody is good all the way through. We all have a dark side.

297

But the memory of my mother is tainted, and it doesn't feel nice.

My phone wakes me from where I slept in the easy chair in the lounge. I draw the curtains as I press accept.

It's Grant. Should I tell him that it's true about my mother's curse? Should I call the whole thing off before something bad happens? Truth is, I'm scared. Magic to enhance your cake decoration or encourage a pot plant to bloom is delightful. The darker side is not what I want.

'Come over tonight. I'll cook,' he says.

'As long as Mrs Craggs and your brother are out.'

'Just us. I'll pick you up at seven. Bring an overnight bag.'

When I put the phone down, all I can think of is that fucking four-poster bed.

I don't need to bake anything today, so once I'm washed and dressed and I've done a few chores, I sit in the kitchen with my laptop and take my hygiene certificate online. It's basically common sense, and I'm glad it's out of the way. A pleasant woman collects the unicorn cake, and Cressida rings.

'I've got a problem,' she says.

'Okay, shoot.'

'I've forgotten the anniversary of the day Jane and I met. Well, not entirely. I remembered when I was butt naked in front of thirty students. Freezing my tits off. I thought, what does that remind me of? Oh yeah, the freezing day I met the woman of my dreams.' She chortles. 'Trouble is Jane will definitely remember. Anyway, I'm stuck here 'til this afternoon. I was wondering if you had time to make me a cake.'

298

'Absolutely. What sort of thing?'

'Oh, anything. Something romantic and chocolaty.'

'Chocolate says I love you like nothing else. When do you need it?'

'Tonight. If you're too busy...'

'All I've done today is a hygiene certificate online.'

'Were there any questions about magpies in the kitchen?'

'Luckily, no.'

'Can I swing by and get it after work? I'll pay extra!'

'You don't need to pay. I'll make a cake, it's my pleasure. And I'm not meeting Grant until seven.'

Cressida is all ears, and I recount the field sex. Which, of course, she finds hilarious. Then I have an idea.

'You couldn't drop in the shops for me on your way over?'

'What do you need?'

'Grant's asked me over for dinner. And the night.'

'Hello...'

'Thing is...' Might as well come right out and say it. 'All my underwear is dire. Could you pick me up some sexy stuff? And not too expensive. I'm totally skint.'

'Yes, child.'

I give Cressida my sizes and congratulate myself on a good idea. Because the truth is I'm going to have to visit Grant wobbling free and knickerless or get some new under-garments. Who buys underwear when they're skint and single? Maybe I should start a company that delivers lacy lingerie at short notice. Speedy courier service for impromptu sex. Fast Elastic? Knickeroo? Deliver O?

There is a corner cupboard in the kitchen that's a very awkward shape. I am sure there must be more cake tins than the ones I'm using. I have two square and one large round tin, but I'd like something to make a tray bake in and a smaller circle tin for Cressida and Jane.

I kneel on a cushion (my knees aren't what they were) and empty the cupboard. It's time this kitchen had a clear out. Twenty minutes later, the contents are everywhere and I'm up to my waist, grabbing the last few items lurking at the back. Some of this stuff is ancient and it's been here for years.

'Maybe I should start a museum,' I say to Ink, who's come to sniff. I back out of the cupboard and manage not to bang my head or drop the last armful of tins. 'Museum of ancient kitchens.' It's only when I'm out that I realise I'm not alone. The door is open, and someone is standing outside. I can't see who because Ink is so close. I haul myself upright among the pans.

'Hello, Lilith.' It's Ida Carmichael-Grey.

'Oh,' is all I can say. Ink's hackles are a stiff ridge of black fur on the back of her neck and the base of her tail. I feel the same.

'I thought I'd pop by,' she says, showing her teeth.

I pick my way through the mess and stand on the doorstep. Ink is beside me. Huge and menacing. Cold air blasts my face.

She pats her immaculate French pleat with a gloved hand. She's wearing a long navy coat and smart flat boots. Tall women always look elegant. She undoes the silk scarf around her neck, expecting to come in. I move aside. Ink's lips curl, revealing hooked fangs.

'You should have more control over your familiar.'

'What do you want?'

'Lilly, it's time we had a little chat. We always seem to get off on the wrong foot.' She takes a few steps as if she intends to sweep into the kitchen. Ink and I remain. I'm almost snarling myself.

She stops. Paces backward despite herself. Hostile Ink is enough to put anyone off, and I have a saucepan in my hand.

Ida sighs deeply. Condescending bitch. 'You got the message about the initiation?'

'Elaine told me.'

'Are you going to ask me in?' She shivers, and my inner need to please and be well-mannered almost takes over. We should have a nice, polite, passive-aggressive conversation over a cup of tea. But social graces don't trouble Ink. She growls.

'I'm in a bit of a mess,' I say, glancing at my junk-strewn kitchen.

'Indeed.' She wrinkles her nose and frowns at Claudia who is giving her bottom a thorough lick from the inside of an oval cake tin.

Hard to tell how old Ida is. She's one of those women who hit forty, found her classic style and then never aged.

'We're willing to overlook the recent incident with Barry Rutherford.'

'He grabbed me!' My fingers tingle.

'You can't use magic just because a man grabs you,' she says dismissively.

'When then? When he's hit me?' When he burns me?

'Don't be so stupid. Barry would never strike a woman.'

'Well, I wasn't about to wait and find out.'

Ida flares her nostrils and re-ties her fancy scarf. 'This is you all over, Lilith. Act first, think later. Well, my dear girl—'

'Don't fucking come here and talk down to me like I'm a child!'

Ida attempts a smile. 'But that's just it. You are a child. You can't go throwing your power around and expect there to be no consequences.' She shakes her head.

'The only consequence to Barry landing on his misogynist arse is that his ego was bruised.' And his arse. Probably.

Ida tuts.

We glare at each other. She forces another 'smile' onto her thin face. 'The initiation, Lilly. Here is the official documentation. Thought I'd best bring it over as you're so disorganised with anything important.' She holds out a small scroll. A scroll. Really? It's very dramatic.

'Thank you,' I say, taking it from her.

'It needs your wand signature.'

'Hang on.' I tread carefully through the clutter on the kitchen floor and keep going until I'm in the lounge and out of sight. In a dark corner, I unravel the thick parchment and read. The words are inconsequential – the strange orts that swirl around and through it tell me more. A spell has been cast on it, and my instinct is not to sign. I take a quick picture

302

of the details with my phone. I'm still unsure what to do. Then I take it back. Will she know I haven't signed it? Honestly, I don't care.

I stand on the doorstep and hand it to her. Without another word, she strides off. In the lane, a large chauffeur-driven car rolls up for her to get in. The windows are tinted, yet I feel eyes watching me as it pulls away.

Her strange three-stranded orts are wisps on the path. I follow where she walked around the cottage. She stood in the front porch and touched the frog door knocker. Then she went as far as the gate into the forest and stopped. Returned the way she came. Nosey cow.

Chapter Forty-Three

After she's gone, I throw myself into tidying up the colossal mess I've made. It's a good use of my angry energy. I can't believe there was so much in that cupboard. I've found great baking tins: three sizes of hearts, a set of numbers and a star. They all get a soapy wash, and I put them on the range to dry. Then I clean the worktop and make two chocolate heart cakes – one for Cressida and Jane and the other for Grant. If he can be corny with flowers, I'll be corny with cake.

Once the cakes are baking, I carry on with my task. 'I'm not the first baking witch in this family,' I say as I snug Ink up with a blanket. My mother baked a bit but not this much. There are muffin tins in every size, fluted flan rings and plenty of biscuit cutters. Trouble is, everything looks useful. Also, this old stuff is better quality than what's available in the shops. I can't throw anything out. I wipe the cupboard and store the washed tins in a more organised way. I even make a list of sizes and shapes and stick it inside the door. Maybe I could make a go of this?

Later, when it's dark outside and I am in my dressing gown after a shower, hair wash and general spruce up, Cressida arrives. I'm putting the finishing touches on her cake, which has their names and chocolate and cream roses.

'That's amazing. I can't believe you made that in an afternoon,' she says.

But I can tell by her face that there is something wrong. 'What?'

'She spells Jane with a "y". I should have said.'

'No problem. I'll quickly fix it. It's not set,' I lie.

'Only if it's no trouble.'

'No trouble. Could you grab me a handful of mint? It's in a pot outside, next to the other door.'

While she's gone, I wave my hand over the cake and imagine how the icing should look. It rises, rearranges into the correct spelling and sinks without spoiling my mirror glaze.

'Smells lovely,' says Cressida, sniffing the mint leaves. 'Oh my god, you've done that already. That's incredible. Like magic!'

Just like magic. I also made the herb grow while she walked around the cottage. I pull off some leaves and pop them into a couple of mugs. 'Mint tea?'

We have a drink and a chat and then I box up the cake. 'Nearly forgot to give you these,' she says, putting a paper gift bag on the table.

'How much do I owe you?'

'Nothing. A cake! Fair swap.'

'Thanks.'

'Thank you. She's always saying I'm about as romantic as a brick. Well, not tonight, darling!'

I see her to the car with the torch. 'Have a terrific shag!' she yells out the window as she drives off.

The underwear is fancier than anything I would have bought myself. And more expensive. Two bra and knicker sets. One is bright red. The other is classic black. Each has a matching suspender belt and stockings.

I go crazy and wear the red. The stockings take a bit of organising, and I feel faintly ridiculous in them. Can't think when I last wore such a thing. When I've got everything on – suspenders untangled, boobs shaken into the plunge bra – I look in the mirror, expecting to hate my fat self.

On the contrary, I'm sexy. I'm no skinny chick, but I look

okay. In the depths of Big Bag I find the devil lipstick Cressida once gave me and pout at myself when I've put some on. Let's hope he's in the mood. Maybe I'm reading too much into 'bring an overnight bag'. Perhaps he just wants to watch telly.

I've ironed a nice frock – black, button through – and I leave the top button open, showing a bit of my racy underwear. If this all goes wrong, at least I made an effort.

He texts to tell me he's on his way. How nice. Ink and I wrap up in our coats and wait in the lane. With a little overnight bag, and the cake in my nicest box, I'm ready.

In the car, I have to concentrate on not grinning like an idiot. I watch him as he drives me the short distance to Fox Lodge. He's spruced up as well. Crisp white shirt and dark trousers. Subtle, expensive aftershave with lemony undertones and a big hint of fuck-me-now.

The lodge gates open automatically and are still softly closing as we get out of the car. Ink goes straight to the Aga and lies on the warm blanket bed. I put the cake box on the counter. One end of the kitchen table is set with a cloth and candles. 'Thought we'd eat in here for the warmth. This house is always bloody freezing.'

'Looks lovely.'

'So,' he says, taking my coat and draping it over a chair. 'What would you like to do first?'

I'm not sure what he means.

'We could eat, chat, drink wine, have sex and then sleep.' He's laughing. 'Or we could sleep, drink wine, have sex and then eat.' He's ticking off the options on his fingers. 'Or, and I quite like this one, we could have sex, eat, drink, chat and then sleep.'

I laugh. The next moment, his arms are around me, and we're kissing. I follow him upstairs. My portrait has gone. Good. He's probably as embarrassed as I am. In the bedroom, a log fire burns and candles glow. He closes the door and leads me to the huge four-poster bed. How many women have held onto these bedposts?

We unbutton each other's clothes. 'Bloody hell,' he murmurs when my dress falls to the floor. He steps back to admire me as he takes off his trousers and pants. He's already sockless. Comfortable in his skin, he stands there smiling. I try not to stare at his tattooed and very erect cock.

On the mantlepiece is a small glass bottle. He tips a few drops of scented oil in his hand and rubs it on his cock. Now I can't help looking. I don't know whether I'm shocked or turned on as I watch his manly hand casually slide up and down the shaft. Holding his manhood, he steps closer. Stoops and kisses my neck. Whispers in my ear with hot breath – 'I'm going to fuck you now, Lilith' – and pushes me onto the bed.

The counterpane is already stripped off. Smooth bastard. I reach to slip off my skimpy red knickers but he says 'No' and grasps me by the hips. He pulls me to the edge of the bed, slides a finger under the panties, tugs them to one side and thrusts himself inside me. I gasp, but he's well-oiled. The bed is the perfect height. Of course it is. He glides in and out, finds my sweet spot and holds my thighs as he pumps me. Maybe it's the anticipation that's built up all day, but he feels damn good. For a while, this is enough. As I get bored, he stops inside me, licks his thumb and finds my clitoris. Gentle but firm, he circles and presses until I'm wiggling and moaning. Then he pounds me hard, and I come with a weird squeak. I've never done that before.

He slides out of me and pulls my very wet knickers off. We get on the bed properly. He kisses my mouth and my nipples through the lacy bra. Then he's inside me again, good old missionary style, and it's so wonderful to hold him and feel the closeness of his breath on my shoulder. I slide my hands over the muscles of his back. Like this, I can move with him, and together we find a rhythm. I clench my pussy and relax, and his breath quickens. I wait a couple of beats and do it again, and this time I have him – in a gasping, shuddering groan. Bingo.

We stay locked together for a moment. Then he reaches for some tissues (man-size). They are a little out of reach, and we have to do an ungainly shuffle across the enormous bed so he can grasp the box. Did Henry the Eighth have this much trouble?

Tissues applied, we lie back in the firelight. The bed canopy is carved with a woodland scene. He pulls the covers over us, and we doze. When I wake, he's gone. I wash in the bathroom. When I come out, he's there in a long blue dressing gown. In one hand, he has my overnight bag and in the other, a glass of wine. 'Dinner in five,' he says.

I've had this bra on for a couple of hours and my tits feel like they're being strangled. I'm glad I brought a friendly old one and comfy pants. I also packed the fancy kimono I got for Christmas.

'That's pretty,' he says when I waft into the kitchen all embroidered peonies and exotic birds.

I sit at the table as he lifts a large red casserole pot from the Aga. 'Beef bourguignon,' he says, lifting the lid. It smells delicious. There is a terrine of mashed potatoes and another with steamed greens. 'Winter food,' he says as he dishes up onto hot plates.

'This is terrific,' I say, tucking in. 'Do you cook a lot?'

'Yes. I like to eat healthy. Cooking from scratch is the only way, really. Easy to do here. The kitchen in the flat is well appointed and *compact*.' We laugh at his estate agent jargon.

'You don't live here much, then?'

'Hardly ever. I have a place in Barrington. This old house belongs to my brother and I, and we can never agree what to do with it. Lot of old family history. We lived here for a bit as kids. When we weren't packed off to boarding school.'

'You're so much posher than me.' I chuckle.

'It's all bollocks.'

Hungry, we eat. Ink is peaceful by the Aga, an empty food bowl beside her.

'I'm sorry about Ink. You must miss her.'

'I do miss her. But don't be sorry. Magical creatures go where they will. And I know you love her.'

'I do. How old is she?'

'Inka? Ink. No idea. It's like they keep coming back – and honestly, it's hard to say if it's the same dog. She seems the same. Sometimes, they arrive as a puppy. Other times not. There's been a big black greyhound in my family for a long time. She's always been slightly mischievous.'

I tell him about Ink stealing a dildo from a woman's handbag in a gift shop. Grant roars with laughter and says, 'And that old coat of hers? We don't know where she got it.'

'It looks handmade. There are charms sewn into the lining.'

'She's a fascinating creature. Magical yet still a dog.' He clears the plates into the dishwasher.

'Ida came to see me today.'

'Yes, cousin Ida popped in here too.'

'She's your cousin?'

'Thought you realised. Rutherford and *Grey*?'

'No. Never occurred to me.'

He pours more wine. 'The Greys are my mother's people. We're all tied up together in business.'

'And the Coven.'

'And the bloody Coven. Would you like something else? I have ice cream. My cooking skills don't extend to puddings. I have a fear of getting fat,' he says, laughing. I won't mention the chocolate cake then.

'No, I'm fine, thanks.'

'Lilith, I'm sorry to bring this up, but while we're on the subject...' He opens a kitchen drawer, takes out the scroll and puts it on the table. 'She said you didn't sign it and, well, you should.'

I put my hand over my glass when he offers to top me up. 'Ahh. Well, I have my doubts.'

'Doubts?'

'About the Coven.'

'I know Ida can come across as a little harsh...'

Bitch is the word that springs to my mind.

'But she's got the welfare of the Coven at heart, and she's not so bad when you get to know her.'

In the candlelight, his orts have a shimmering beauty and renewed strength after the sex. Good job sex is not where I get my magical strength. My mind strays to his tattooed cock.

'Lilith! The scroll. You should sign it. Otherwise, you can't attend the initiation until next year.'

'I need you to explain a few things first.'

'Okay.' He leans on the table, watching me with dark eyes. 'They haven't put another binding spell on me, if that's what you're looking for.'

'How did you live with such a thing?'

'I've been a Coven member since I was a child of nine. Their rules are a part of life for me.'

'Don't you ever question this stuff? It's all so... weird. So controlling.'

'When I was a younger man, I tried to change a few things. But it's an old establishment that has survived in the modern era. You'll come to appreciate it as I do. And you don't have to be a part of the daily politics of it. That side is best left to those who enjoy that sort of thing.'

'Like Ida.'

He presses his lips together.

'Tell me about this threat – the dark, or whatever the fuck it is. What's that all about?'

He sighs. 'Come on, let's leave talk about the shadows until morning.' He reaches over and takes my hand in his. He's so warm. 'Could you sleep now? Or do you want to watch the TV?'

I'm exhausted. He's right. Why spoil a pleasant evening talking about scary stuff? I'll ask again in the morning. We plod up the stairs together and take turns in the bathroom, which feels oddly intimate.

'This is one hell of a bed,' I say.

'Yes, one of the Rutherford family heirlooms. Came from the big house.' He lifts his arm so I can lie with my head on his chest. The fire crackles, and the shadows flit about the room. 'You feel soft,' he says, stroking my back. We're both naked, although I brought a nightie with me. The door opens slowly and closes again. 'I wondered how long it'd take you,' chuckles Grant as Ink hops onto the bed. She wanders about, treading on us and making us laugh, then settles at my back. Grant flicks a blanket over her.

Chapter Forty-Four

F ox Lodge is quiet and cold in the morning. The fire has gone out and I can see my breath. I'm alone in the warm bed, and the fanciful carvings of wild animals stare with beady eyes. How unnerving. I'm glad I didn't notice them last night, or I wouldn't have slept.

I take a shower and consider the other set of new underwear. It looks bloody uncomfortable, and I put on the friendly stuff with jeans and a pink sweater. I've forgotten to bring socks and panty liners, but I have my HRT in the miniature jam pot and wrinkle cream. I fold loo paper into a homemade panty liner – a much-needed precaution. I don't trust my pelvic floor. Who does after forty? Then I pack my bag, pull up the bed and draw the curtains. Grant and Ink are walking over the back lawn. It looks like they've been jogging.

'Morning, sleepyhead!' Grant greets me in the kitchen. Ink is all skinny wriggles and Grant kisses my cheek. He drinks a glass of water and switches on a fancy coffee machine. I lean on the Aga next to Ink. The kitchen clock says it's 10.30am. He's in shorts and a vest top. Unshaven and slightly sweaty. I could shag him again right now, and he bloody knows it.

'Coffee?'

'Tea, please.'

He tuts with a twinkle in his eye. He pours water into a small teapot, finds a pretty cup and saucer, puts a drop of milk in a matching jug and sets it all on the table. Then he makes a tiny espresso, which is a huge palaver even if it does smell delicious.

We eat toast made from healthy granary bread. There is butter. He uses low-fat spread. No wonder he looks so good.

'That's changed!' I say and then wish I hadn't. The feather mark is perfect again. Like it's newly made.

He shrugs. 'When I behave myself, it renews.'

'And have you? Behaved yourself?'

'What do you think?' He leans over and kisses my neck, giving it a little nip, creating a shiver of desire. 'It's not my most interesting body art.'

I'm blushing like a schoolgirl.

'Right,' he says. 'Twenty minutes and I'll be back.'

I check my phone. Cressida has sent a picture of herself and Jayne with the cake. They look very happy. On the family Chatteroo there are pictures of the twins asleep in their salopettes. I finish my toast, clear things into the dishwasher and start it up. Then I put on a coat and wander in the garden. There are forsythia and early miniature daffodils since last I was here. New leaves are ready to burst on the trees as soon as the days lengthen and warm. I'd like to cut back the perennials in the herbaceous border. Give the standard roses a quick prune.

'You can still come and garden here, you know. If you want to, that is?' He's all smart in a suit and tie.

'It's a lovely garden.' I'm not sure I'd ever come here on my own again, though. I wouldn't want to bump into Barry – or Mrs Craggs, for that matter. 'What became of your last gardener?'

'Donald got old. Died a few months back. We've had a lot of trouble replacing him.' He turns away and looks across the lawn. 'Some people stay the same for years and years. So strange when they're gone. I still expect to look out the window and see him cutting a hedge or weeding. When we were kids, he grew enough veg that we never had to buy any. And strawberries that tasted amazing.'

I stand beside him. Put my hand in his. 'Did your parents garden?'

He laughs. God no. My mother liked her fingernails too much. No, it's all Donald.'

As we walk into the house, I look at my battered hands.

'I have to head over to the office. I'll run you home. Unless you want to come to Barrington?' He opens the door for me to go in first.

'I could do with a trip to Barrington. I've still got some books from the witch library.' And I'd like to have a nose around the posh cook shop on the high street. 'But I need to be back this afternoon.'

'What are you baking?'

'Golden wedding anniversary cake. They're not collecting until tomorrow morning, but I'd rather not rush.'

'Come with me. I only need to be in the office for a few hours. We could have lunch. There's a nice café I know. Then I'll bring you home.'

He's turning on the coffee machine again. 'Need another shot before we go. Office coffee is...' His grimace is hilarious. I park myself on a chair while he messes with the coffee grinder. 'Want some more tea? Or a *proper* cup of coffee? I can do you a latte?'

'I'm fine, thanks.'

On the table is the scroll. Neither of us have mentioned it. I haven't asked about the dark force, or if Barry went to see Mike in the penthouse and I promised myself I would. Seems a shame to spoil our jolly mood, though. Maybe I'll ask about it in the car.

Ida's weird three-stranded orts cling to the scroll. They are hard to see in the bright morning light, but they're there. I trace my finger in them to see if I can feel something. Yes, there is a slight chill. I lean over and sniff. No, they don't smell. I pinch a wispy thread between finger and thumb, lift it and place it on my tongue. It's slightly bitter, which is not surprising.

Grant is watching me with his espresso cup halfway to his mouth. He probably thinks I'm nuts.

'Funny how Ida's orts stay for so long,' I say.

He drops his cup, and it smashes on the flagstones. Ink jumps up from her nap and barks.

'You can see orts?' He's got an arm around Ink to stop her treading on the broken china. 'Are you sure?'

'Yeah. First noticed it at the meet-and-greet ball. Ida has a weird three-stranded thing going on. You have a golden glow and Elaine leaves a pink trail where she walks.'

Grant is clearly shocked, but protecting Ink's feet takes priority. I fetch a long-handled pan and broom and sweep the floor. Grant vacuums the whole kitchen in case any shards escaped. I mop up the coffee.

'That's a rare gift, Lilith. Why didn't you say?'

'I didn't realise I was unusual.'

'I've never met anyone who could see them.' His eyes are wide as he strokes his chin. 'Mine are gold?'

'Yes. You have a golden shimmer around you.' He smiles

at the floor. I think he's embarrassed. And pleased. How sweet.

'I never knew that I even had orts. Not everyone does.'

I don't tell him his brother's are green and creepy. 'What do they mean, the different kinds and colours?'

'No idea. I only heard about it in passing. Ort interpretation is not everyday magic. I bet Mouse has a book about it. Ask him?' He kisses me on the lips. 'You're a rare witch, Lillith.'

We go back to North Star Cottage so I can drop off my bags, get some socks, pick up the books I borrowed and check on Claudia and Maud. On the kitchen floor, rolled up in a heap next to my basket, is Grant's expensive coat. I stuff it in a bag for life to bring with me. Then I walk through the cottage trying to remember what I've forgotten. Nope. Nothing springs to mind.

In the car on the way to town, the radio plays. It's nice. Cosy, in fact. He drops me outside County Hall.

It's weird being back, and I head straight up the stairs for the library, Ink streaking along at my side. When we're alone in the corridor, she ditches her lead, and I follow her to the library door. Mouse is sitting in one of the wingback chairs by the fire. 'Lilly!' He comes to greet me, but Ink gets there first. 'Hello, hello,' he says, and we laugh when she flops on the rug in front of the fire. I look over my shoulder.

'It's alright, there's no one here,' he says. 'In fact, I didn't expect anyone today, what with the conference.'

He takes the books back like they're old friends and puts

them in his room with a small box of cookies. I try to see what it's like inside as the door swings open. Does he live here, or is that my imagination?

'So, Lilly, I hear you've been making a nuisance of yourself.' His eyes are bright with curiosity.

'Oh, I'm confused. Not sure if I should join the Coven.'

Mouse raises his brows but doesn't comment.

'I wondered if you had a book about the marks. The feather marks?'

'Coven brands,' he says, nodding. 'What else?'

'Orts.'

'Really?' He taps his fingers on the table where the huge Grimoire rests. 'Can you see them?'

'Yes.'

'Honestly?' It's almost as if he doesn't believe me.

'Yes.'

'Rare thing. I've not met another with the gift for many years. Tell me what yours are like?'

'I don't know.'

'And mine?'

'Pale grey, much like smoky string.'

He harrumphs like he's heard that before and goes to search his bookshelves. While I wait, I note the many orts floating above the parquet floor.

He drops three books into my lap and goes through his door again. When he returns, he's carrying a large leather-bound journal. 'I'd like this back. Keep it as long as you need, but I want it back. This is the only copy.'

'Yes, of course.' I lift the cover. It's handwritten.

'Never got this one published, but I will bequeath it when I die. You see, the first thing to know about being an ort observer is that you must never tell another lest they use it against you.'

I close the cover carefully. 'Thank you. Thank you for sharing your knowledge with me.'

'Secret knowledge, Lilly.'

'Yes.'

I put the books in a jute bag.

'And don't, whatever you do, tell Grant about his golden glow. It'll only make him more big-headed than he already is.'

Chapter Forty-Five

I nk is reluctant to leave Mouse's warm fire, but I don't want to hang about any longer than I have to. 'What's the conference?' I ask as I clip on Ink's lead. Not that it makes any difference to me.

'It's the Alliance of Witches' annual get-together of covens great and small. Important people making dull speeches about what they think should get done, get changed or be abolished As soon as they've had a good moan, everything can carry on as before. Coven politics is best avoided.'

'Thanks for the books, Mouse.'

'Anytime. Take care, Lilith Blackwood.'

It's freezing outside. All the puddles are iced over, and I wish I'd eaten more than toast for breakfast. I have another hour to kill before meeting Grant. Ink and I go to the cook-shop, but they won't let me in with a dog. How annoying. It's the only shop I want to go in, and leaving her outside is not a good idea. She always gets up to something. Maybe I'll pop back later when Grant can keep an eye on her.

On my phone, I find the nearest dry cleaners. 'Good deed for the day,' I say to Ink. The shop smells horrible, and the heat hits us as we go in. Ink sneezes dramatically. A tall fellow comes from the back.

'Can I help?'

I can hardly breathe. I don't know how they stand it. 'Yes. This coat, please,' I say, pulling it out of the bag.

'Express service or regular?'

'What's the difference?' I sneeze. It's one of those violent ones that come from nowhere.

'Eight hours or four days?'

Damn, I've wet myself. And it's the one day when I'm not wearing a panty liner.

'Regular, please.' I'm breathing through my mouth now, but this is an evil smell you can taste with your throat. Ink has shoved her nose under my jumper. I pull it over her head, and the man looks at me as if I'm crazy. He checks the label. Bloody hell, Grant's initials are embroidered in gold over the inside pocket. Must be a boarding school thing – the need to have a name tag in your clothes.

'You are?'

'Blackwood.' He writes it on a ticket and pins it to the collar. Picks off a few leaves and twigs. I should have given it a shake.

Trying to hold my breath, I watch him make out another ticket.

'Any marks?'

I shake my head. What can I say – yes, it's covered in spunk and grass stains because I had mad, passionate sex in a field in broad daylight?

He tells me the price. I'd gasp if I wasn't trying not to die from the fumes. I root to the bottom of Big Bag for the envelope of money and grab a couple of notes.

Outside on the pavement, clutching the dry cleaning ticket, I gulp fresh air. I'm light-headed and damp. Grant's coat cost me a fortune and I feel robbed. What the fuck are they cleaning these coats with? Gold dust? I would have left it on the kitchen floor if I'd known it would cost me the price of three celebration cakes. I head for a big high street chemist on the corner. My wad of loo paper is holding on, but I need to sort myself out ASAP.

The chemist says no dogs. They won't let me in even though Ink has on her 'Therapy Dog in Training' disguise.

'Sorry, love. Guide dogs only,' says the security guard, tapping the sign.

I'm wondering what to do next when I spot my son-in-law ambling along with his hands in his pockets. 'Brian!' I call. He wanders past and I have to grab his sleeve. 'So glad I spotted you. Just hold Ink for me while I pop in here. I won't be long.' Before he has a chance to protest I give him the dog lead and dash off.

It's a huge chemist that sells everything. I ask a member of staff to buy what I need, pop to the toilet as quick as I can and rush for the doors. Brian is petting Ink. 'You never said you were training her to be a therapy dog.'

'It's a long story. How was your trip?' I almost expect to see him with a broken leg. Skiing is the last sport I imagine Brian ever doing.

'They're not back yet,' he says, rubbing his chin. Ink's still wagging her tail to say hello as if I've been gone for hours. Daft dog.

'I thought you'd all gone.'

He shuffles his feet. 'No, just Bell and the kids. Said she needed a bit of "me time".'

'Well, it's good to have a break.' What am I saying? That's a crap thing to say. I give Ink a dog biscuit from my pocket.

'Yeah, gave me a chance to get on with my Master's.'

'Oh, that's good.' He's been taking a Master's with the Open University since before they were married. 'You okay?'

'Yeah, just getting some of the chores done before term starts. They're back tonight.'

He leans in and kisses my cheek. 'Lovely to see you.'

I watch him walk away. Funny how telling a person's walk can be. Brian's is dejected.

Rain is forecast later, and people are exercising their dogs in the park to beat the weather. Ink has a canter around the open green space. Her fluid run is lovely. A few dogs attempt to chase her, but she outstrips them easily and comes back panting. We walk to the other side of the park up the hill. A bench at the top has a pleasant view, and I admire the church spires and the red brick buildings of the university. Barrington is a handsome city. It's calm up here, and my mind wanders. Memories of picnics with other mums and toddlers seem like only yesterday.

There are purple and yellow crocuses and early daffodils. The birds sing, and a rhododendron bush is noisy with chattering sparrows. Ink leans against me for warmth. Here, with the dog and the prospect of lunch with Grant, I'm happy for about ten seconds – until my phone chirps.

On the Chatteroo is a picture of Mike, Belinda, Jason and the twins drinking hot chocolate. Behind them is a spectacular mountain view. The twins have milky moustaches. Sweet. But who is taking these pictures?

I know the truth. A picture never lies, they say – and sure enough, the evidence is there as I scroll through the photos. A handbag on the table. A glimpse of a well-shod foot. A reflection in a window.

Theodora.

That bitch is on holiday with my family. The fact that

she's fucking – and probably always has been fucking – Mike is bad enough. This is even harder to bear. A hurt in my chest lodges deep within me. I put the phone away. No point torturing myself. I sit hugging Ink, trying to breathe deeply. I've read it's supposed to help. At least I found out while on my own. Brian obviously knew.

I should be pleased for them, all having a delightful holiday. Proud of myself that despite everything, my kids still have a bond with their father. We're divorced, and I must be, if not happy, at least resigned that Mike will be with someone else. And it's not as if I like Theo. They are welcome to each other. I ought to find joy in my 'blended family'.

I'm not that noble.

I feel like shit.

Beside the flowerbed hangs the shadow of an ort. Strange how I can tell when another magical person passed by. It moves. Blown by the breeze, the wisp of grey darkens, turns black and sinks onto the path. I lean forward on the bench to get a closer look. I've not seen one like this before. Usually, they waft about and disappear. This one has a purpose. A dark stain spreading over the concrete toward me.

The sparrows stop chattering. Ink wines and pulls on her lead. I can't move. Black tendrils encircle the bench. Ink jumps up beside me. She's barking, but I cannot hear. The black slither is a cold hand grasping my foot. Dark ice seeps up my legs. I try to scream to Ink. No words come. I'm paralysed and drowning. Sinking into an evil gloom I cannot fight.

Fear overwhelms me as it fills my body, and I know when it reaches my head, I'll be gone.

It's twilight when I wake up. I'm freezing cold and shaking. Grant is lying on the ground, holding me close. Ink is here too, breathing hot, doggy breath in my ear.

I start to panic and struggle. 'It's alright. I've got you,' says Grant. I stay still, trying to piece together what happened.

'Something tried to get me.' I pull back in his arms to look at his face, and Ink licks my cheek.

'Something did get you,' he says, stroking my hair. 'How do you feel?'

'Cold. Hungry and annoyed. What the fuck was that?' I'm struggling out of his arms – or trying to.

'Give yourself a minute,' he says.

'How long have—'

'I've been here an hour. But you've been here about two.'

'Oi. Get a room!' someone shouts across the park.

I pull away and try to stand, but I'm stiff. Grant hauls me up. My limbs are heavy and won't obey. We sit on the bench. Ink puts her head on my lap. 'Good girl, Ink,' I say, glad of her calm reassurance as I attempt to quell my rising panic.

'She came to find me.'

I'm shivering now. Uncontrollably.

'If you can manage it, the best thing would be a hot drink and some food.'

Leaning against him, I stagger down the hill and into the nearest coffee shop. He sits Ink and I at the back beside a radiator while he orders from the counter. When he brings a tray over and hands me a mug of tea, I'm shaking so much I can hardly drink. I'd have a good cry if I had the strength.

'I've ordered us soup.' He looks frozen as well. We sit there in our coats.

The coffee shop is almost empty. A mother reads while her toddler sleeps beside her in a pushchair, and a man taps away on an expensive laptop in the corner.

Vegetable soup arrives with a hunk of crusty bread and we tuck in. The waitress returns with a bowl of chopped chicken and a water dish for Ink. We eat, stopping now and again to peel off a layer of clothing. By the time we've finished, we all feel better, and Ink naps on my coat.

I'm about to ask what the hell happened when the coffee shop door opens and Ida Carmichael-Grey walks in. She struts straight to us. Raincoat over her arm. Smart fitted floral dress in blues and greys. Same flat boots. Same immaculate hair.

Grant stands, which is annoying.

'What happened?' she says to me, throwing her coat over the chair and placing her large, expensive handbag on the table. 'Coffee, please.'

Grant clears our soup bowls and goes to the counter.

'I came as soon as I could. Grant says you were attacked in the park.'

She must have been at the conference. She sits, her pale blue eyes expectant. I say nothing and she checks her watch. From under the table, Ink growls.

'Are you going to speak to me, Lilly, or have I wasted a journey?'

I'm befuddled. What did happen?

Grant places a tiny cup and saucer in front of her. She takes a sugar sachet and tips a few granules into the cup. Grant stands by the table.

'Please sit down.' I say, and he looks to her for approval before doing so. Ridiculous.

'You seem to invite trouble,' she says, stirring her coffee. I have an overwhelming urge to tip the rest of the sugar into her espresso.

Ink really hates her. These days, I trust the dog's judgement more than most people's.

'Whether you like me or not, it's my job to protect everyone in the Coven.'

Lofty intentions.

She takes a sip and grimaces, then lowers her voice. 'Every day we are under threat, Lilly. Tell me what happened so I can understand what we're up against.'

'Some weird thing crept over me. Sent me unconscious.'

'Describe it.'

Recounting the experience sets my heart racing. Ida listens without interrupting. My hands are shaking so much I fold my arms.

The waitress bustles over and gives the table a quick wipe. 'Is there anything else I can get you?'

'No,' says Ida, handing her the espresso. 'Take this away. Your coffee is disgusting.'

The girl opens her mouth to speak. Ida glares at her, and she scuttles off.

'How do you feel now?' Ida leans nearer. 'Is there any lessening of your power? Do you feel weaker?'

I shrug because I honestly don't know.

'You'd feel it if you'd been reduced. That's something, at least.' She looks at Grant.

'How would I know?' I ask.

'It's painful. Not at the time but after.'

Ida opens her handbag. 'I assume you still haven't signed the initiation agreement, Lilly. So I brought another.' She lifts out the scroll and opens it on the table. 'Take out your wand, Lilly, and sign. I have a meeting to get back to, and I can't mess about here anymore.'

'I haven't got it.' It's in the gardening coat, where it always is.

Ida stands and turns to Grant. 'Get it done. Message me when you have it. Next time, she might not be so lucky.' She puts her coat around her shoulders. 'And don't leave her side. Let's get through tomorrow without any more incidents.'

Grant hails a taxi, which we take across town to where he's parked, and then we go to the cottage. It's dark when we arrive.

This has been the worst attack. I have no bruises, but the thing – whatever it was – got inside me. It was like claws in my head trying to control me. I'm afraid as never before. Ink was there. We were in a public place. But it still happened. Each time it has come for me, I've managed to shut myself down somehow. It's like I have an instinctual safety mode. I'm unsure how much longer this can work. I get my wand from the coat on the back of the door, and Grant opens the scroll on the kitchen table.

'What do I do?'

'Tap it.'

Bethany Blackwood's pale young face stares into the kitchen. Grant turns toward the window, then says softly, 'Lilly, it's going to be alright.'

I hold the wand over the parchment. Bethany shakes her head. But a ghost cannot protect me, and I need this to stop. There is a resistance when I hold the wand near, like repelling magnets. Weary, I tap, and Grant rolls it up. He's on his phone and waits by the garden gate until a car comes to collect it.

That's it, then. I'm going to join the Coven. Now I've decided, I'm relieved.

Chapter Forty-Six

After a hot bath and cheese on toast, I go to bed. Grant makes up the fires, takes care of the creatures, locks up and joins me. I spend the night wedged between a big bloke and big greyhound.

Maybe I need a king-size or an antique four poster.

In the morning, Grant is already dressed and is busy with

his laptop at the kitchen table. No wonder. It's ten o'clock. I take my tea upstairs. After everything that's happened, I need some space. I shower. Pluck the chin hairs, replenish the HRT patch, moisturise the dry bits and apply anti-inflammatory gel to my knees. No idea why my knees have it in for my sex life.

My (witch) craft room is full of Jason's computers, video games, sketch pads and files. I expect he will be home sometime today. Grant is obviously staying. I'm not even arguing this time. What I'm going to tell Jason is another matter. Should I put Grant in the spare room? Why am I embarrassed to have a lover when they've been on holiday with Mike and Theo? I bet they didn't sleep separately.

With a few old cushions on the hall window ledge, I get comfortable. This used to be my reading nook when I was a child. It's raining outside, and my tea is cold. I reheat it. The books Mouse gave me float up the stairs and stack themselves on the floor. Magic can be useful when you want to be alone. If Grant was not here, I'd take the books to bed or sit in the easy chair downstairs with a rug and Ink to keep me warm. But I'm hard-wired not to look lazy. It's the scourge of my generation. We were the women who tried to work while shouldering all the household chores. 'Have it all' women raised on the notion we could earn money, deal with the childcare, cook and clean the house. We just ended up with more guilt. Guilt if we worked and guilt if we didn't.

I read until lunchtime. Grant is stirring a pot over the

range in the kitchen. I suddenly remember the golden wedding anniversary cake I haven't started.

'Oh, for fuck's sake!'

He almost drops the wooden spoon. He's not entirely comfortable with women swearing. 'I made soup.' He sounds apologetic. He must think I'm cross because he's cooking in my kitchen.

'That's great. I just remembered I'm supposed to be baking.' I scrabble around in Big Bag for my phone. There is only one email. Mr Richards is asking for the cock cake. He's found a better picture with more detail and assures me that the cake does not need to be as large as his cock. That's the trouble with anything online – the perverts can get hold of you. I delete the message and block him. Goodbye, Mr Richards. I haven't got time for your dick pic.

Valerie is due to collect her mum and dad's cake at five for their tea party. This gives me four hours. A voice in my head shouts, 'BAKE!'

There is a message from Jason to say they are all back safe and he's staying at the flat with his dad. I'm relieved and annoyed in equal measure and make more noise than is necessary getting out my baking equipment. 'It's a sponge. If I get it in the oven quick, I think I'll be okay,' I say, cracking eggs into a bowl. Thirty minutes later, the large heart cake is safely in the oven, and Grant and I eat lunch. Vegetable soup and cheese sandwiches. It's really good. I could easily manage seconds, but I don't want to seem like a piggy.

Grant washes up, and I make cute golden roses out of

buttercream icing. It's pleasant in the warm kitchen with the animals snoozing and classic FM humming away in the background. But it's time to address the elephant in the room. I still don't know what has attacked me three times.

'I need you to explain what exactly happened yesterday.'

Grant twists the tea towel into a knot. 'It's simple, really. There's light and dark in everything. Good and bad. Witchcraft is no different. Some practise dark magic.' He hangs the tea towel on the range. 'The trouble with the darker side of witchcraft is that it requires direct magical energy.'

'Which is what exactly?'

'Energy taken from another.'

'Okay. I don't feel any weaker.' I snap my fingers and send a rainbow of glittering sparks across the kitchen. Grant smiles. Holds out his hand to catch some.

'You're a powerful midwitch, Lilith. I think you naturally put up a barrier to stop it happening.'

'Surely I'd know?'

'Not necessarily. A lot of magic is instinctual.'

He sits at the table and traces a finger in the icing dust. His orts glow. Gold orts are rare. I've learnt a lot from my reading session.

'So who are they? Another coven?'

'It could be one of two. Or even both, at different times. Did you feel any differences in the attacks?'

'No. They were all awful.'

He laughs. Alexa tells me the cake is ready, and I lift it

from the oven and test it with a skewer. Pop it back in for five more minutes.

'Smells amazing. Chocolate is the best.'

'You were telling me...?'

'Yes. Two covens in the UK practise dark magic. The Truts and the Walsteds.'

'Odd names?'

'They both go by the names of their founding families.'

'Who is the nearest?'

'That's the problem. These covens aren't centred in one place. No doubt to stop them being persecuted. Members are scattered everywhere, and they're very strict about keeping their meetings secret.'

I get a cake rack from the cupboard, put it on the table and turn out the cake. So much doesn't add up. He's still holding back. Or maybe I'm being paranoid. I drop the hot cake tin in the sink. Then I put my arm around his head and pull him to me. There's something nice in the way he holds me around my legs. The warmth of his hands. His smell. Grant is a tactile man.

'Doesn't the ACC keep track of these two dark covens?'

'Well, they try. But I think their policy is not to get involved.'

'That makes sense, I suppose.' I wonder if he shaves his head because he's bald or because he's grey.

'What about those men that came here last year? When you made me hide. A man and his son. Did you know them?'

'No. Never saw them before,' he says.

He's lying. I can feel it through my fingertips and in my mind. How strange.

I wash my hands because they feel grubby. Then I peel off the baking paper and set the heart on the rack. It is getting dark but the rain has stopped. I slip on my backdoor shoes – a pink crock and a blue half wellington boot.

'Where are you going?'

'I'm taking this cake for a cooling walk. Can't put the icing on until it's cold.'

He shrugs on a coat and follows me. 'It's freezing out here!'

Ink's in her coat and is snuffling about in the borders. I like twilight. I put the cake on the stone bench beside the path and stand with him so he can wrap his coat around me. We kiss. Which is nice, but I'm not in the mood.

'Are you sure you didn't know them? It seemed like you did.'

'No. Didn't know them.'

Lie.

I put my arms around his waist under the coat to keep warm. This would be sexy if I wasn't so disappointed with him.

'I don't understand why they didn't see your magic?' I say.

'Few people can see orts.' Truth. I can feel the truth, which is white and clear. This is so weird.

'Did you ever sleep with Theo?'

'No.' Another lie. 'Why are we back on this? Why are you so jealous of her?' He frowns.

This skill would have been so useful on Mike. Pity Grant is a lying bastard as well.

I break away and get the cake. 'I'm not jealous of her. I'm annoyed.'

'Why?' He holds the kitchen door for me. A liar with lovely manners. Well, that's something I suppose.

'Lots of reasons.' My cat. My ex-husband. You. For a moment, he looks sad and worried. Then he smiles and sexy, fuck-me-now Grant is back in the room. Deceitful bastard.

'Get some logs in. I've got a cake to ice.'

While I ice the cake, Grant taps away on his laptop and makes work-related phone calls in the lounge. I'm sprinkling on a little edible gold glitter dust when Ink gets up and opens the door for Valerie. I put the cash into a cracked blue jug on the window, happy I finished it in time and she liked it so much.

No more baking for a few more days, except for the teashop scones. Good. I need to concentrate on my magical self. But it's past 5pm and Grant has finished his working day – just when I could do with a bit of thinking time.

'Shall I cook, or would you like to go out?' He's rubbing his head and wincing.

'What happened?' I ask.

'I was making up the fire and the poker hit me.'

That's because I'm annoyed. I pat the cottage wall.

'Let's go out.' Neutral space might be a good idea.

Upstairs, I freshen up and tidy the books and cushions on my reading nook window. The sea glass Ink dug from

Bethany Blackwood's grave falls on the floor. Magic is instinctual, according to Grant. Sure enough, as I think about seeing the feather, it appears. I hold it in the light. A feather and the word 'beware' is clearer than ever before. I turn the sea glass over and realisation dawns. The reverse is the same because the feather is inside. This is not an etching. This is my mother's Coven mark. Somehow, she removed it and trapped it within the sea-kissed glass.

I hold the sea glass to my heart. This must have cost her. Magic has consequences. Not the everyday stuff – making a plant grow, tweaking your cake decorating, brewing a tea to cure a cold. No, that is inconsequential. But the big spells, yes. Reversing what the Coven had done would have required a surge of power. That would have had consequences. But what?

'Do you fancy a curry?' Grant calls up the stairs.

'Great.'

'I'll see if I can get a table at Cumin.'

My magical ability has changed and matured since last I touched the sea glass. It has a weight to it and something else. I stand in the dark, close my eyes and concentrate. There's a pull. It's slight, but it's there. The sea glass is attracted to something. I carry it in my palm, my hand held out, and follow the sensation. It gets stronger as I walk, and it leads me to the secret cupboard where the locked book is hidden.

'Okay, they could only fit us in at seven-thirty, but I said we'd be there. You nearly ready?' I put the sea glass in my pocket and give it a tap. I'll deal with this later.

Chapter Forty-Seven

The roads are empty on the way to Market Forrington. Grant hums to the radio as he drives. He parks in the street near the restaurant and takes an umbrella from the boot. We walk with Ink between us. Hounds hate getting wet.

'Mr Grant. How nice to see you again,' gushes the

manager as he ushers us to a booth at the back. Ink checks for crumbs under the table and stretches out on the thick carpet. Cumin is already busy.

The menu is huge. God, this place is expensive. No wonder I've never been here. None of the options are familiar. My experience of curry is a ready meal from the supermarket.

The manager is back. Grant orders beer and I ask for sparkling water. I need to keep my head clear. It's going to be a long night.

'So, do you come here often?'

He smiles. 'Used to.'

How many women has he brought here?

'Shall I order for us both?' he says when a waiter brings the drinks.

'Sure.'

Is it that obvious I'm a curry virgin?

Grant has a long chat with the waiter about this dish and that. I hope this lot doesn't blow my head off when it arrives.

He checks his phone briefly, puts it in his pocket and chats about the housing market. He is happy and charming. The candlelight enhances his good looks and his orts. He is a handsome man, and he knows it.

A tall blonde woman in a slinky dress gives him the eye as she returns from the ladies' room. He smiles back. Another rogue. I attract them. Bad men are the story of my life. He holds my hand while we wait for the food.

'Lilith,' he says, smoothing his thumb over my knuckles. 'I'd like to ask you something.'

'Okay...'

He's smiling, looking at the tablecloth. 'Will you be my girlfriend?'

How very old-fashioned. I laugh, and the food arrives before I have the chance to answer. It's a complicated business involving lots of little bowls that are kept warm over candles. There are side dishes and sauces and different kinds of rice. Grant explains what everything is and adds some to my plate. I'm not really listening. Orts wisp across the swirly red carpet.

I know whose they are. But I have to check.

'You haven't answered my question,' he says, dark eyes twinkling.

'Hang on,' I say, getting up. I wander over to the other side of the restaurant. Sure enough, sat in a booth looking oh so smug is Theo.

'Madam? Madam, you've lost your way?' The waiter thinks I'm trying to find the ladies'. He's right, though. I have lost my way.

Theo is telling the waiter exactly what she'd like. Definitely not her first posh curry.

'Madam?'

I walk on. Curiosity killed the witch's cat. But I've got to know for sure.

'Mum!' It's Jason. He's leaping out of the booth to give me a hug. 'What are you doing here?'

343

'I'm here with a friend.' I manage to smile at Theo and Mike, which is a heroic effort.

'Come and join us,' he cries. Bless him. He thinks his parents are above bitter animosity.

'No, love. Our food's arrived. Good trip then?' I look at the three of them. They are tanned and healthy. Mike's high-lights are fresh and his little wiglet blends in perfectly. Is Call Me Charlie still doing his hair?

'I didn't know you liked curry,' says Mike in a 'what are you doing here' voice.

'Neither did I.'

'Don't let your meal get cold,' says Theo. Absolute bitch.

I return to our table. My plate has gone, and Grant nods at the waiter, who scuttles off and brings it back under a warming tureen.

Grant is unaware that my ex-husband and his ex-lover are here, so I say nothing. The food is delicious. Everything he's ordered is perfect. At least he's a sophisticated bastard.

'So will you?'

'What?'

'Be my girl?'

I don't think of myself as a 'girl'.

'If you like.' I'm going into this with my eyes open. And at my age, there have to be compromises. He's a liar, but he's good-looking and a fabulous shag. He knows I'm a witch, and that's helpful. And I have an advantage - I can tell when he lies.

I move my leg so it touches his. I'm wearing Belinda's big

old black boots so I can't do anything wildly sexy like slide stocking-clad feet up his trouser leg. Even so, he seems quite pleased with the contact and puts his hand on my knee. Ooh, that frisson of sex—But no, I'm too full of food. We play the flirting game, though. Why not?

'Tell me about the initiation tomorrow. Will I be okay? You know, afterward?'

'You'll be fine,' he says, patting my leg. Another lie. Interesting.

'I mean, what happens? Will I feel tired?'

'Yeah, I think a lot of people do.'

Truth.

A large group of people come in. There is a lot of chatter and flapping of wet coats. In the kerfuffle, our candle blows out. Our corner is much dimmer without it. When no one is looking, I snap my fingers and relight it with my spark.

'Witchflame,' says Grant, moving the candle into the middle of the table. 'You have a lot of rare gifts.'

'Just as well I've got this one. Never can find the matches.'

'There's a reason you can't find them.'

'Tell me.'

'Matches – the heads are made from sulphur.'

Clearly, he expects me to understand. I shrug.

'Sulphur repels magic.'

'Really? I didn't know that.'

'It's why most people can't use magic in County Hall.'

I remember my feelings of impotence when I was kept there against my wishes.

'But some magic was there. Ida. She used magic.'

'She's a powerful witch. So are you. At the end, you managed to use your power.'

He rubs his arm. Our legs are still touching, so I know he's telling me the truth. But the Coven mark doesn't like it. Fascinating.

'This was great,' I say. It's true. I've never eaten anything so tasty. A flurry of waiters descend on us. They clear the plates and sweep every crumb and grain of rice from the cloth with a silver pan and brush.

'Would you like anything else?' asks the waiter, laying another menu on the table.

I've had enough, but Grant discusses the options with the waiter then holds my hand again.

'Why didn't you ever marry?' I ask.

He looks at our hands. 'Two reasons. It was considered unwise because of the kind of witch I am and where I get my energy. They think we're incapable of fidelity.'

'Were you faithful to the woman who moved to Italy?'

'Yeah.' His gaze is steady. So is the sensation of his lie.

'And the second reason?'

'The family curse... Well, it weighs on your mind.'

'But your brother married.'

'Oh, he thought he could counteract it. Believed he was strong enough. And his wife was not a witch so he thought she'd be safe.'

'It could have been a coincidence?'

A flash of anger flicks over his handsome face.

'What about your brother and the rest of your family? Won't they be annoyed you're dating a Blackwood witch?'

'It will be our secret,' he says, and his dark eyes glitter.

The blonde woman is back. 'Her bladder must be worse than mine,' I say as she sashays past. Her sharp heels mark the carpet. She smiles at Grant, who responds with a subtle lift of his eyebrows.

Theo is making her way to the ladies' room. She's deliberately taking a strange route so that she doesn't pass our table. I have an idea. Orts are not the only thing I have read about today. 'Just be a minute,' I say, grabbing Big Bag and heading for the loo.

I make a play of brushing my hair. The blonde woman is examining her face in the mirror. It looks okay to me. How old is she? Forty? Younger than me, anyway.

'Are you seeing him?' she asks as I root in Big Bag for lipstick.

'Who?'

'Er, Grant Rutherford?'

In the cubicle, Theo stops peeing. Presumably, she's listening.

'Grant!' I pretend to laugh. 'No. Our families go back a long way.' Since they burnt my ancestor at the stake in medieval times. 'He said he recognised you.'

'Really.'

She smooths her dress and clicks out. Good. They can have a nice flirt while I tackle Theo. I wait, but she's silent.

Probably waiting till I'm gone. I push the door, let it swing to and stand quietly.

Her eyes are wide when she leaves the cubicle. Not like Theo to be disconcerted. She washes her hands deliberately.

'What do you want, Lilly?' she says, drying her hands on a paper towel, her composure regained.

I wave at the door, locking it. She steps backward holding her handbag like a shield. 'Don't touch me!' she says.

'I'm just going to take back what you took.'

Theo stumbles in her flirty little ankle boots. 'I'll scream!'

'I don't care.' And I don't. I'm perfectly calm as I grab hold of her arm and push back her white cashmere sweater.

'Please don't!' Her eyes are wild. Someone rattles the door.

'One moment!' I call, all sweetness and light. I grasp Theo's bare arm with both hands and twist in opposite directions. What we used to call a Chinese burn at school. I've absolutely no idea what I'm doing, and I hope the book I read is accurate. Theo finds me pretty convincing and lets out a dramatic little wail.

'Give me what you stole, Theo. Or I *will* hurt you!'

'I never took anything from you. Don't you remember?' she simpers.

'Not me, you bitch. My cat.'

'The cat?' She has no regard for my familiar.

'Claudia. You took her ability, and I want it back. Are you going to return it freely, you thieving witch?'

She swallows. I've never seen her look so worried, which

is good. If she doesn't return Claudia's power voluntarily, I don't know how to make her. That was in the next chapter. I give her arm another twist for encouragement.

'Wait, wait! Let me find it...' She closes her eyes. Her eyelids flutter, and a thin line of green vapour rises from her arm, forming a marble-sized ball that floats in the air. From Big Bag, I grab my tiny jam jar and tip my emergency HRT supply into a side pocket. Then I scoop up the green mist and put on the lid. It floats like a miniature planet. How strange.

Theo is running her arm under the cold tap. It's a bit red, but she'll survive. The door handle rattles again, and there is an irritated knock. I wave a hand at it, and two women burst in.

'What do you think you're doing!' says one of them, giving me a haughty glare.

'Yes, we've been waiting ages. You're not supposed to lock this door.'

'Oh shut the fuck up and have a pee,' I say, walking past.

Theo follows me out. 'You've changed,' she bleats.

'You haven't.'

Chapter Forty-Eight

Grant is laughing with the blonde woman. She minces off looking pleased when I arrive. He exchanges a 'what now' look with Theo as I pet Ink and sit.

'Try this, it's really nice,' he says, pushing an oversized plate toward me. On it is a small mound of ice cream sprinkled with pistachio nuts and gold leaf. Heart-shaped crispy biscuits are scattered around the edge. Two spoons wait. Grant is a romantic, share-my-pudding guy once again.

'Did you know she'd be here?'

'Who?'

I give him a look.

'Why wouldn't she be here? She only lives up the road. Try it.' He offers me a long-handled spoon.

Ink is sniffing Big Bag and wagging her tail. I stroke her to calm my frayed nerves. The ice cream is silky and not too sweet. Subtle flavours of rose and vanilla. 'Lovely,' I say.

We eat, and he moves his feet so our legs touch, and Ink rests her head on top of Big Bag.

'What time does it start tomorrow?' I ask.

'Not too bad. Ten o'clock. We should leave at nine. Dodge the traffic. Or we could stay at my flat in town and walk to County Hall.' His phone vibrates. It's on the table beside him. Can't blame him for playing with it. I've been gone for twenty minutes extracting stolen magic from my frenemy.

'That was Ida,' he says, glancing at the waiter for the cheque. 'She wants to know if you'd like me to present you?'

'Meaning?'

'Usually, parents or a family member present the initiates.'

'Yeah, sure.' I won't be asking Theo.

Grant stretches out his arms and arches his back like a satisfied cat that got the cream. He bashes off a quick text and flicks his gold credit card onto the platter when the waiter arrives. Ink stands, gives herself a shake, and I put her coat on then mine.

Grant chats with the manager, and I try not to look at my son, Mike and Theo. What's the etiquette? Leave? Pop over and say bye? Out of the corner of my eye, Jason rises. Over he comes, all jolly. Bless. He shakes hands with Grant. How nice. Ink is delighted and causing havoc as she does the skinny wriggle and says hello to a few customers for good measure. She's loving the attention.

'I'll pop over tomorrow, mum. Get some of my stuff.'

'Okay, love. If I'm out, you know where the key is.'

Seems like Ink has decided to greet the whole restaurant. Some of the waiters follow and try to shoo her away from the customers.

'Ink. Ink, here.' I say. Dog's gone deaf and trots after Jason.

'She'll come,' says Grant, steering me by the elbow. At Cumin they like to give you a good send-off, and smiling staff and a lovely woman in a beautiful sari wait by the door.

I whistle Ink. Her recall is better that way. I didn't intend it to be so shrill. Heads pop over the booths to see what's happening and then turn toward a loud 'A - wooo,' and the familiar voice of my ex-husband shouts, 'Fucking DOG!'

Ink hurtles into view, sending a waiter crashing into a serving trolly. She bounds toward us, shaking her head. There's something in her mouth that she tosses in the air and catches. A woman in a nearby booth shrieks 'Rat! Rat!' and stands on her seat. Now everybody is on their feet.

I feel the need to explain and rush over for the sake of the restaurant's reputation. 'She's just killing my ex-husband's wiglet thing,' I say grabbing the woman's sleeve. 'And that's just her happy growl,' I add before Grant drags me outside.

She's still got it when I settle her on the back seat of Grant's car. 'Give,' I say, and she dutifully drops it into my waiting hand. I put the choking hazard into my pocket.

'So what do you want to do?' asks Grant as we drive off.

'About what?'

'About tonight. My flat in town?' I'm glad he's not bothered by Ink's antics. Then again he's probably used to them.

'That'd be good. But I kind of wanted to put something smart on, and I've got nothing with me.'

'It is a bit short notice.' The windscreen wipers swish. 'We could stop off at yours and get your stuff, then go back to mine. Save all the driving in the morning?'

This gives me an idea. 'Only if you don't mind?'

'No trouble.'

I take my phone and the jar of stolen magic out of Big Bag when I pretend to look for a hanky. When we pull up outside North Star Cottage, it's spitting with rain. 'You turn the car round. I'll only be two minutes.' I leave Big Bag on the seat and say, 'Did Ink have a piddle when we came out of the restaurant?'

'Can't remember.'

'I don't think she did. Come on, Inky dog. It's a long drive to Barrington.' Ink jumps out and we go through the gate. Grant drives a few hundred yards for a wider turning circle. By the time he's alongside, I've cast a spell to keep out intruders. Ink's had her pee, and we're already inside. I lock the door and put my hands on the wall.

'No one to enter here, friend, foe or family. My house is locked, my boundary sealed above, below and all around. Let no one pass without my permission.'

Ink shakes off her coat. I lift Claudia from the blanket bed onto the table, take the jam jar from my pocket and unscrew the lid. She gives it a sniff but is not interested. Maud hops onto my shoulder, and Ink presses against me and wags her skinny tail.

The magic knows who it belongs to and floats out of the jar. Claudia meows. She's more interested in getting her supper. The iridescent green ball lands on the table and rolls toward her, and Claudia stares – fascination in her blue eyes. The ball teases, swishing back and forth. A flash of paw lands on top of it. For a moment, she is still. She sneezes once. Then she sits tall and straight and regards us. I tickle under her chin and she looks into my eyes, knowing and clever. My cat familiar has returned.

I feed everybody, stoke the fires and make a pot of tea. Outside, a car horn sounds. Oh dear, Grant Fucking Rutherford has realised he's been tricked. Big Bag kept him fooled for forty-five minutes. Well done, Big Bag.

Chapter Forty-Nine

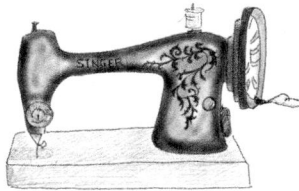

M y phone chirps. I'd like to ignore it, but I'm always worried it might be one of the kids. It's Grant. I can't be bothered with a long, drawn-out conversation. I send him a message: 'Sorry. Need space and thinking time. Go home. I'm fine. I'll let you know what

I'm going to do in the morning.' Might as well keep him guessing.

'You know I can't go home. You're not safe,' he replies.

Well, that's increasingly a matter of perspective.

The phone rings. Grant again. The cracks on the screen are a perfect tree now. I pour myself a nice cup of tea and switch the phone to silent. 'Right, Maud, let's have that key.' I climb onto a chair and then the table. Search the top of the dresser and the bread basket nest. The tiny key for my mother's locked book and a sapphire engagement ring are under a shiny piece of Christmas wrapping paper. I leave the ring where it is. Never seen it before. Something to worry about later.

From the secret cupboard, I retrieve the book and bring it to the kitchen table. I pour more tea and check the witch ball. Grant's car is still in the lane. It's such a filthy night, a part of me wants to ask him in. Then I think of the inevitable curry farts. Maybe it's for the best.

Claudia gives her whiskers a thoughtful wash. From my pocket, I take the sea glass and put it on the table, where it slides of its own volition next to my mother's book. I turn the key. The book opens. The words dissolve, and new writing appears.

I knew you'd work it out, Lilly, and I hope it has not taken you too long. You'll understand when you read this Book of Truth *that I could not risk anyone but you learning what I must tell...*

I sit in the kitchen all night and read the story of my

mother, her witchcraft and what she did to keep me safe from the Coven. She was a seer and always knew my magic would arrive in midlife. She also knew she would be long dead by the time it happened. So she left me a magical trail to follow and learn from.

As dawn breaks, I dress in warm clothes. If I can escape the Coven's clutches until the Spring Equinox has passed, I will be safe – at least until next year. Wand in hand, I walk around the garden's edge and speak a chant my mother advised. When I am back on the path, Grant is standing in the lane.

'Lilith!' he cries. 'Stop being so stupid. We want to protect you!' His face is taut. Behind him, Coven members emerge. Church Lane is full of cars. I never heard them arrive, which is creepy. I should have started this earlier.

Some stand and watch. Others huddle behind Grant. The orts of their spell twist in green spirals above their heads. The small crowd only strengthens my resolve. I will not let these people bully me or take my powers against my will. Ink stands in front of me. Brave dog. I put a couple of blackwood leaves on my tongue and feel their strength.

I place my hands on the earth and ask for protection. Tendrils of life seep into me. I reach to the sky and send forth sparks of light. A great dome forms over North Star Cottage and the garden. It sparkles with rainbow colours like a bubble. As I admire the beauty of magic and nature, I realise my orts are this shimmering rainbow. I spread my hands before me, giving thanks for the luminous colours.

In the lane, the witches have stopped casting spells. They stare.

'You can't stand against us alone,' someone cries out.

Take a good look, witches. I am not alone. Here I am with my familiars. Magpie on my shoulder. Huge, sleek black dog in front of me. Claudia brushes against my leg. She has become a panther. Clever cat. In the shadows, I sense the green-eyed fox and the ghosts of my ancestors.

Ida Carmichael-Grey steps forward. She grips her jewelled wand, her knuckles white. She's muttering a spell. Behind her, witches and thralls form a triangle, each holding the next.

A wave of hate washes through the barrier I have created. But I'm not waiting to see how they will cast their collective spell. I raise my hands and feel the power of nature and life and all the women of my name. A great breath fills my lungs and my voice sings with a thousand witch voices.

'I am the Blackwood midwitch. You will not intrude here. Be gone!'

A gust hits them. They fall and tumble, blown by my witchwind.

I stand on the path while they leave. Cars drive away. Most look back with fear as they scuttle off. Grant holds the car door for Ida. His expression is dark. 'I thought we could have had something together, Lilith.'

'We still can.' I beckon him. Ink wags her tail. For the briefest of moments, I think he might join me. One hand is on his arm where the Coven mark hurts.

'I can fix that,' I say.

Grant gets into the car.

When everyone has gone, I remain. The birds sing, and there's a gentle rustle of new leaves. The sun shines on my face. Like the solitude, it is a balm. I thank the earth, the old yew tree and the green-eyed fox who stands by the gate into the woods. Claudia changes to her cat self. Just as well. There isn't room for a panther in my kitchen. Ink becomes a regular greyhound. Maud gives my ear a friendly peck. Bethany Blackwood and the others fade away.

The barrier only needs to stay over the cottage for twenty-four hours – until the Spring Equinox has passed. I keep it for two days. I need to be alone.

I put Jason off collecting his things with a lie about a sore throat I don't want him to catch. Then I re-read my mother's *Book of Truth* and the spellbook I found in the loft last year. Knowledge is key.

I reclaim my craft room. Stack Jason's things in the corner of the big bedroom. There is plenty of space if he needs a desk. I can't imagine he will stay with his father for long. My door is always open but we'll need to set some house rules when he returns.

Grant's bouquet, delightful while it lasted, is dead and smelly. Pulling off the cellophane (I don't want that in my compost), I notice the foil gift bag from the raffle in the kitchen window. I'd forgotten all about it. The meet-and-greet ball feels like a lifetime ago.

Over a cup of tea, I unwrap the gift inside. A mobile

phone. I've never had a new one. Usually, I repurpose a dated model the kids have finished with. I put it back in the bag and slot it into a gap on the dresser. Truth is I'm attached to my old phone especially now the tree on my screen has grown leaves.

I garden until it rains, then sew in my witchcraft room. Like much else, my machine is old and belonged to my mother. It's a Singer with a turn handle and is amazingly heavy. I make a little pouch for the sea glass. It's essential to keep it with me for protection against the dark shadow the Coven sends. When I'm done, I put it around my neck on a ribbon and tuck it under my jumper. Winter clothes will keep it hidden, and hopefully, by the summer, I will know what to do about the Allingshire County Coven. For now, my mother's Coven mark will guard me.

I have a good rummage through the scraps and make Ink a new coat. Red velvet with a soft lining of fleece. Of course, I cast a water-repellent spell on it and sew fresh charms into the lining. Now that my magic is stable, the charms are easy to find: the top hat from the Monopoly set (it's why everyone wants it); a sea shell; a holey stone; one of Maud's feathers; a whisker from Claudia; a blackwood leaf; and needles from the yew tree.

'What do you think, Inky dog?'

She sniffs the coat deeply. I think she approves.

Chapter Fifty

The next morning I need to walk to Foxbeck.
Deliver scones into the tearoom and get some
groceries. I pull on boots and pick up my basket.

What have I forgotten? I put my hand over the sea glass in its little pouch around my neck. Nothing.

Ink follows me outside. After the night's rain the spring sunshine is bright on the wet garden. Ink gives herself a shake. Her new red coat is on, and she comes to be petted and told how beautiful she looks.

I lift the barrier with a wave of my wand. The bubble bursts, and I follow Ink along the lane. She does look beautiful. The red suits her black fur, and I'm pleased she has chosen to wear it. Will she have it after I'm gone and she's another witch's familiar? I hope so.

Spring is here and the air is fresh and cold and full of birdsong. The trees are covered in soft new leaves and the banks of the ditch are splashed with yellow primroses. I pick two bunches, surrounding the flowers with the leaves and take one posy to my mother's grave. Maud perches on her gravestone as I give silent thanks for her foresight and wisdom. Then I go to the very edge of the graveyard and give some primroses to Bethany Blackwood - the daughter of the young woman who was burnt at the stake. Not for the first time I wonder where her mother's remains are.

Fox Green is busy. Everyone has waited for the rain to stop. I hand in the scones and then head for the grocery shop, getting my list from my pocket.

'Excuse me!' An old man catches us up. 'I've been trying to get in touch. The people in the café said it was you. The Fox Bake lady.' He pats Ink. 'I sent an email, but I'm not very good with computers. I'm Bill Richards. I wondered... If you have time, you're probably very busy... I'd like a cock cake.'

Oh god, it's him.

He's reaching inside his coat pocket. 'I have a picture. It's a bit blurred.'

He hands me a photograph. I hardly dare look.

'Brings back memories. Me and the Mrs, we used to be breeders.'

The picture he's thrust at me is of a cockerel.

'Isn't that the most beautiful cock you've ever seen?'

'Yes, Bill,' I say, relieved. 'He's an absolute joy to behold.'

Nice Mr Richards explains that the Fancy Bird Society which he helps run with his wife will soon be fifty and they're having a tea party to celebrate. I take down the details and tell him where I live so he can collect it in two days.

Ink manages to stay out of trouble while I buy groceries and then we head home. I'm thinking about dropping off the shopping and then walking to the beach as it's such a lovely day when I stop. Beside me Ink takes a step back.

A dark stain moves over the road, killing the sunshine in the puddles as it slithers nearer. I put my hand over the sea glass. The shadow can't hurt me now. I could walk by and leave it there, looking for the uninitiated. But I have had enough coven nonsense, and it's high time we all moved on with our magic.

From my basket, I take a jar. Funny how you always know what it contained long after the label has washed off. Dill Pickles. Now a frog. I lift him out, put the jar on its side on the ground and wait with the frog cupped in my hands over the jar. Sure enough, the black stain slides in. Before it can escape, I let the frog go and twist on the lid. The hex swirls like an angry storm cloud.

The frog shines green and gold in a ray of sunshine. 'Thank you,' I say, and the hapless creature, unaware that it is a natural magnet for hexes, hops off.

We're nearly home. Maud lands on my shoulder, and Claudia sits on the garden gate. It's surprisingly warm in the sunshine. Ink has taken off her coat. I put my hand on her smooth back. For the first time in so long I am content and, more than that, I feel safe and in charge of my magic.

Don't get me wrong. I'm not so stupid to believe the Coven has given up. Of course there will be more trouble. But that, as they say, is another story, for another day. For now all is well and I'm going for a beach walk. Then I'll get some washing on the line and bake a cock cake.

Free short story

Thank you for reading.
If you can take a moment to leave a review
I'd be very grateful.

Join my mailing list for a free short story and writing updates.

www.djbowmansmith.com

Acknowledgments

Grateful thanks to my husband for his unfailing belief and support. My two lovely daughters for their wisdom and kindness. My sister-in-law for her constant encouragement. And, of course, the clever and knowledgeable editor, Anna Sharples without whom none of this would be readable. Find her here: www.sharpsightedgrammar.co.uk

About the Author

DJ Bowman-Smith writes witchy paranormal women's fiction. She's passionate about giving mature female protagonists the strong voices they deserve.

She lives with her husband on England's south coast and has two grown-up daughters. When she's not conjuring up magical mayhem on the page, you'll find her creating her own artwork (because apparently one creative obsession wasn't enough) or baking because her husband loves cake.

She finds much of her inspiration in the everyday: overheard conversations, people watching and walking Evie whippet on the beach. Magic is everywhere, if you know where to look.

She loves connecting with readers who share her passion for stories with grown up protagonists and midlife humour, so don't be shy about finding her on social media or joining her mailing list—she'd love to connect.

www.djbowmansmith.com

Printed in Great Britain
by Amazon